DRAGON CASTLE

DRAGON CASTLE

by JOSEPH BRUCHAC

Dial Books for Young Readers
an imprint of Penguin Group (USA) Inc.

DIAL BOOKS FOR YOUNG READERS
A division of Penguin Young Readers Group
Published by The Penguin Group
Penguin Group (USA) Inc., 375 Hudson Street, New York, NY 10014, U.S.A.
Penguin Group (Canada), 90 Eglinton Avenue East, Suite 700, Toronto, Ontario, Canada
M4P 2Y3 (a division of Pearson Penguin Canada Inc.) • Penguin Books Ltd, 80 Strand,
London WC2R 0RL, England • Penguin Ireland, 25 St. Stephen's Green, Dublin 2,
Ireland (a division of Penguin Books Ltd) • Penguin Group (Australia), 250 Camberwell
Road, Camberwell, Victoria 3124, Australia (a division of Pearson Australia Group Pty
Ltd) • Penguin Books India Pvt Ltd, 11 Community Centre, Panchsheel Park, New Delhi
- 110 017, India • Penguin Group (NZ), 67 Apollo Drive, Rosedale, Auckland 0632,
New Zealand (a division of Pearson New Zealand Ltd) • Penguin Books (South Africa)
(Pty) Ltd, 24 Sturdee Avenue, Rosebank, Johannesburg 2196, South Africa • Penguin
Books Ltd, Registered Offices: 80 Strand, London WC2R 0RL, England

The publisher does not have any control over and does not assume any responsibility for
author or third-party websites or their content.

Designed by Jennifer Kelly
Text set in Sabon

Printed in the U.S.A.

1 3 5 7 9 10 8 6 4 2

Library of Congress Cataloging-in-Publication Data
Bruchac, Joseph, date.
Dragon castle / by Joseph Bruchac.
p. cm.
Summary: Young prince Rashko, aided by wise old Georgi, must channel the
power of his ancestor Pavol the great, and harness a magical dragon to face
the evil Baron Temny after the foolish king and queen go missing.
ISBN 978-0-8037-3376-3 (hardcover)
[1. Princes—Fiction. 2. Wisdom—Fiction. 3. Kings, queens, rulers, etc.—Fiction.
4. Dragons—Fiction. 5. Fairy tales.] I. Title.
PZ7.B82816Dr 2011
[Fic]—dc22
2010028798

FOR ALL THOSE
WHO KEPT SLOVAKIA
ALIVE IN THEIR HEARTS

The Wall Hanging

A MONUMENTAL TAPESTRY decorates the wide back wall of the Great Hall in Hladka Hvorka, my family's large old castle. The tapestry has been there since the castle's earliest days. No one knows who wove it. Perhaps, some say in jest, it wove itself. That idea may not be so far-fetched if one believes the legend that Hladka Hvorka was constructed—or grew up out of our high round hill—in but a single night.

The sequence of scenes depicted upon that wide weaving isn't easy to describe, even for me. It's not just because of the bright intricacy of its texture, the way sparkling threads of silver and crimson, russet and gold, cerulean and jet, azure and amber seem to not merely reflect light but glow as if lit by fires from within. Nor is it merely due to its sheer size, double the height of a tall man and encompassing a surface the length of a strong spear cast.

It is, to be frank, frustrating to try to describe the imagery held by the Hladka Hvorka tapestry because the shapes within its weave seem to change as I study them. Just when I think I'm perusing a pair of juggling lads, I realize I'm looking instead at two lissome maids, who gaze back at me with dismissive eyes!

And therein lies the more disturbing aspect of our gigantic tapestry—at times it seems more aware of me than I am of it. *Nie! Do not look at me*, it soundlessly commands, and I find myself unwillingly averting my gaze.

By the head of the dragon! Quite unsettling.

However, as I've looked at the tapestry often, I've discerned at least one or two recurring motifs.

First and foremost, of course, there's the epic journey and eventual triumph of our ancestor Pavol, dragon conqueror, scourge of evil, founder of Hladka Hvorka and the ensuing Reign of Peace we yet enjoy. We also may observe his noble steed, his friends and allies, and so on.

(Interestingly, the gold thread that outlines Pavol appears later in the tapestry, where a tall, youthful shape hesitates before a doorway. In similar fashion, the red thread associated with the deceptive dragon also resurfaces there.)

Secondly, of course, there's Pavol's adversary, the

Dark Lord. The jet black silk that outlines him also seems to loom up and then subtly disappear throughout the wide weave—unpredictable as the late spring frosts that may wilt our crops just when we assume winter's cruel reign has ended. Quite disconcerting.

Whenever I look at the great tapestry it makes me wonder. I find myself wishing I understood more. So few real facts about our great ancestor's story have come down to us today.

Perhaps I'll never know.

Pyrva

RUN, SON, HIS mother said.

Hide! His father's last word to him.

He had always done as they asked. And though the grim look on Otec's face and the tears in Matka's eyes made him want nothing more than to remain with them, the slight, six-year-old child did as they commanded.

He allowed his father to lower him out the window until it was but the drop of a child's height. His small feet landed lightly on the packed earth. He ran swiftly across the back courtyard, where a small confused group of their servants huddled like chickens that have seen the fell shadow of a hawk.

Some of them nodded uncertainly to him. All of them were looking to the front wall, but none attempted to man it. After all, who among them knew enough to mount a defense—even if they had been armed? Suddenly they were all pushed aside by a round, aproned whirlwind that came rushing out through the kitchen door to intercept him. Maria, the cook. She grasped the boy's thin arm, hugged him fiercely to her huge bosom. Then she thrust a cloth in which several warm kolac were tied into his shirt before pushing him on his way.

Old Strom, the carpenter, stood with his broad back braced against the postern wall. He said nothing, merely nodded at his hands held together in front of him. One step into those cupped palms, a quick boost, and the boy was atop the parapet that had never been raised so high as to withstand an attack. It was more of an aesthetic feature than a defense. After all, castles are expected to have ramparts, even one such as theirs—St'astie Dom, the House of Happiness, where the gates were left open day and night to admit tradespeople, wandering musicians, and any ordinary folk in need of the help his big-hearted parents would always provide.

What use had they for defenses? Who would attack them? They were the kindest of rulers, generous and undemanding of the common people, friends to all. That was why, it was said, that the Silver Realm, the place of the Fair Folk that can never be found on any map, lay so close to their tiny kingdom. Though the Faerie people never directly interfere in the doings of mortals, the fact that the aura of their glittering realm could be seen from St'astie Dom implied that they looked with favor upon that little land of kindness and peace. The Fair Folk were pleased to be bordered by such guileless, gentle humans.

So, too, had been the other larger dukedoms and principalities around them. Until recently, courteous visits from their various royal neighbors had been commonplace. But it had been two seasons since any visitors from other kingdoms had graced their home.

All that had come were dire rumors, which the boy's parents had not spoken about to him. However, his ears had been keen enough to pick up their whispered conversations about the calamity such stories said had come to the lands around them. A dark warlord, one whose only desire was to crush and conquer, slaughter their leaders, and then rule those lands with a fist of iron. It did not matter how small or poor any principality might be. The very fact that it was there was enough to draw the attention of that evil one. It was so terrible a story that surely it could not be true.

Only a story, not reality. That was what they had hoped, if not believed—until this day. Then, was it only a hour ago? Krajat, the woodcutter, had stumbled through the open gate. Terribly wounded, he told with his last breath of the grim army that approached, led by that same monstrous conqueror they had hoped was mere fantasy.

The boy and his parents had looked then to the north. And there they saw the black storm cloud sweeping down off the mountain, that same thunderhead said to ride above the dark warlord's army.

The boy dropped from the parapet to the soft earth below. As he rose from the ground, he risked a quick glance to either side. No sign back here of the besiegers. And why should there be? The front gate was wide open, as always. Closing it would have been impossible without breaking the rusted hinges or wrenching the metal free from its pins. He pushed away the thought of his mother and father sitting as he knew they would be, side by side in the simple chairs that served as their thrones. They would be holding hands as they waited.

I should be with them, he thought. But he had to

do as they had told him to do. His mother's words had been urgent, his father's command simple and direct. No time to pause and think. Run! Hide! He wiped his eyes and ran. Within thirty strides he was in the embrace of the welcoming woods.

CHAPTER ONE

Don't Worry

"DON'T WORRY." MY brother, Paulek, smiles at me and goes back to sharpening his sword. "Remember what Father says. Worries never dug a ditch."

Hah! Easy for him to say. He's never used a shovel in his entire life. All he ever worries about is finding time to practice his swordsmanship, riding his horse, and looking like the proper heir to our little kingdom. As if looks could take the place of rational thought! Why, I sometimes wonder, am I the only one in our family who ever seems to entertain a thought as anything other than a transient visitor? Why is it that when our lord and creator Boh was handing out brains, my parents and my brother apparently got in line behind the hummingbirds? If it were not for my taking charge, nothing would ever get properly done around here.

By the head of the dragon! How would they ever get along without me?

And where are my parents?

"Brother," Paulek says, responding to the question I didn't realize I just asked out loud. His voice is as calm as only that of one who never fits more than one idea in his head at a time can be. "You know that Father and Mother can take care of themselves."

Hah! again. Has he never seen our good father standing out in the rain and looking up in wonder? Just standing there until I came running out with a cloak for him to put over his head? And what did Father say in reply to me when I observed that he was getting soaked to the skin?

"Lovely storm, isn't it?"

Has my brother never noticed that our dear mother is so innocent that she never has a cross word for anyone, even when they burn the porridge or forget yet again to repair the broken glass in the chapel window? She doesn't even seem to realize that there are actually things in this world that can do injury! Just last month I had to pull her away from stroking a bee as it rested on a sunflower. And what was her remark to me?

"Rashko dear, that bee would not have hurt me."

I suppose there has to be at least one responsible

person in every family, even a royal one. But why does it have to be me? And where in the name of Peter and Paul and all the other Blessed Svatys have my errant parents gone?

You might wonder why I am so concerned. After all, it was only two nights ago that they rode off—without even telling me that they were going or why they left in such haste in the middle of the night. It was only after they had failed to appear for both breakfast and the midday meal that I realized something was awry. I admit that eating is one of my own favorite pursuits, but few people enjoy food as much as do my parents and my brother. The way they eat, you would think that each mouthful was manna like that the Lord sent from heaven to Moses and the wandering Israelites.

Nie! I wish that image of lost wanderers had not come to me just now. If my parents had been leading those Israelites, they never would have made it out of the desert.

"Our parents are gone," I remind Paulek, trying not to panic. "It's been two nights now."

His response is predictable. He holds up his hand and counts off the nights on his fingers. "*Raz, dva.* One, two. *Ano.* That's right, Rashko." Then he smiles again and points up.

"Did you notice?" he asks. "Those little swallows

in that nest on the north tower are finally about to fly from their nests."

What's wrong with him? I know that, despite his size and his strength, he loves little creatures. But this is no time for watching birds. By the head of the dragon! Doesn't he realize he should be upset about this? Why should all this fall on my shoulders alone?

And that's not all. More had just been added to my burden in the last hour by that supercilious self-important messenger, who just left. Paulek had taken no notice when Georgi, the castle steward, whose deeply wrinkled face both shows that he has served our family forever and belies his surprising strength, came to tell us of the uninvited arrival outside the walls of Hladka Hvorka. My brother was too busy sharpening his sword. So it was left to me to follow Georgi to the gate and accept the message—and the insulting way it was delivered.

"Shall I read it to the young lord?" the foppish courier had sneered, looking down from his mount and speaking his words in a deliberately slow and overemphasized manner—as if addressing a lack-wit.

"*Nie*. I am literate enough to read quite well on my own, thank you," I replied as I broke the impressive wax seal on the thick parchment scroll and quickly perused the imperious words emblazoned upon it in a glowing flowery script so golden that it almost appeared to pulse on the page.

The Great and Honorable Baron Temny
Lord of the Twelve Lands
Informs You That His Excellence Will Soon Grace
Your Presence

Had I not been feeling such a mixture of impatience and distress I might have studied it longer. Despite its overblown language, the scroll was beautiful, indeed strangely attractive. But instead I curled my lip in displeasure, rolled it back up, and glared at the herald.

He seemed surprised. Had he expected me to clasp my hands to my chest and chuckle with glee?

"I've read it," I said, handing it back to him. He took it with ill grace and then went bouncing off on his palfrey, leaving me with a deep feeling of foreboding that has increased rather than lessened since his departure.

Who, I wonder, is Baron Temny? And what twelve lands is he lord of? Surely not the kingdoms, each with its own set of rulers, that surround our small, sleepy land? But when was the last time we heard anything from them, isolated as we are in our small valley with the mountains on four sides and the Silver Lands of the Fair Folk on the other?

"Paulek!" I try not to lose my composure. "Listen to me. We are about to have guests. Important ones, apparently."

This time my words sink in through his thick skull. My brother becomes as delighted as I am disconcerted. He actually puts down his sword.

"Guests?" he exclaims. He claps his big hands in delight like a child. Despite the fact that he is a year my elder and though but sixteen the second-tallest person in our kingdom, my brother oft displays such a shocking lack of dignity that I must be twice as serious to make up for it.

"Paulek," I plead, "please listen." But I might as well be speaking to a wall. A blissfully happy one.

"*Dobre, dobre!* Good, good! We must have a feast, a big one to welcome them. Right, Rashko? As Father says, the welcomed guest is always the best. Perhaps there may be some formidable fighters among them. Then we can have a sparring match or two. *Ano!* What fun!"

And off he goes to tell the servants what to do to get ready, even though I let Georgi know before attempting to speak with my brother. I have no doubt our competent old retainer already has things as well in hand as anyone can.

"Rosewater for the baths, Grace!" my brother shouts, a huge grin on his face. He waves at the servants already bustling back and forth to carry out various tasks. "*Chytro!* Quickly! Grace, fresh linens in the guest quarters! *Vd'aka.* Thank you. Charity, Cook needs to make extra bread. Too much is never enough for company, you know! Move along now, Grace. Janko, that's a good lad. *Dobre, dobre, dobre!*"

As if they don't already know how to do everything for our fortunate family twice as well as most of us can do for ourselves. Paulek disappears around the side of the chapel, still waving his hands like a choirmaster who thinks he's leading the chorus but is actually three verses behind the singers.

Amazingly, our servants never seem to resent the many demands made, ever so politely, true, by my parents and Paulek. If anything, they respond with a kind of amused courtesy. I'm the only one who's ever outraged.

Might it not be easier to be an orphan like our famous ancestor Pavol and have no parents or siblings to worry about?

"How do you put up with it?" I said to Georgi just last week after watching him help Paulek put on a pair of boots exactly like those I had just pulled onto my own feet all by myself.

He said nothing until Paulek, oblivious as always, was out the door. Then, with more of a paternal look on his face than I'd ever seen on my father's, Georgi leaned forward, laying his finger beside his nose to let me know that what he was disclosing was just between him and me.

But what he whispered to me was puzzling. "They need less help than one might imagine, young sir."

Then, to confuse me even more, Georgi tapped his fingers together and patted me on the shoulder, adding, "They are not thinkers like you, young sir."

Thinking of thinking, I think I am about to lose my mind. If the message that discourteous courier delivered was true, our uninvited guests will arrive in time for the evening meal. That's less than three hours. What should I do? Prepare for their arrival? Continue looking for my delinquent sire and dam? Who knows what they might have stumbled into! Stumbled into?

An unbidden and highly unwelcome image suddenly comes to my mind. The moat!

In old stories, such as those Baba Anya told Paulek and me when we were little, castle moats always hide fearsome creatures. Their dark waters are full of predatory fish or great snakes or reptiles, floating menaces waiting to devour anyone foolish enough to attempt to swim across.

Our moat is full of floating menaces too, but none of them are living. I doubt even the hardiest reptilian horror could survive long in its noisome depths. The springs have never had sufficient flow to overcome the stench of the sewage dumped into it daily from our privies.

In my fevered imagination I see my hapless parents returning in the middle of the night. Absentmindedly they forget that the drawbridge is up. They both tumble into those horrid waters. Then—the image is as inexorable as a bad dream from which I cannot wake—they sink beneath its surface, too dignified to shout for help.

This time I don't just think the old oath that harkens back to the founding of our line. I blurt it out.

"By the head of the dragon!"

I sprint to the stables and grab the long pole-hook that Edvard, our junior groom, uses—rather too infrequently—to fish things out of the thick brown water. I rush to the edge so fast that I almost lose my balance and fall in myself. Frantic, I set my feet in a solid swordsman's stance. I start stabbing, probing, prodding. Greasy bubbles rise to the surface and break, releasing gases so foul that my eyes water as I begin to lever things out and flip them onto the shore.

Nothing living, of course. Not from this poisonous stew. A worn jerkin. A coil of rotting rope. A broken-legged stool. A tangle of rotting chicken bones, guts, and feathers. Then the hook catches on something heavy and dead and man-sized. A fist clenches itself inside my belly. The submerged body is stuck on something, but I bend my knees and put my back into it. A shoulder breaks the surface and a sob escapes my throat. My eyes blur with tears.

Then I see the horns, the collar around its neck, the silent bell clogged with brown, slimy weeds.

A hand rests itself on my shoulder. "Sir," a familiar voice says, "you've found Matilde. Poor old blind goat. We all feared the worst for her when she vanished a week ago."

I turn to look down at Georgi's untroubled face. He lifts the pole from my grasp with one hand and twists it to flip the goat's corpse up from the moat's brown, grainy surface and onto the far bank.

Despite his slender frame, old Georgi is one of the strongest people I know. I've seen him pick up a horseshoe and absentmindedly twist it into a circle. (And that is no easy thing to do. It took me two tries to bend that iron back into its original shape.) Though Georgi's face is as wrinkled as a date and he's as bald as the top of a mountain, he's still straight and supple as a birch tree.

I'm now a head taller than our loyal aged overseer, but I still look up to him. He's unfailingly polite, always self-contained. I've never seen Georgi either angry or visibly delighted. Of course, I have caught a twinkle in his eye every now and then when my parents or brother have done something particularly foolish.

Like that time last summer when we were in the market. One of the vendors, a Russian jeweler who had not been to our little land before, was clearly trying to deceive my father. My father should have known that. Word had already been spread that the man was a cheat. Angry glances were being cast in his direction. But because the man was built like a bear and armed with a brace of knives slung across his chest, no one had done anything.

"Here, noble sir," the jeweler said in an unctuous voice to my father. He displayed the brooch in the palm of his right hand as he held up two fingers of his left. "Fine bargain. Only twenty pieces of silver."

I almost spoke up then. Even though I was young, I could see that brooch was worth no more than half that amount. But Georgi elbowed me in the ribs. I suppose, like me, he wanted to see how my poor innocent father would deal with such deceit.

"Oh," my father replied, a happy smile coming to his face. He plucked the brooch from the man's hand and pocketed it. "Only two pieces of silver?

Agreed." He dropped two silver coins on the man's table.

"*Nyet,*" the Russian merchant said, spreading all ten of his fingers twice to indicate the actual total. "*Nyet, nyet.* More than that."

"You want me to take more?"

It amazed me just how confused my guileless father became.

"*Vd'aka, pan.* Thank you, sir." My father reached out with his broad left hand—his right hand resting on the hilt of his sword—to scoop up the entire contents of a tray filled with rings. "These will do nicely," he said, patting his sword hilt as he eyed the glittering palmful. "*Dobre.*"

Then, before the startled merchant could speak another word, my father turned and walked away.

The Russian stood there, his mouth open as he stared at the empty tray. Even though it was obvious to me that my father had no idea what he'd just done, that cheat had just been paid back in kind. All through the market people were nodding at my father, their pleased expressions turning into even broader smiles as my father casually passed out rings to each of them.

For a moment it appeared the Russian was about to follow my father and protest. Or perhaps he thought to do more. His right hand was twitching toward one of those two knives. That was when Georgi stepped in front of the man and grasped the jeweler's shoulder with such strength that the cheating merchant gasped. Georgi leaned close and whispered a few firm words in the man's ear. The color drained from the burly Russian's florid face. Within moments he had packed up his cart and departed rapidly from our marketplace and our land, never to be seen again.

Good old Georgi. Who else could turn a moment of confusion on my poor father's part into an act of justice?

It's a measure of how distracted I've been by the strange absence of my parents that I haven't thought to seek Georgi's counsel. Not that he would have told me directly what to do. Georgi has this way of offering diffident suggestions, hesitant hints that— when followed—may lead one to a conclusion.

"The junior groom will bury poor old Matilde, sir," Georgi says. He pats my hand reassuringly. "No need to worry yourself about her. But just now, I do believe there is something else at which you might want to look." He motions with his head toward the window forty feet above us. "Up on your father's dresser."

Dva

THE BOY RAN till he felt himself reaching the limit of his strength. Still, despite the knife of pain in his side, he urged himself farther. Just ahead was the crest of the hill that rose up from the middle of the old forest like the head of a bird from its nest.

From that spot, he knew, St'astie Dom would come into view. He could see what happened. Perhaps it would not be that bad. Then, when it was safe again, he could return to his home and his family.

A tall ancient pine rose from the top of the hill. The stubs of its dead lower limbs were like a ladder. He had climbed it often before. Despite his fatigue he struggled his way up it again. More than once he almost lost his grip and came close to a deadly fall. He paid no heed as his clothes caught and tore on sharp branches, as his fingernails broke and his bleeding palms were blackened by resin and bark.

His breathing was ragged and painful as he reached the top, wrapped one arm around the trunk, and parted the green-needled branches aside so that he could see. His home lay there in the heart of the valley. It seemed, from this distance, a small structure made from a child's blocks. But the black cloud that now loomed overhead was still large. It glowed and flickered as if it were a living thing threaded with fire.

In front of the castle a mass of black ants seemed to have gathered, waiting behind one mounted figure that stood a long spear cast ahead of them.

"The Dark Lord," the boy whispered. Far as it was from him, that figure was amazingly clear. Though it was impossible from his great distance, it seemed as if the boy could make out the arrogant features of the man's face, see the sneer on his lips.

Now, the boy thought, he will call for our surrender and it will be over. Perhaps he and his parents would have to live as peasants or servants to their new ruler. But that would not be so bad if they could just be together.

However, such was not to be.

The Dark Lord raised his hand, his palm glowing as if it were a burning brand. He lowered it and great gouts of lightning came pouring down from the black cloud.

Every bolt struck the castle. By the time the great roar of thunder reached the shocked boy in his tree, it was over. St'astie Dom was gone, obliterated, wiped from the face of the earth along with every living being within its walls.

The boy let go his grip and fell.

CHAPTER TWO

The Invitation

ON TOP OF my father's dresser?

As I start to rush away I think I hear Georgi mumble under his breath.

It stops me in my tracks. "What was that?" I ask.

"Nothing, young sir," he replies, "just clearing my throat."

Georgi's face is composed, devoid of any expression other than his usual readiness to please. I believe, though, that he did say something. Was it that old proverb I've never understood? "Pity the one whose heart is bigger than his eyes"?

I hardly pause as I pass the great tapestry that tells the story of our mighty ancestor Pavol. Usually, whenever I start to walk past it, it stops me and I study it for long minutes, feeling that somehow its mysterious weave holds a special message meant for me alone in its images of Pavol, the mighty dragon he defeated, his magical pouch, and all the other rather curious figures—including armed men, revelers at a feast, and some sort of fair with Gypsy jugglers and the like.

But not today.

I pound up the four flights of stairs, reach the open door that leads into the royal chamber. The first thing I notice is that the bed is still unmade. Then, as I take a few steps into the room, I see, just beyond the bed, a dust cloth left in the middle of the floor. Strange. Though they come from overly devout and underly imaginative parents, Grace, Grace, Grace, and Charity, the four sisters who are our chambermaids, are neat as pins. They never fail to make our beds and would not dream of leaving cleaning things lying about.

Then my eyes discern something stranger. It shimmers from atop the largest chest of drawers to the left of the bed. It's a smooth subtle effulgence of light. None of the flickering one would see from a candle. I step slowly toward it.

Why am I thinking of a moth being attracted by a flame?

I stop short, lean forward to study it.

Though I've peered in their bedroom at least twice in the last two days, I've not noticed it till now. Of course, I'd not been seeking a shimmering scroll small enough to fit into one's palm. I'd been looking about for two wayward adults. Why would I have looked atop the highest dresser? Was it a place where I might have found either of my parents perched? Well, perhaps.

I resist the urge to trace its golden script with my fingertips. Where have I seen writing like this before?

I lift my left hand slowly toward the edge of the thing. The card quivers in my hand as I pluck it up gingerly between my thumb and forefinger. Best not to grasp things of magic too hard or too long, for only magic has this look and feel. I flip it onto the bed.

I read it—but only once, and silently at that. Speaking words scribed in such a script might cast a glamour over me as strong as that which I now believe bemisted the already foggy minds of my dear parents. I close my eyes, but I still see those lines.

Come Thee, Come Thee
O'er the Way
To a Ball So Fair and Gay

Though I kept this perilously seductive card in my grasp for no more than a heartbeat, I feel its effect on me. True, I don't pack an overnight bag, saddle up my horse, and ride unceremoniously away as did my parents. However, its magic works another way. Suddenly, as I think of my parents, I am actually able to see them.

It's as if I am looking through a window in the midst of the air. Before me is a landscape of fantastically beautiful trees and flowers, graceful arching towers, and frozen fountains of shimmering, singing waters. A fair field of folk are there, all heartbreakingly gorgeous. My parents are in their company. Father and Mother are, I note with a bit of pride, nearly as physically attractive as any of the Faerie. Further, they are so solid, so self-contained that they stand out in that crowd. They look regal. I can understand why they would be welcome as ornaments at any party, even one thrown by Fair Folk.

It's clear to me in this moment that, unlike other mortal beings enchanted by the Faerie Lands and unwilling to leave them, my parents will certainly come back home. After all, we are of Pavol's blood, a lineage favored by those of the Silver Lands.

I can imagine my father's reaction as he read that invitation. Rather than being ensorcelled and glamoured, he felt honored. I can imagine him saying to Mother as he showed it to her: "What a nice invitation. Shall we accept?"

And then her response: "Well, dear, it would be the neighborly thing to do."

I'm guessing that its only undue effect on them was to hasten their departure, make them absentminded about letting their worried son know where they were going.

I breathe a sigh of relief. They'll not be seduced by drink or gluttony or the pleasures of the flesh that have proven so ruinous to other mere humans who've entered the silvery realm to either never return or drift wanly back as withered shells of their former selves.

The image shimmers, bringing them closer. Now I can hear their conversation.

"Would you not like a cup of this punch?" a tall, graceful lord in shimmering robes is asking Father.

"*Vd'aka,* thank you, gentle sir," my father replies. "But I'm not thirsty now, y' know."

Then I hear my mother. She is politely chatting with a group of women whose effulgent beauty is striking. Yet Mother's gentle loveliness still stands out. One of them proffers her a tray of sweets.

"How kind, but I am not at all hungry. Ah, those little golden snakes do such a lovely job of holding up your hair, my lady. Their hissing is rather musical."

My father's voice draws my attention again. He's swapping hunting yarns as a group of broad-shouldered Faerie lords lean in to listen.

"*Ano, ano,* yes, yes. I am sure that a griffin is challenging game to go after, but there was this great black boar in our woods."

I've heard such conversations a hundred times before. All is well. But then I suddenly remember what I have been told about the Realm by Baba Anya. Time passes differently there for mere mortals. The Fair Folk, it is said, are untouched by the ravages of years. They are like us in some ways. In fact, legend says, a mortal man or woman may even marry one of the Fair Folk. Their children, neither fully Faerie nor mere mortal, may choose to live in one land or the other. According to one of Baba Anya's more fanciful tales, such offspring of the two peoples are benevolent and seek to do good—though usually in hidden ways. Also, if they choose to live among humans, those doubly heritaged ones are unusually long-lived.

However, when any normal human ventures into the Silver Lands, that unfortunate mortal is pulled out of time. A week there may be a year here. Mortals who enter the Realm for what seems a brief visit may return home to find that everyone they know has grown old and died.

I cannot imagine my parents making that mistake. But even a brief stay at a party such as this may mean they'll be gone for a fortnight. Time for far too much to happen in their absence.

I look more intently at the picture in that airy window.

My father is speaking again, this time to the tallest of the Fair Folk, one who wears a diadem of diamonds.

"*Vd'aka*," Father says, "thank you for inviting us to this party."

A frown furrows the brow of the Faerie lord. "I sent no invitation."

What? A terrible thought comes to me. "*Nie!*" I shout. "No!"

My father and my mother start to turn their heads in my direction.

The scene vanishes. For a moment the room around me seems to spin as I try to regain my bearings.

I close my eyes, trying to see them again at the Faerie ball. I hear the music faintly, smell the delicious delicate odor of the food and wine of the Fair Folk. Then, like smoke blown away by a sudden breeze, it's gone.

I quickly open my eyes, brace my hands to keep from falling. I'm leaning over the bed, my face almost touching the treacherous surface of that false invitation. Its pull dizzies me.

I force my legs to move, backing away until I feel the edge of the open window with my outstretched hand. I turn and lean over the sill. The wind that touches my face rises up from the moat.

Dank, odiferous, vile. Excellent. Just what I need.

I breathe its disgusting stench in and out several times until the allure no longer overwhelms my senses.

Thank the lucky stars that my brother was not the one to find that card first. Then there would have been three missing members of our family.

"Rashko!"

My brother's feet thudding up the stairs accompany his voice. He'll be here in a heartbeat. I grab the dust rag and toss it on top of the bed just as Paulek enters the room. The cloth covers the card. Paulek will not see it. The day when pigs can fly will arrive long before the time when my brother picks up a soiled cloth.

"*Bratcek!*" His big hand slams affectionately into my arm. Paulek has never known his own strength. If I were not as big and muscular as he is—despite the fact that he calls me "small brother"—that friendly blow might have dislocated my shoulder.

"Rashko," he continues, "I've come to tell you that . . ."

He pauses. My brother's sky blue eyes are glazing over more than they usually do when he tries to form four sentences in a row. Even from its place of concealment beneath the dust rag, that treacherous invitation card is attempting to exert its pull upon him. I grasp him by the elbow, steering him out of the room and shutting the door behind me.

Georgi is waiting in the corridor. The apologetic look on his face tells me he tried without success to head my brother off before he reached the room. I wonder how Georgi, who also saw that treacherous invitation, was able to resist its pull. That dust rag was probably dropped in the room by Grace or Grace or Grace or Charity as Georgi hustled her out before the spell could claim her.

Good thing, that. I shudder at the thought of a mere chambermaid, enthralled by enchantment, attempting to enter the Silver Lands. The Fair Ones have been said to express their displeasure at such uninvited intruders by turning them into uglier-than-usual toads.

I nod at Georgi over my brother's shoulder. I saw it.

Georgi nods and holds up his ring of keys.

Zamkni to! "Lock it," I mouth.

Georgi nods again.

I probably do not need to be secretive. Paulek is oblivious to subtlety. He hardly notices Georgi's presence unless he needs something. It's not that my brother is unkind. He simply accepts that he's privileged.

"Just the way it is, y'know," he would probably say.

Then he'd quote one of Father's silly proverbs.

"Tradition and law are sisters," or something of that sort.

I groan inwardly. Why am I the only one in our family with any common sense?

As we make our way down the stairs Paulek remembers why he was seeking me out.

"Our company is almost here." He grins. "I've seen the dust cloud from their horses coming down the road!"

"Nie." I groan. Out loud this time. I thought it would still be hours before they arrived. Did those brief seconds I spent gazing into the Realm make time pass more quickly for me?

Unfortunately, I pause just a little too long to ponder that question. My brother's friendly elbow not only comes close to cracking a rib, it nearly knocks me down the stairs.

"Come, brother," Paulek laughs, reaching to grab my wrist. "You know what Father says. Visitors always bring new tales."

Yes, I think as I allow him to drag me down the stairs. No doubt about that. But will they be stories with happy endings?

And what sort of visitors lure your parents away with false and ensorcelled invitations?

Traja

As THE BOY fell he caught a glimpse of the shining lands whose borders changed from day to day and moment to moment. For the land of the Fair Folk occupies the fifth direction—that one other than the usual east, south, west, and north. Now, though, its silver light flickered and then vanished.

The Fair Folk, he thought, have seen the destruction of my family. They will show themselves no longer to our conquered land. They are sad.

His body struck a branch so cushioned with needles that it stopped his fall for an instant, almost like a wide green hand trying to catch him. However, he did not grasp at it with his own hands. Instead he allowed himself to slip limply from its embrace.

Let me join my family, he thought, falling again.

But the arms that caught him before he struck

the ground were not green nor those of a tree. They were human and as heavily muscled as the chest that he thudded into. It knocked the wind from him and for a moment he gasped like a fish out of water, his traitorous body still struggling to breathe despite his wish to let his life end here.

"Child," a deep voice said. "It is not your time to die yet."

CHAPTER THREE

Two Friends

THE FIRST THING I think when I reach the ramparts and discern the size of the cloud coming across the valley toward our tall hill is that "invited guests" may not be the right words for a body of riders large enough to throw up so much dust.

Army of invaders is more like it.

The second thing that comes to my mind is to wonder about the whereabouts of our dogs, Ucta and Odvaha. A party of men that large may have a pack of dogs with them. Great vicious wolfhounds, perhaps, loping beside their destriers. If such dogs should encounter my two faithful friends, it would not bode well.

For the wolfhounds.

Where are you? I think.

Here.

Here.

Their minds answer me from the direction of Stary Les, the forest of great trees that begins near the foot of our hill and to the left of the main road.

I look over at Paulek. He's bouncing up and down in excitement as the ominous cloud of dust grows closer. As always, only I can hear Ucta's and Odvaha's silent voices. He loves them as much as I do. There's no doubt their devotion to him is just as strong. They'd give their lives to protect Paulek. But his relationship is different and has been from the start.

I remember the day we first met them. I was ten years old and Paulek was eleven. Both of us were certain that nothing in the world could ever harm us. Each of us was well-armed with bows and arrows over our shoulders and short sword at our sides. We were already accomplished horsemen. Our mounts were fine, spirited steeds. We thought ourselves two knights out to do great deeds. Perhaps we'd find a dragon to fight as our great ancestor did long ago.

To be honest, I was not that eager to find a real dragon. It wasn't as if we were carrying Pavol's legendary pouch. I knew my older brother and I were playing at being knights. Paulek, though, really thought he was one.

Still, each of us had been well enough trained by

then to shoot an arrow through the knothole in a piece of wood sixty paces away. The sword training we'd received from our father and Black Yanosh had made each of us—big for our ages and strong as we already were—a match for most grown men.

Before we left, Georgi came out with something wrapped in cloth.

"Young sir," he said, knuckling his forehead and holding the bundle up, "you and your fine brother might have need of this."

"Come along, Rashko," Paulek said, pacing his horse back and forth. He was impatient to set out on our valorous quest. "No time to waste. Remember Father's words. The arrow not fired never strikes a target."

I reined my horse in to take what Georgi handed me. It was warm and the good smell that came from within was familiar.

"Bread and bacon, young sir," Georgi said.

"*Dakujem,*" I said. "Thank you."

A knowing smile came to his face as he placed his finger alongside his nose. "Meant to be shared," Georgi replied.

I placed the bundle into my saddlebag and then forgot about it as we rode along. It was a beautiful day. A balmy breeze came down from the Tatras. A golden eagle described great circles in the sky above us. The warm spring light shimmered from the leaves of alders along the small singing streams.

Despite the lovely day, finding great deeds to accomplish proved harder than we had expected. Our parents' reputation combined with their light-handed rule of our diminutive dukedom had done little to improve the opportunities for knight errantry. There was no obvious iniquity. Not a single maiden in distress being kidnapped by dark villains. No huge, bloodthirsty monsters threatening the lives of the peasants diligently working their fields.

In Mesto, the small town at the center of our land, all was equally and boringly at peace. People went about their business unmolested by ogres, trolls, or evil beings of any sort. Merchants smiled, waved for us to stop. I was tempted. Some sort of fair was going on. I saw bright-colored wagons and the painted shapes of an eye and a hand on a flag—the sure sign of a fortune-teller. A troupe of entertainers was just setting up near the blacksmith. I especially wanted to stay and watch the Gypsy jugglers, but Paulek was impatient.

A thought had come to him. Undoubtedly it was a bit lonely after wandering companionless through my brother's mind.

"I have an idea!" he said, slapping his palm to his forehead.

I almost fell off my horse. Even at ten I knew how rare a statement that was from Paulek.

"I know just where we can go," he continued.

That was when I got worried. "Just where we can go" could only mean the one place that we should not go. It was. . .

"Cierny Les," he said. "That's where we'll find some excitement."

How right he was. I groaned inwardly. Cierny Les, the Black Forest, in the north of our dukedom, was nothing like Stary Les, the Old Forest. Stary Les, close to our castle, had once, before the arrival of our famous ancestor Pavol the Good, been a place of deadly peril. Now, though, it was as safe as an old family friend.

"Our parents told us that those who are wise always avoid Black Forest."

Wrong thing to say. I bit my tongue as soon as I uttered those words. I'd forgotten what passed for logic with my brother.

"Of course," Paulek said, a pleased grin on his handsome, innocent face. "But not those who are brave! As Father says, 'Wisdom and adventure seldom travel together.' Thus there must be some sort of adventure there. Let's go!"

Off he went, me trailing behind him and hoping I had learned enough of Cesta from Uncle Jozef to save my reckless brother from his own eagerness.

"Cesta" means the Road. I suppose I should tell you a little about it, since Cesta—and Georgi's parting gift—was so important that day. So here is a bit of what old Uncle Jozef taught us about the way.

The Road teaches us to give one thing for another.

That, as I said, is a little about Cesta.

That is how Uncle Jozef has always taught the way. He answers questions with simple sayings. Simpler than even one of my father's proverbs.

Or Uncle Jozef gives even less than words. Only a gesture. Such as pointing to his nose or knocking his knuckles against a water jug. Then he leaves me stewing in my own juices for days and weeks, trying to figure it out.

Until suddenly, in the most obvious way, Cesta becomes clear to me. I see the path to follow. For a moment, at least.

Then I think about it and it becomes even more complicated.

Suffice it to say, my foolhardy brother and I stayed on the path Paulek had chosen. We rode on over hill and dale, across brook and stream, down valley and up, until we came to the edge of the Black Forest. We'd left all ways but one behind. Before us the narrow twisting path that dove down beneath the old, ominous branches of the oaks into the dark silence where no birds sang and the shadows grew strong.

"Dobre, dobre," Paulek chortled. "This is perfect. There has to be adventure here."

"Ano," I replied.

How else could I have answered him? Other than we are doomed as doomed can be?

We did not have to venture far. We rounded the first corner in the wood and suddenly there they were. They stood in the center of the path. They were huge and menacing. Each of them was twice as large as a bull mastiff. Their coats were black as coal and their eyes red as flame. Their sharp, gleaming teeth were bared. The tense muscles in their shoulders rippled as they crouched, ready to spring. Their deep-throated growls made the air seem to throb.

My right hand began to slide slowly down toward the side where my short sword hung.

Although he has never been imaginative enough to be terrified—he always leaves that up to me— Paulek was impressed enough to rein in his horse. He looked over at me—as he always does when he gets us into trouble.

"What now, Rashko?" he asked in a calm voice. As if I would know?

Surprisingly, I did. My hand continued past my sword hilt to the saddlebag with Georgi's package in it. I pulled it out, unfolded the cloth.

"Tu," I said. "Here."

Then I tossed each of the wolves a piece of bacon wrapped in bread. One thing for another.

Each of them caught their bread and bacon in midair and gulped it down. Then they began to wag their tails.

"Oh," Paulek said. "Nice doggies."

My brother, as I have mentioned earlier, has always loved animals. It was Paulek and not me who was always bringing home little bunnies or fawns from the woods. I was the one who returned them to the places where he found them after my mother explained that their parents would be worried about them. Having two puppies to pet—even ones big enough to rip his throat out with one bite—was much more fun than playing at being a knight errant. Before I could say a word, Paulek had hopped off his horse. By the time I climbed down both giant wolves were on their backs, their tongues hanging out as he rubbed their stomachs.

"What shall we name them, Rashko?" he said.

"Ucta," I said without hesitation, not knowing why but knowing it was right as I caught the eye of the one with the white marks on his chest and front paws. "Honor."

Ano, I heard back, a low growling voice in my mind.

"And you," I said, looking at the one who was

sable dark as night, as deep an ebony as the thought of blackness itself, "you are Odvaha. Courage."

Ano, kamarat. Yes, friend, it answered.

All plans for adventure vanished from Paulek's mind. He couldn't wait to get back to share our new friends with my parents.

"Will they come with us?" he asked me.

Ano.

Ano.

"Yes, they will."

Tails wagging like the big dogs we would tell everyone they were, they followed us home.

We soon learned that not only would my parents accept them without question as two lost doggies looking for a pair of boys to be their masters, but that Ucta and Odvaha would be our most faithful friends. They were always ready to go anywhere with us and, if necessary, to risk their lives for ours. All that in exchange for a gift of bread and bacon—or something a bit more than that. Cesta being Cesta.

THE CLOUD OF dust has reached the bottom of our hill. I see banners and figures emerging from it. The insignias on the two flags are not ones I've seen before. The first one pictures a black cloud beneath which a red-mailed fist holds a twisting yellow serpent in its grasp. The second banner features the grim image of a black sword thrust through a bleeding heart. My guess is that their owner is not a proponent of gentle debate. That guess is strengthened by the fact that those flags are flying from the glistening steel tips of two long lances. Also the two broad-shouldered men holding those lances have the cold faces of killers. Plus there are at least thirty other armed and just as hard-bitten mounted troopers behind them.

How lovely.

They all seem a bit disappointed that our draw-bridge has been ratcheted up since their messenger's departure. Georgi and I made sure of that. It's a good thing we did. I see no friendly intent in the scarred and helmeted faces below—as well as sufficient weaponry to wage a small war or two. There are crossbows and bundles of quarrels, bows and quivers of arrows, long swords, lances, balls and chains, pikes, and enough knives to supply a bevy of butcher shops.

The lanky herald who visited us a few hours ago impatiently kicks his heels into the side of his mount and makes his way to the front of the mob that is glaring up at Georgi and me on the battlements.

"Hello, the castle," he calls, cupping his hands around his mouth. "Lower the drawbridge. We are friends. We come in peace."

Now, why do I doubt that?

Styria

THE BOY LOOKED up at the broad face of the bearded and burly man who had saved him from having his brains dashed out by the rocks of the hillside. The boy was used to kindness, having seen it all his life in the faces and actions of his parents. He saw a similar kindness, marked by sorrow, in the rough features of his savior. And there was something else here that the boy had never seen before.

Grimness, the boy thought. Kind though those eyes might be, somehow the boy knew that the one who held him as easily as the boy could hold a feather would make a formidable foe.

The big man, who was built like a bear, placed the boy on his feet.

"There," the man said. Then he waited, his hands on his knees, bent over in a stance that was almost deferential toward the small figure dwarfed by his massive body.

"They killed them all," the boy said in a small, clear voice. He wondered why his voice was so calm, why he was not crying.

"*Ano,*" the man agreed. His face looked more sorrowful now.

"Will you help me avenge them?" the boy asked.

"*Ano a nie.* Yes and no," the man said. "I will help you help yourself."

The boy nodded, not totally understanding, perhaps. Or perhaps he did, for even at that young age there was something in him that was remarkable.

"It will take time," the man said. "Years for you to learn the way."

Another nod.

"Then we will begin."

The man straightened up and held out a hand. The boy took it. The man started to walk and then paused when the boy tugged at his hand.

"You knew my parents?"

"You may say that. They were good and kind."

"Who are you?"

"You may call me Uncle Tomas." The man held a thick finger up to his lips and then pressed it forward twice as if making marks in the air. "Two things you must promise me now."

"*Ano,*" the boy agreed. There was no hesitation. The man who called himself Uncle Tomas marked that and nodded.

"First, you must always listen."

"I will always listen."

His small voice was as solemn as that of a knight taking an oath on his sword.

"Second, you must never again speak the name you were given by your family. There are other ears that might hear it. From now on, you will have another name. From now on you will be Pavol."

"Pavol," the boy said.

CHAPTER FOUR

Lowered Defenses

"By the head of the dragon!" someone next to me whispers in an awed voice.

I look over to my left. Zelezo, our castle black-smith has come up to join me in the battlement. In fact, nearly all of the others who reside in Hladka Hvorka have climbed the steep stone stairs up to the forward rampart to peer down at the well-weaponed force glaring up at us. Cook is there as well as Jazda, our groom, and his twelve-year-old son, Hreben, the stable boy. Our four maids, Grace, Grace, Grace, and Charity. Janko and Juraj, our two serving boys. Georgi and myself. Twelve of us in all. The only others not in sight are Brana and Dvihatch, our two elderly gatemen—who have remained at their posts in the barbican—and Black Yanosh.

I'm not surprised that he is missing. Nor do I think for a minute that he is unaware of the threat outside our walls. It is Black Yanosh's way to make himself scarce at times such as this. Watch and wait, see the weakness of any opponent before showing your hand.

Thinking of hands, aside from myself and burly Zelezo, who's holding his hammer, the hands of the rest of us are empty. We are most certainly not an army.

Nothing unusual about that. Like all of the generations of Hladka Hvorka since Pavol the Good, my parents have never seen the need for any sort of army. Their only wish, an innocent one, has been to rule well and be left alone. Our lands are not on any main route to anywhere. The road that leads up here ends at our castle after passing through the one gap in the High Tatra Mountains that circle us like the embrace of stone arms. Thus there's been no history of armies marching back and forth through here on their way to conquering someplace else. No one in any of the twelve surrounding kingdoms and baronies has ever shown any interest in our lands, which are fertile enough to support our people, but produce nothing of any greater worth than wheat, vegetables, a few cattle, and the honey that is our valley's one export and the only thing that seems to draw outsiders up here. Our family has inherited wealth enough to support us and help those in need, but we have never shown ourselves to have the sort of riches that would inspire greed.

There are certain wild rumors that Hladka Hvorka hides some sort of great secret, hidden here since the time of Pavol the Good. But the thought of making such a long journey and then having to confront my mother and father has always discouraged fortune seekers. For some reason, despite my parents' openness, good nature, and generosity, people often appear to be a bit awed by my mother and father.

It is not just that my parents are both direct descendants of a man who defeated a dragon or that my mother is reputed to have magical powers and a touch of Faerie blood. There are also some rather fantastic stories of things they supposedly have done. All of which happened before Paulek and I were born. None of which I quite believe.

Can you imagine my gentle mother calling down lightning to strike a water demon that had taken up residence in the swamp of Bahno Diera, where it was luring people to the edge of the water to drown them? Or my father wrestling an ogre that had been stealing sheep? My father is strong, I admit. But it is difficult for me to believe that he lifted such a creature over his head, walked to the edge of a cliff, and then asked (in a reasonable voice) if it would prefer to descend into that valley which led to the pass out of our land on its own feet never to return again or take a, one might say, faster route. Purportedly, that ogre indicated in a carefully polite voice that walking was its preference.

However, though such legends of my parents' prowess are probably exaggerated, Father and Mother have shown themselves now and then to be, in an absentminded way, rather formidable.

As are the moat and the thick walls of Hladka Hvorka. It would take a far larger force than the one I see below us and extremely sophisticated siege engines to breech our defenses. Although most of those within our walls are not trained warriors, everyone has been taught what to do if the time might come when we would need to defend ourselves here.

Unlike most castles, there are no structures made only of wood within the smooth, doubly thick walls of Hladka Hvorka. Visitors frequently comment that our castle seems to not have been built but to have grown out of the living stone of the hill itself. It's a comment that I always find amusing. I am sure there is a reasonable explanation for the organic appearance of our home. Perhaps some technique of making a stone-like substance that can be poured and shaped—some process forgotten with the passage of years. In any event, fire arrows can do little damage.

I mentally tally our assets. We have two wells of clear, sweet water inside the castle. There are enough stores of food and firewood to allow us to remain inside here for months and outlast any invaders. The moat is wide and deep. The parapets of the castle have been well made, with embrasures to shelter defenders from the arrows of any attackers. And we have bows and arrows in our armory that could be fired down through the arrow slits in the embrasures. A few of us know how to use them to deadly and discouraging effect. Especially my brother and I. But thinking of Paulek, where is he now? He's not on the battlements with the rest of us.

No matter. We'll be fine for now as long as we do not . . .

"Lower the drawbridge," a clear, friendly voice calls from the main courtyard below.

I spin around to look. It's Paulek, of course. While I was lost in thought, he went down to the gatehouse.

I descend the stairs as fast as I can.

"Zastav!" I shout. "Stop!"

My voice goes unheard over the rattle of the great chains, the screeching of metal as the portcullis is raised, followed by the earth-shaking *ka-whomp* of the great iron-bound planks of the bridge as they thud down onto the other side.

Too late. But even if I'd called out louder, would I have been obeyed? I'm the younger brother. With our parents gone—and what a time for them to be missing!—he's in charge. And if Paulek makes his mind up to do something, I cannot just tell him no. With a little time, I can manage to convince him to do what is best. But there is no time for that now. The entire mounted host, led by their two bulky flag bearers, comes clomping over the bridge and into the main courtyard in the heart of Hladka Hvorka. All I can do now is step aside. As he passes me, the helmeted flag bearer on the right turns his head to leer down at me. Part of what looks like a long scar on his cheek is just visible through the helmet.

"*Dobry' den, pan,*" he growls. "Good day, sir." His guttural voice is as thick with sarcasm as it is with some sort of accent. Austrian, perhaps. Many of that nation are mercenaries.

Then he spits at my feet. I let it spatter on my right boot, not giving him the satisfaction of stepping back. I hold his gaze until he is so far past me that he needs to turn his head or lose his balance.

This is not good.

I look around for Paulek. I'm not quite certain what I am going to say to him. I'm angry and worried at the same time. Now that these armed men are inside, our defenses down, they may attack us at any time. I feel the weight of the sword at my side. Perhaps we might still stand a chance if we take action quickly enough. I can sense Black Yanosh somewhere nearby. I picture him thoughtfully stroking his mustache as he watches.

We are here.

The voices of Ucta and Odvaha are close, no longer in the woods below the castle. Unseen and cautious, they've followed the soldiers and are just outside the gate, waiting for my call. But I can do nothing until I find my brother.

"Vitajte kamarati," a welcoming voice shouts. Paulek's voice.

He's standing halfway up the steps where he can be seen. His arms are held open. There's a big smile on his face, probably because he is always looking for sparring partners. Lots of these men look to be formidable fighters. Plenty of new opponents for him to cross swords with in what he thinks would be comradely combat! Ha!

"Welcome, friends," he repeats in his deep, resonant voice. "Welcome to Hladka Hvorka. I am Prince Paulek. I greet you in the name of my father and my mother, who are both, er, away at the moment."

It's a properly princely greeting. Paulek both sounds and looks regal as he poses there. With his best gold-embroidered cloak over his broad shoulders, he is impressive indeed. His height, his muscular arms and legs and broad chest make him even more impressive. His handsome features are not at all diminished by the hook nose that has characterized every male in our family since Duke Pavol the First.

Now, if only he could think as well as he looks.

The lanky herald dismounts, struts forward to stand below Paulek, then does an extravagant bow, sweeping off his feathered cap as he does so.

"Young man," the herald says, "we thank you for your welcome. And now it is my pleasure, my honor . . ." He pauses, then shouts his next words as if they were meant not just for our ears but for all the land around: "TO INTRODUCE HE WHO IS BELOVED BY ALL, A LION AMONG MEN, THE GREAT BARON TEMNY!"

His declamation is followed by the loud thuds of the mounted men pounding their fists against shields and striking the butts of lances against the stone of the courtyard. As one they chant their leader's name.

"TEMNY! TEMNY! TEMNY! TEMNY!"

It's impressive. I've now moved across the courtyard and mounted the steps to stand near my brother and get a better view of the ominous spectacle being acted out before us. A figure in lacquered armor on a prancing chestnut steed is crossing the drawbridge and passing through our gate. Mist—and where did that come from?—swirls around him. He's all in red—save for his left hand, which is encased in a silver gauntlet. Because his helm is cradled under his left arm, I can see his face. It's as disquieting as the raised sword held high aloft in his right hand. His vulpine features are narrow and the small teeth shown in his wide smile appear as sharp and pointed as those of a weasel. His close-set eyes are shaded by eyebrows that join together in the middle of his forehead and are as thick and red as the long hair that falls down to his shoulders. The look in his blue eyes, which dart constantly back and forth, is far from magnanimous and honorable. Vicious and hungry, I'd say.

From the length of his legs and the size of the horse he's riding, he's at least as tall as Paulek and I. Though his raised right arm seems almost skeletally thin, there's enough strength in it for him to hold high that heavy blade without wavering.

He sweeps the sword down so that it is level

before him. The shouting and thudding of fists and lances suddenly stops. The sword points, interestingly enough, at my chest. But only for a heartbeat. The baron twirls and sheathes it in a motion that is as elegant and threatening as was its previous position.

"Young princes," he trills. His voice is higher than I'd expected, but as smooth as oil. "*Dakujem*. Thank you."

He then makes a wide gesture with his right arm, as theatrical as his herald. The two of them must spend a bit of time practicing in front of mirrors. His hand ends up thrust toward the gateway, palm up, fingers extended.

"And now I introduce to you my dear and lovely daughter, unmatched in grace and beauty, the fairest of innocent flowers, the delightful Princess Poteshenie."

I look out of the corner of my eye at Paulek. His mouth is open in eager anticipation. All his defenses are lowered.

Not good. Not good at all.

Another mounted figure appears on the other side of the moat, as if conjured up out of the curtain of mist that rose there after the baron's entrance. The mist swirls as the white horse moves, picking its way delicately forward. Then the white cloud parts to reveal a slender figure dressed all in virginal white sitting side-saddle, a veil modestly covering her face. It's a graceful, carefully demure entrance. But her arrival seems as foreboding to me as the baron's. I also wonder what is moving inside the large wicker cage fastened to the back of her saddle.

The princess halts her palfrey beside the baron. She pauses, for effect. Then she languidly lifts up her hand. It's a long, finely shaped white hand, the sort a courtier would kneel to kiss in a chivalrous saga. She pushes back her veil and lifts her chin to reveal her face. Oval, perfect, framed by long, lustrous hair that is as red as the baron's. Even from fifty feet away I can smell her perfume. Its scent is so heady that it makes me a bit dizzy. Her pouty lips are pursed, slightly parted, moist and trembling. She lowers her chin and lifts her eyes to look up at us.

Come to me. Come to Princess Poteshenie, the princess of happiness . . .

Zobud! The breathless voices of Ucta and Odvaha speak as one. *Wake up!*

I blink my eyes. My vision, which had begun to blur, is clear again. I look toward the drawbridge. My wolf brothers are there, sitting up on their haunches, alert and ready.

Dakujem, I think to them. Thank you.

I turn my gaze back to Poteshenie. For the briefest moment it seems as if the princess herself becomes indistinct. It's as if the air moves and reshapes itself around her. Something trembles there, like those nearly invisible strands of spider's web that sometimes catch across one's face. Do her loveliness and youth seem to fade? The moment passes too quickly for me to tell. I blink my eyes and she is just as she was before. Exquisitely beautiful, perfect . . . too perfect.

I no longer feel drawn to her. From the subtle displeasure in her eyes and the way she presses her lips together, she knows she's lost me. Her look hardens even more as she turns back to look over her shoulder at my two four-legged friends. She knows it was their voiceless call that snapped me out of her spell. I'll not be caught by her again. Attractive as she may appear on the outside, I see that what's within this princess is not at all lovely. She's as alluring as a plum with a worm in its heart. I no longer find her attractive at all.

But not Paulek. His mouth is wide open now. His eyes are glazed.

"P-P-Princess," he stammers. Then he descends the steps like a sleepwalker, kneels before her, reaches up and takes that perfect hand to kiss it.

Everyone is looking at the two of them.

Except for the baron and me. His appraising gaze is taking me in from head to toe. And I am measuring him.

His dark eyes glitter like those of a snake. I feel as if I can read his thoughts.

There's nothing you can do to stop this, he's thinking.

Paulek, though, is oblivious to this. He is still staring, mouth wide open, at the princess. The baron turns to look at my brother. His thin lips curl up at the edges. Again, the baron's look is easy to read.

We have this one hooked.

The baron looks toward Georgi. Our faithful majordomo is standing with his arms at his side, his eyes subserviently focused on the ground. The baron nods his head dismissively.

A mere servant.

The baron looks at me again. My right hand taps the hilt of my sword.

He shakes his head, no longer so pleased.

The baron flexes his fingers inside the silver gauntlet wrapped around his pommel. The leather creaks in protest. Then he turns his eyes away from mine.

By the head of the dragon! We are in trouble.

Thinking of trouble, Princess Poteshenie has now

dismounted from her horse. She's fiddling with that large wicker cage on the back of her horse, lifting up the door at the front of it.

A dark-furred creature leaps out, hisses and spits at us. Then, swift as an arrow from a bow, darts off around the side of the keep.

The princess claps her hands in delight. "Oh, see how happy my sweet little innocent pussycat Laska is to be free!"

Little? If that spitting ball of malice is a cat, it is the largest one I've ever seen. It's the size of a lynx, but with a longer tail.

Hysterical squawking erupts from behind the keep. It comes to me just where the princess's sweet little monster was headed. Our hen yard.

I know it is rude to take off at a run just when a visitor has arrived, uninvited or not. But those chickens are the source of our breakfast eggs. However, by the time I reach the yard it's too late for half our laying hens. Blood and feathers are everywhere. Slaughtered bodies are strewn about the straw. Their surviving sisters are perched on top of the coop, squawking in terror. In the center of the carnage, Laska squats on her haunches, contentedly chewing the head off our rooster. I slowly start to reach for the pitchfork that leans against the coop.

Before I can do anything, Princess Poteshenie's voice comes from behind me. She's also followed those sounds of feline-initiated slaughter—likely quite familiar to her.

"*Milacik, pridi!* Darling, come!"

One last bite to sever the head, which she drops by my feet in what could only be described as a contemptuous fashion. Then the purring assassin stalks past me to leap up into the protective arms of her mistress.

THE BARON IS sitting patiently on his horse. Paulek is also waiting. His eyes focus on Poteshenie as she walks past him to place Laska back into her cage and close the door. Then, as she turns, a perfumed handkerchief falls from her sleeve. It would seem like an accident if I had not seen her artfully placing that kerchief there so that it would descend at the twitch of a wrist.

Paulek almost falls over his own feet in his eagerness to leap forward and pick it up.

"P-Princess," he says. "You dropped this."

She lifts one hand to her mouth, purses her lips. "Oh, how gallant. *Vd'aka*. But you must keep it. Keep it to think of me."

Paulek cradles the kerchief in his hands as if it were a baby. I think I am about to throw up. I almost say something, but the baron speaks first.

"My friends," he says in a loud voice that draws all eyes to him. "My gracious friends!" He holds out his hand. "Truba!"

Truba, the herald who had announced their arrival, opens a saddlebag and produces a large piece of parchment. He carefully unrolls it and then ceremoniously passes it up to his master.

"Our invitation from your parents," Temny announces. "Would you like to examine it?"

Yes, I would! I step forward to take it.

The baron, though, casts a quick appraising glance at me and shakes his head. He turns to the other side to deposit the document in the hands of my brother. Not that Paulek reads it. He is too busy smelling that perfumed handkerchief and staring like a mooncalf at Princess Poteshenie. She has now lowered more of her veil to expose her perfect profile as well as her décolletage.

Truba plucks the parchment from my brother's fingers.

"I shall now share with all assembled here, the most gracious invitation we received from your ruler," he declaims.

My dear Baron Temny, my dear old friend,

The ardent desire of both my dear wife and myself is that you should come posthaste to Hladka Hvorka. You and your small group of loyal retainers shall be welcome to the fruits of our hospitality for as long as you wish to remain.

Although we may not be here when you arrive, we know that our sons shall make every effort to offer their assistance and provide for your every need.

Further, as we have so often discussed in the past, your visit will provide the opportunity for your beloved daughter to finally meet her future husband, our own son Paulek.

There is more beyond that. Truba's lips are still moving, but I'm not hearing his words. I'm too shocked.

Truba has finished. He is giving the scroll back to Paulek.

"Read," Truba says, placing a palm on Paulek's shoulder.

This time, Paulek actually does hold the gilded document in front of his face. Amazingly, it's drawn his attention away from the princess. His gaze is glued to it. His lips are moving as he silently mouths each word.

Is it also ensorcelled? I look over his shoulder. All

too familiar golden letters on the parchment glisten. Perhaps because I'm prepared, their power does not affect me. And, as I start to scan the words, I note something else about this deceptive invitation that is not quite right. There's nothing in its language that matches my father's plain way of speaking.

Truba snatches the parchment away from Paulek before I can study it more closely. He quickly rolls it up and slips it back into the saddlebag.

"Of course," Paulek says, his voice a monotone. "Of course."

My brother's voice becomes louder as he turns to look at all of us. "We must make our honored guests and my bride-to-be welcome!"

Pat

DAYS FLOWED INTO weeks, weeks into months, months into seasons, and seasons into years. They flowed the way small snow- and rain-fed rivulets in the High Tatras join larger streams, then rivers in their rush toward the sea.

The boy whose name was now Pavol grew quickly into a tall, strong youth. Perhaps it was from the work of wood cutting that Uncle Tomas put him to or the good food that Uncle Tomas's wife, who bade him call her Baba Marta, stuffed him with each day.

Perhaps too it was from the teaching they gave him. There were the physical challenges Uncle Tomas put before him—which included not merely the work of a woodsman but also running for miles without rest, wrestling, and swordplay, though the "blades" they used were made of wood, not steel.

Strategy and planning were also part of what Uncle Tomas taught, how whether one is stalking a dangerous animal or about to lead an army into battle, the wise man is the one who has a plan and is prepared.

Those physical lessons given him by Uncle Tomas were reinforced whenever the third of his teachers came to visit—the elderly Gypsy who simply called himself Gregor and only appeared when the leaves were about to fall. Though Gregor looked to be an old man, he had the suppleness and strength of someone far younger, and he always had a few new tricks to show the adopted child of his two old friends.

Pavol loved Gregor's visits. He thrilled at the wrestling contests between Uncle Tomas and Gregor. Tomas's bear-like brawn was always matched by Gregor's ability to twist and turn, to find a way to escape and then unbalance his bigger opponent. As Pavol grew older, Gregor began to teach him some of those same techniques that could turn another's power to his own advantage.

Strength, Gregor said, is not always stronger. One who tries to overcome everything with mere force alone may end up fooling himself.

Those teachings from Uncle Tomas and Gregor were reinforced by the stories Baba Marta told each night, legends of bravery and good deeds, tales of the rewards to be reaped by one who was patient and steadfast. She challenged Pavol with proverbs and riddles that were often as hard to get at as the meat in a thick-shelled nut.

He also read. Rough-hewn as Uncle Tomas appeared on the outside, beneath the homespun clothes and the great muscles beat the heart of a scholar. The dom that he and his wife, Baba Marta, shared with Pavol had a secret room, one that no one would ever guess existed when they looked at the little house from the outside. Within that room was a great store of books and scrolls, not only in the language of the land but also in Greek and Latin, Arabic, and other tongues. Literature, histories, magic and medicine, philosophy and mathematics were stacked on heavy-laden shelves.

Pavol absorbed all these lessons the way dry earth soaks up the rain. He accepted the bruises, the aching muscles that Uncle Tomas's back-breaking work and pitiless training inflicted upon him, the way Baba Marta's stories sometimes made his brain feel as if it were tied in knots. He struggled to master the reading of one language after another, sounding out each new word aloud at times, fighting his stubborn way into the mysteries of musty tomes until they opened vistas to him he had never imagined before. He learned, and learned to love learning.

One thing, though, was the most difficult for him

to master. It was a lesson that his teachers reminded him of every day, especially when they saw a certain look come to his eye. It was the lesson of patience. It truly was the hardest for him—especially because of the reign of iron under which the land still suffered.

The Dark Lord himself had left their little kingdom soon after wiping out what he assumed to be all of its royal family. Though there were still tales here of treasure to be found and magic to be mastered, their land lost some of its allure when the lights of the Silver Lands could no longer be seen. With the death of his parents—and over the next months, all those still loyal to them— that fifth direction had vanished. True, the dragon was said to remain. Though the dragon had not been seen for years, the tales all agreed that it slept still in its cave high atop the tallest peak. But even the Dark Lord had no stomach for battle with a creature said to be invincible.

The departure of the Dark Lord had not meant the end of tyranny. He left others in charge who saw to the collection of taxes and made sure that any spark of resistance was quickly and brutally quenched. Though that brutal tyrant was not there, his eye remained always on the land.

Seeing what had been done, what still was being done to the land his parents had cared for so lovingly, was as bitter as the taste of wormwood. But

Pavol forced himself to accept the part that both his guardians told him he must play and play well until the time, the right time, came at last.

To be safe until that day, there was only one part he could play. And though it grated upon him, it was a role that he played whenever he was out of the company of his two wise guardians—that of a harmless fool.

CHAPTER FIVE

In the Courtyard

I'VE BEEN KEEPING watch since dawn. I'm looking out a high window in our castle over our soiled courtyard below. Its white stones usually glitter in the sun. Georgi makes certain that it is kept as clean as a freshly washed plate. But that is far from true of its western quarter today. It's been burned with campfires, scuffed with boots that have mucked through mud and horse manure, littered with the belongings of the baron's little army, as well as those rough, unkempt ruffians themselves. They've occupied that entire section near the main gate, leaving only a ten-foot-wide aisle in front of the guest quarters where the baron, his daughter and her cat, and his herald have been lodged. Though it is past mid-morning, the baron and the princess have yet to show themselves. Are they just sleeping late or are they up to something in there?

They'd planned to stay in our castle. But Georgi somehow turned their attention toward our guest lodge. It's a finely built single-story structure of well-dressed stone with several large rooms, each with its own fireplace, bed, and furnishings. It's placed just within the walls, where the barracks might be in another castle. But, like all those who occupied Hladka Hvorka before them, from Prince Pavol on down, my parents have never felt the need to keep an army.

"Much more comfortable, convenient to your men," Georgi explained, tapping his fingertips together and lowering his head subserviently. "More private."

"Will it do for us . . . my daughter?" the baron said. He turned to the princess, who was studying something that she held between the palms of her left hand.

"Tu je to!" she said to herself in a pleased voice.

Here it is? What did she mean by that? I wondered.

Then she smiled and her next words made even less sense.

"We are close enough . . . my father," she said.

Close enough to what?

I could not stay to try to hear more. While Georgi was negotiating their lodgings with Baron Temny and his enigmatic daughter—with no help from my brother, who just kept staring at her—I needed to be busy elsewhere.

First, I made certain that all the outer doors to the great hall of Hladka Hvorka were closed and barred from within to discourage our visitors' troops from tromping in and taking it over. And probably using our furnishings as firewood.

Next, as they led their steeds toward our stables, I ran ahead of them. I opened the door and was greeted—as I had hoped—by the welcome sight of empty stalls.

"*Zmiznite*, disappear," Georgi had whispered to Jazda and Hreben as soon as the little army poured through our main gate.

They had done their job well. All seven of our horses had been led out the back of the stable to the rear wall of Hladka Hvorka. There, by pressing the right stones, Jazda opened a door in what seemed a solid wall and lowered the small concealed drawbridge that is big enough for one horse at a time to cross. Our herd, watched over by our stableman and his son, was now safe in a field far from the sight of the castle.

"Where your mounts? Where your stable boys?" growled the bald-headed ruffian, the one with the livid red scar on the side of his face.

One of Father's proverbs came to mind. "Let your teeth hold back your tongue." Instead of answering, I looked at him blankly as if I couldn't understand his question.

The scar-faced man stared at me for a moment, then shook his head in disgust. "*Dumbkopf! Blazon! Fool!*"

He pushed roughly by me to lead his horse into the stable, where he and his band of blackguards had no choice but to rub down their own mounts, feed, and water them without help. Not at all what they'd expected as our honored guests.

Guests, indeed. I shake my head, thinking again of that "invitation."

The few lines I'd read before Truba smoothly snatched it away had been enough. That brief moment of scanning the duplicitous document was enough to convince me that it had *not* been penned by *my* father. I could never imagine my parents inviting anyone to stay as long as they wanted. They enjoy visitors, but never for more than two or three nights. As Father puts it, "Fish and visitors start to smell after a few days."

Plus, most tellingly, there were no words misspelled. Quite unlike my father.

I look up at the sun. It's now close to noon. Still the baron has not yet roused himself.

What *are* they doing in there?

The only one of their little party of four to emerge thus far has been Truba. The lanky herald strode imperiously into our castle—likely asking for yet more hot water, food, and drink to be brought to them. Then he returned to our guest quarters.

Temny's men, however, are all too visible. They've been awake since dawn, long enough to raid our depleted hen yard. A dozen of our fattest hens are now turning on spits over cooking fires they've kindled with the firewood taken from the kitchen—without as much as a by your leave to Cook. The greasy smoke that now hangs over our once airy courtyard is a good match for this rabble. Some of them, I note with distaste, are even too lazy to trudge out to the plank over the moat. They're using one corner of our courtyard as a latrine.

The ruffians haven't seen me watching them. They're too busy eating, drinking, dicing and quarreling and making bets as they toss knives at a log they've propped up.

Wait!

Some of their heads are turning—the way the more vigilant in a pack of jackals concealed in tall grass react when an antelope comes to drink from the water hole. What have they seen?

Oh no! At the far eastern side of the courtyard a slender young woman in a brown dress has just come out of the castle. It's Charity. She's only four-teen years old, the youngest of our serving girls. Her arms are full of clean linens. Meant, I am sure, for the baron and his daughter. Probably what Truba came in to demand. Everything else brought to the baron's party was delivered by one of our serving men. Georgi's been careful not to send a young woman—or a lad, for that matter—out through that dangerous rabble. But this time, perhaps out of boredom or curiosity, Charity has taken it upon herself to do the task.

She was clever enough to not try to cross the courtyard, quietly making her way along the far wall toward the side entrance to our guest lodge.

Unfortunately, she failed to avoid notice. Even more unfortunately. the one whose eye she seems to have caught most is the Scarface. He seems to be Temny's head bully. More unfortunately still, I am four stories above them. I ask myself what I should do. I don't get an answer.

A pleased smile crosses the thick lips of Scarface. He turns his head back to his left toward the guest lodge. Temny himself is standing in the doorway. The baron lifts his left hand lazily, nods, and flicks his little finger in Charity's direction. Then he vanishes back inside, having set the stage.

Scarface looks over at his companion with whom he's been dicing. It's the other of the two flag bearers from yesterday, the blond-haired hulk with a long spade-shaped beard. Scarface holds out his hands, palms up, gestures like a servant offering a bowl of fruit.

Your turn or mine?

"Go, Peklo." The blond ruffian makes a rude gesture with his fingers. "You get that wench. But the next one's mine."

Peklo's smile turns into a wide grin showing yellowed teeth. He tosses his knife aside and rises eagerly to his feet.

By the head of the dragon! I turn and dash down the stairs, fearing I will be too late.

In a way, I am. By the time I burst through the courtyard entryway, the scene is playing out without me. Georgi is already here. He must have been watching just as I was. Despite the fact that he's burdened by a large pot and two long cloths slung around his neck, he's managed to place himself between Charity and Temny's men before Peklo could get to her.

Peklo reaches around Georgi to grab Charity's shoulder. However, before Peklo's rough fingers can grasp her, Georgi trips. The steaming contents of the iron pot pour down Peklo's chest. The iron pot lands on the burly man's forward foot.

"Arrgggh!" Peklo roars, hopping on one foot while trying to wipe hot soup from his front.

It's rather an amusing spectacle, but I keep myself from laughing out.

Peklo's companions, though, who saw it all happen and assume it's just an accident, are roaring with mirth.

"Peklo, save some of that soup for us, you greedy beast."

"First bath you've had in a month!"

Georgi hisses a word into Charity's ear. White-faced, she nods, runs swiftly back across the yard and through the servants' entrance to the castle. There's a thud and the rattle of a bolt as she slams and locks the door behind her.

I relax and lean back against the wall. My sword is belted around my waist now. I'm close enough to come to Georgi's rescue if necessary. But I have a feeling my help may not be needed.

"Oh sir, good sir," Georgi is saying. "*Prepac, prepac.* Sorry, sorry. So clumsy of me. All that fine turnip soup Cook prepared for you and your men."

"Acchhhh!" Peklo replies, still hopping. "Acchhh!"

His vocabulary is clearly limited by his rage and

the pain in his big toe. He reaches out for Georgi like a praying mantis grabbing at an irritating fly.

At this point any other servant who spilled soup all over a violent man would flee or cower down to absorb blows from said scalded ruffian. But Georgi is not any other servant.

"Oh good sir, here. Allow me to dry you."

Georgi ducks under Peklo's grasping hands, and deftly loops one of those two long cloths he is carrying around the angry brute. Another loop, then another. It pins Peklo's huge-muscled arms to his sides. He's unable to strike, grasp, or strangle.

Georgi holds the ends of that wrapped cloth in place with one hand that is, as I've already mentioned, far stronger than anyone who does not know him would suspect.

"Allow me to clean your face, good sir."

As he awkwardly wipes Peklo's face with the other cloth, I cannot help but observe that Georgi is doing an excellent job of getting more of the soup into the bully's eyes.

I fold my arms, keeping one eye on the crowd of toughs at the far end of the courtyard. Not one of them has stirred to assist their leader. They're even more amused.

"Y' look like a baby all wrapped up in his swaddling clothes," one wit shouts.

"Let your old nurse wipe your bum, Peklo!"

"Oh, good sir," Georgi babbles in his most servile voice, rubbing boiled turnips into Peklo's ears. "So sorry, sir, so sorry."

"*Volne mi!*" Peklo screams. "Free me!" He staggers back and forth, trying to extricate himself from the cocoon of cloth.

"*Ano,* good sir," Georgi steps back and pulls hard at the cloth wrapped about Peklo. Peklo spins like an oversize top, ending up on his knees. By the time he rises to his feet, Georgi is gone.

His face red, not wanting to embarrass himself further by trying to pursue a clumsy servitor, Peklo rises and stalks back to his men. They're silent now.

"Something funny?" Peklo says in a deadly calm voice.

He clubs his fist into the face of the one who shouted out that remark about Peklo looking like a baby.

"Any other jokers?" Peklo growls.

Nearly all of them, including the man he struck, now spitting blood and a tooth onto the stones of the courtyard, turn away to avoid his angry glare.

The only one still smiling is the blond hulk, who fingers his beard as he looks up at his companion. He clearly views himself as Peklo's equal. Now that I think of it, when the baron arrived, Spadebeard was the one who stayed closest to Temny's side.

"Where's your lass?" Spadebeard asks with an insolent chuckle.

"Shut up, Smotana," Peklo snarls. "We deal with them all. Later."

Perhaps they don't know I can hear them from where I lean against the castle wall, a spear's throw away. My hearing is much sharper than most.

"True enough," spade-bearded Smotana agrees. "The baron has promised us the lot of them, and our master always keeps his word. But if you like, we could seek out that old bald fool and break his neck now."

Peklo nods his head. "*Jah*. But I settle the score, not you. I break his bones good."

I doubt it. Though Peklo may keep his eye out for any glimpse of the fool who dowsed him, there'll be no score settling today. No one is better than Georgi at remaining unseen.

"That lass looked tasty," Smotana says. "And there's at least one or two more in there, or I miss my guess. How long will it be until we get the go-ahead?"

"When the master and our, ah, young mistress grow strong enough," Peklo says. His voice is unsettlingly calm now.

"Ah," Smotana says. He shows his teeth in an even wider grin and nods his head as he continues to stroke his beard. "Of course."

What little amusement I was feeling at the way Georgi handled Peklo had now left me. I slip back around the corner with a sick feeling in my gut.

Are we all doomed?

Sest

ON THE SEASONS flowed. The snows of Zma
melted into the sweet promise of Jar, then the long
hot days of Leto, until finally again it was Jesen, the
time when the leaves turn and fall from the trees,
the very season in which the boy now known by all
as Pavol had been born.

And like the small trees in the forest, he had
drawn strength from the passing of seasons and
years. Though he was still slender, there was no mis-
taking the strength in his arms grown hard-sinewed
from the woods work that was his daily labor. His
years upon the earth now numbered sixteen and he
was taller than most men.

As he had grown and changed, something else in
the land had done the same. First as a flicker like
foxfire in the night, then as a glow like a flame near

burned out, the light of the Silver Lands had begun to show itself again, that fifth direction that had vanished on the death of his parents was returning. Not everyone could see it, but it was there once more.

Baba Marta was the first to point it out to him. Then she told a story of the Silver Lands, how those who lived their long lives there were pleased when humans lived in peace, how they watched the lands of mortal folk but did not interfere—though now and then a lord or lady of Faerie might fall in love, true love with a mortal. Then, if that love was returned, the couple had a hard choice to make. If they would live together, one must pledge to give up all that had been known and familiar before and go to that true love's land to share long life or swift mortality by his or her side.

"What if they have children?" Pavol asked.

Baba Marta smiled at that. Was her smile because his question proved to her how truly her boy was now becoming a man? Or was there a bit of sorrow in the expression that crossed her face?

"Ah," she replied. "For them it is different."

And that was all she would say.

CHAPTER SIX

Why Climb the Tree?

WHY CLIMB THE tree when the apple is about to fall into your hand?

That proverb of Father's comes to mind as I consider how things have gone since the arrival of our aggressive guests. Three days have now passed since they marched through our gate.

Why, you might ask, haven't those well-armed interlopers who vastly outnumber us just thrown us into the castle dungeon? Well, we've never had a dungeon in our castle. Who needs a dungeon when you have no enemies to place in one?

We do have the castle cellars. But no one—aside from our family—ever goes there. And that space is well filled . . . with other things. True, we might have built some sort of jail aboveground inside the castle walls, but Father thought it much more practical to use the space for a larger stable.

The lack of a dungeon aside, why haven't they just taken over?

After all, force has long been a means of establishing legitimacy in the twelve kingdoms around our tiny and peaceful domain.

Now that I've had a little time to ponder things, I think I partly understand why Baron Temny held his men back from attacking us after entering our castle. Though I cannot quite put my finger on it, I sense that the man does not completely trust his own strength. I cannot say why, but something seems missing in him. There is none of the calm certainty in him, for example, that is so much of my brother Paulek's character. I cannot imagine a battle that Paulek would ever run from—even one where defeat seemed certain.

The baron, though, seems reticent to fight. More weasel than lion. Direct conflict is the approach of one whose bravery is greater than his guile and who does not yet trust his own strength. The baron is not a warrior looking forward to combat. Despite the sharp sword he brandished that first day, a straight-forward thrust is not the baron's way.

Sit back, set events into motion that will confuse or discomfit us—such as stationing his unruly troops in our courtyard and bewitching my brother. Observe our weaknesses. Then, like a clever predator creeping close and closer, strike when success is certain?

Yes, that may be it.

I still do not understand, however, those words spoken by the princess as she studied whatever she held in her hand. Some sort of amulet, perhaps? What exactly were they close enough to?

And what about Peklo's remark regarding Temny and Poteshenie growing strong enough? Strong in what way? Physically? Magically? And what would make them stronger? Perhaps merely by being in our castle, by being close enough to something here, they are gaining power the way a tree draws strength from being rooted into fertile earth?

In terms of strength, there's no doubt that they've found *our* weak point. It is the easily influenced mind of my besotted brother!

Aside from that first kiss on her extended hand, Paulek has been kept at arm's length by the princess. She and the baron are playing a game with him, giving my brother only brief glimpses of his bride-to-be, a few words to tantalize him.

"When we are married, we will always be together, yes?"

A smile, the flutter of her eyelashes, her hand reached out so that her fingertips brush his flushed cheek before she pulls back with what is intended to sound like a modest giggle. Then the ever-present baron whisks her away. It's so obvious to me. Can't Paulek see the way Temny is dangling her in front of him as if she were a sweet and Paulek a child being coaxed into doing the bidding of a manipulative adult?

I tried talking to him earlier today.

"Brother, are you sure this betrothal is the right thing?" I began.

In reply he plucked a white, heavily scented handkerchief from his pocket.

"Look, Rashko, the princess gave me this. Doesn't it smell wonderful?"

I managed to control myself and not say that its scent reminded me of the spices used by awful cooks to cover the fact that their food has gone bad.

"Paulek, don't you think you're rushing things?"

I might as well have been talking to a tree, for at that exact moment the princess appeared at her window and gestured to him.

"Look, Rashko, there she is."

And with that, deaf to any further words I might utter, he left my side to go stand beneath the window and stare up at her.

With Princess Poteshenie as my brother's intended, the baron is not an interloper, but a relative-to-be. As Paulek's wife, the princess would become a legal

heir—should our parents not return—to our kingdom.

The thought of that makes my skin crawl.

I do not know much about marriages. Why should
I? I'm only fifteen. It is always the older brother who
marries first. But I do know that everything about
this potential marriage is wrong. If my parents had a
say in this, it would be short and direct. In a word,
Nie! No!

Despite their obtuseness, my parents always
recognize honesty and integrity. They would have
seen through this crew of—whatever they are—in
a heartbeat. They would never have allowed those
heavily armed men to cross the drawbridge. They
might have invited the baron and his princess—but
not their retinue—in to dine, bringing them through
the sally gate when a single wide plank can allow
one person at a time to enter. No forged invitation
from Father would have been produced. One word
from Mother would have broken or prevented whatever spell it is that was cast over my gullible brother.

I imagine what it would have been like at the end
of that dinner.

"Such a pleasure to have met you."

"We do hope your charming daughter finds a suit-
able young man for herself."

Then Temny and Poteshenie would have been

escorted from Hladka Hvorka and lodged not in our guest quarters but in the small drafty cottage outside the castle while my parents went to bed early.

At cock's crow the next morning, Georgi would have brought them a cold breakfast and firm good wishes for them to have a pleasant journey as they departed our valley.

My father, though his sense of humor is a bit limited, would likely have chuckled about it all later.

A SWORD TAPS my arm. It wakes me from my musing.

"*Bratcek,*" Paulek says, "are we not going to spar?"

Spar? How can he even think of that at a time like this?

But it is not a bad thing. I've noted over the last three days that this practice yard seems to be the one place where my brother is able to think about anything other than the princess. I follow him down the stairs and through the archway onto the yard.

Two days ago, the only way I was able to pry him away from staring out his window at Princess Poteshenie sitting in the garden below was to suggest a match. Even as far gone as he is in infatuation, the thought of blow and counterblow, steel ringing against steel is still able to get his attention.

My hope is that while we fight I may talk some sense into him.

Perhaps even now before we start?

"Brother, don't you think you are too young for marriage?"

Paulek knits his brow.

"Shouldn't you get to know her before you take such a big step?"

He scratches his forehead.

"Remember what Father always says, that one must take slow steps on unfamiliar ground because it might prove to be a bog?"

Paulek stares down at the blunt sword in his hand.

Unfortunately, I have just asked him three questions in a row and topped them off with a proverb. It's a burden too heavy for his thoughts to lift.

"Bog? But the nearest bog is on the other side of the forest."

"Paulek, do we know these people well enough for you to agree to a marriage?"

Paulek lifts his eyes to mine. He looks worried. "*Bratcek*, are you jealous?"

"No, far from it. Not at all."

A happy grin as broad as a sunrise over the High Tatra Mountains spread over his face. His big left hand thuds into my chest. "*Vyborne!* Wonderful. Then all is well. On guard!"

And before I can say another word—or fully regain my breath—his sword is swinging at me and I am barely deflecting it with my own blade.

"*Utok!*"

No time for persuasion or argument now. I raise my weapon just in time to catch the gleaming blade that descends as swift as a falling star toward my head.

Clang!

"*Udriet!*"

And again!

Clang!

"*Velmi dobre!*" Paulek shouts as his feet shuffle forward on the floor of the high-fenced practice field. "Good! Good defense, small brother."

Defense? Standing within sword's length of a grinning madman who thinks that attempting to bash his innocent brother is an enjoyable pastime? To be fair, though, Paulek would feel terrible if he really did injure me. The strength of his attacks have only increased over the years as my ability to defend and fight back has grown. He prides himself on having been the one—even more than Black Yanosh—who has done the most to turn me into a skilled swordsman. As our wise old teacher has often said, to know how to attack, first learn to defend.

And defense is what I need to put my mind to

right now. Blunt blade or not, Paulek is strong as a bull. Any one of his blows may break bone if I fail to either deflect or dodge it and it connects with something other than my much-dented shield and helm. I have to put my mind to this. No time now to worry about my missing parents or the hungry grin on the face of Baron Temny. At least Paulek is his old self while we're here, and he's trying his best to help his beloved brother grow as a fighter by endangering his life! A smile starts to come to my own face as the two of us engage in our dangerous dance.

"*Utok!*"

Thwang!

"Nicely taken, brother!"

Luckily, Paulek has never been one to think silently as his mind runs through the various techniques we have both been taught by Black Yanosh. Our persistent (and still hidden) weapons master has spent eight weeks of every year with us since Paulek was seven and I was six.

"*Utok! Udriet!*"

Attack! Strike!

No matter what Yanosh has tried, including stuffing a gag in his mouth, Paulek has never been broken of the habit, in the excitement of battle, of stating what he is about to do a split second before doing it.

"*Utok!*"

Swoosh!

The wind stirred by the deftly executed crossing downstroke of my brother's blade swishes past my nose as I jerk my head back.

"*Udriet!*"

Thwang!

My right arm is jarred by the powerful, perfectly placed backhand blow that could have broken my shoulder had I not taken it on my shield.

"*Udriet!*"

Thud! The sound of the hilt of a quickly reversed sword as it strikes the center of an unguarded stomach.

"Ooof!"

A body hits the ground hard. A suddenly regretful brother drops his shield and sword to kneel and apologize.

"*Prepac!* I'm sorry, Paulek."

My older brother sits up slowly. As always, there is no anger in the look on his face. In fact, he looks pleased that I've bested him.

Lately, unless I try really hard to control myself, things just happen. I don't know how or why. One moment Paulek is pressing the advantage and I'm doing my best just not to get maimed. Then, the very next second Paulek is flat on his back and I'm standing over him.

If Black Yanosh were here and not still lying low,

he would be looking at me with one snowy eyebrow raised, his leathery right hand stroking his small, elegant mustache.

"*Znova,*" he would say. Again.

That is all Black Yanosh ever says whenever one of my lucky moves manages to knock down my brother. I never have met anyone who speaks fewer words than our old weapons master.

I help Paulek to his feet.

"I'm really tired," I say. "You've completely worn me out."

Paulek smiles. The fact that I put him on his back yet again has not bothered him at all. He delivers a loving punch to my chest. More bruises.

"*Ano!* Yes, I take pity on you now, eh?"

Paulek goes back into the main castle. I have no doubt where he's going. Our sparring over, the entrancement has returned. He's heading back to his perch, where he can stare out the window onto the garden. Perhaps if he is lucky—or so he thinks—he'll catch a glimpse of the princess strolling about with that vile pet of hers in her arms.

Making my way around the main courtyard, I hug the walls, staying behind whatever obstacles I can find to prevent Temny or his men from noticing me.

I needn't have worried. As usual, the baron and the princess have hidden themselves in the guesthouse. I hear some sort of chanting from within. The cloud of smoke that's been constantly rising from one of the chimneys since their first night here now has a green tinge to it.

The baron's men seem unaware of me as I slip quietly past them. They're all engaged in their usual pastimes of dicing, betting on knife throws, and arguing over who is most obviously cheating. They're cooking the last of our depleted flock of hens. When we have dinner tonight with the baron and the princess, chicken will not be on the menu. They're also still drinking from the casks of wine that Georgi brought them. The arrival of strong drink was greeted by the rabble with considerable delight.

Even Peklo forgot his original plan to break Georgi's bones when he saw our clever head retainer roll out that first cask. Not our best wine, of course. Far from it. But good enough to turn their attention away from other things. I wonder if Georgi might not have put a little something extra into those casks. Not poison. But something that might, in some ways, calm their urges.

For now they do seem to have forgotten the young women of the castle. Not that remembering them would do them any good. Aside from the princess, the only female still inside our castle walls is Cook. After Georgi's rescue of Charity, she and all the other females were spirited out the sally gate with instructions to go to their relatives' homes in Mesto and remain there until things are again safe at Hladka Hvorka.

But will things ever again be safe? Will any of us?

And what can I do, even with Georgi's help, to save us all from whatever the baron has in mind?

I wish I were older.

I wish my parents were here.

I wish I knew how to make my wishes come true. But I don't.

The only thing I can think to do right now is to get away—for a little while at least—from this place that feels less like home each day. I slip out the open gate, cross the moat, and walk down the slope until I reach the beech trees of the old forest.

Sedem

GREGOR WAS BACK. Just as he had done every autumn before, when the caravan of his Gypsies arrived in their land, he left the bright-painted wagons of his comrades to come and spend time with Pavol, Uncle Tomas, and Baba Marta. This time, however, there was a difference.

Gregor walked through the door of their dom with a sack over his shoulder that clanked as he walked. He dumped out its contents. A pair of swords and two shields.

Old, Gregor said, but still good.

And that day they began Pavol's training with weapons of steel. By the time he was fourteen he had mastered all that Uncle Tomas knew of swordsmanship and waited eagerly for each autumn when he knew Gregor would come back and show him even more.

Pavol also treasured those visits as a special opportunity to learn more of the world around them. The Gypsies traveled through every land, more or less unseen by the rulers. Even the Dark Lord seemed not to notice them. Perhaps it was because they were so clearly without wealth or property or position in any society other than their own. Or perhaps they had their own special glamour that kept them concealed from his fell gaze. Wherever they went, the Gypsies listened and learned. As a result Gregor's stories were full of lore and legend and information. Many of the tales, especially those of the foolishness of the wealthy and powerful who sought to cheat the Gypsies and ended up being tricked themselves, delighted Pavol.

The stories of Gregor that he listened closest to, though, were not the ones that pleased him. They were the tales that filled him with both despair and anger—the sad chronicles of the doings of the Dark Lord.

"How can I forget what he did to my family?" Pavol asked.

"You cannot and you should not," Gregor replied. "Memory," he said, tapping his head, "is a treasure greater than gold."

Then it was Pavol's seventeenth year.

Just as in past autumns, Gregor's visit was like a

birthday gift for Pavol. The ageless old man once again brought his stock of stories to share. He sat with them around the fire until late in the night. He praised Baba Marta's wonderful food. He showed Pavol a new series of wrestling moves that ended with a spectacular throw, demonstrated another subtle technique to strip the sword from the hand of an attacker.

This autumn, though, something was different. Pavol saw it in the way his three teachers cast appraising glances his way. Something was up.

"Is it time?" Gregor asked.

"It is," Baba Marta said.

"*Ano,*" Uncle Tomas agreed.

CHAPTER SEVEN

Problems

THERE'S A CLEARING in Stary Les that is a perfect circle. One of my favorite spots in the world, it's there that I first saw a hoopoe, a bird so ridiculous and delicate at the same time that it brings a smile to one's face. Its tall crest swaying on its head, it hopped down from the high branches to perch in front of my face and insist that I share my bread with it.

It was in this clearing too that a fox came up to me and placed its paw on my knee as I sat without moving. I can think of nowhere that seems more vibrant with life. There's always music here—not just the songs of the birds, but from the branches and leaves that chorus with the wind as you enter it along the trail that seemed to keep itself clear. I always feel the place welcoming me whenever I approach. The beeches at the wood's edge bow toward me as trees do when their tops are pushed down by the wind. Even today, when there's no breeze.

I run my hand up and down their trunks. There's not even a scar left where the blade chopped through.

"It won't happen again," I whisper.

Two years ago I failed to come quickly enough one morning when Paulek wanted to practice. No one else was available or foolhardy enough to spar with him. So Paulek lumbered his fourteen-year-old bulk down to the armory. There he chose not a practice sword but one honed sharp enough to shave with. Then he went to my clearing to do his training.

At first I think he was delighted to be able to deliver such precise killing strikes with a real battle weapon and watch his bloodless mock enemies fall about him.

To the right! *Utok!*

To the left. *Bit!*

By the time I realized what he was doing and came running down to him from the castle, I was too late. Young trees lay all around him, lobbed off waist-high by his razor-edged blade.

"Paulek," I said in dismay. "Look!"

We looked about us. Stary Les had never been coppiced for firewood or harvested for timbers like other tame woodlands. The Old Forest is always left uncut. It's kept as a preserve for wild creatures, its roots holding the headwaters of the small river that always ends up flowing, though the end direction may change, into the Silver Lands. In Stary Les, we always walk lightly. It conferred a kind of blessing upon our family. It's the place where the great Pavol spent his years of growing up. A holy place. A place defiled by my brother's heedless deed.

"Oh my," Paulek said. "What have I done?"

Somehow, though, his voice did not have the dismay in it that mine did. Instead, he turned to me and said with a smile, "Rashko, you'll fix it."

Patting me once on the shoulder, he headed back up the hill without a backward glance. Though I quickly realized I had to be wrong—for my brother has never been clever enough to be devious—it seemed for a moment as if he had done all this on purpose to set me an impossible task.

"Fix it?" I said to myself. *"Ako?"* How?

Then, without thinking, I reached toward the first fallen beech.

It was, of course, impossible. As the proverb goes, there is no way to uncut a tree.

I don't fully recall what occurred then. All I remember is that one moment I was bending toward that sad, lopped-off sapling, and the next I found myself in the midst of a grove of whole young trees that swayed about me in a sort of dance. There seemed nothing strange at all about it to me at the time. Nor did the voice I heard in the wind saying *dakujem,* thank you, sound at all unusual.

I just nodded to the trees and said *"Prosim."* You're welcome.

I was tired, though. And somehow, though it had been mid-morning when I went running down to the wood, the sun was now setting. I trudged back up to the hall where my brother and my parents were awaiting my arrival at the dinner table. All three of them wore the same smile Paulek had on his face as he deserted me. None of them said a word, but they nodded at me as if I had passed some sort of test. Strange.

Then Cook came out with not one but two huge plates of steaming, stuffed pirohys mixed with just the right amount of milk and sheep cheese. The aroma was so wonderful that I thought I would faint with delight. I reached out with both hands for the food, eating with a greater appetite than ever before. Then I stumbled up to our room and fell asleep halfway across my bed before I could take off my clothes or remove my boots.

I'M NOT TIRED now, even after that long training session with Paulek.

However, even here where the touch of branches and the trees' soft singing usually soothes me like the caress of a grandmother's hands, I can't relax. Too many things are happening.

How can I get my parents back home? I've not ventured again into their chambers where that invitation still rests. Things have been happening so fast that at times it seems as if I am in a whirlpool, the world seems spinning around me. Thinking back, I know that I felt a link, however brief, between myself and my parents. They were aware of me, about to speak. Could I contact them again through that charm-charged card?

A sort of plan is starting to approach me, like distant footsteps climbing the stairs toward my mind.

"Young sir!"

Whatever idea I was about to have runs back down the stairs, out the door, and into the mist of my returning confusion.

It's Georgi, of course. Only he would know where to find me at a moment like this.

"Your, ah, guests," Georgi says, "need you."

I swallow the curse that comes to my lips, clench my fists, walk a few paces away, look up, and silently count to ten.

Georgi waits patiently, head bowed over steepled hands.

"You know that proverb, Georgi? Guests and fish start to stink after three days? But what if the fish is already rotten when it's placed on your table?"

He smiles. It's a knowing smile I first recognized—to his surprise at the time—when I was a very small child.

I was three years old. My father was about to ride out to hunt down a dangerous beast, a sort of monster boar that had been killing cattle.

There he was, tall and splendid, his bow over his shoulder, a long boar lance in his hand, leaning down from the back of his tall black horse.

"I say, Georgi, did y' happen to see where did I put my good hunting knife? Y' know, the one with the bone handle?"

It was the third time in a row—I'd learned to count that winter—Father had asked that question

Georgi's patient answer was the same as the two times prior. "In the sheath on your belt, sir."

And, just as he had done the last two times, my father nodded, totally unembarrassed. *"Ano, dobre,"* he replied.

Then he kicked his heels into his fine steed's sides and he was off, riding as if he and the animal were a single being. Despite his inability to cogitate, my father has always been a centaur in the saddle, a knight like those in the books I was already beginning to read. Though perhaps more forgetful than one of those perfect heroes.

"*Ano*, sir," Georgi said in a soft voice to my father's back. And then that little smile came to his face.

"Do we amuse you?" I piped up.

Georgi looked down, as if he hadn't noticed me standing there. Of course he had. Georgi somehow always knows where all of us are at any given time and is able to appear as if out of nowhere whenever one of us needs his assistance—whether or not we realize it.

"What do you mean, young sir?" he asked.

"If the word 'amuse' means what I think it does," I replied in a very serious voice, "I mean that we make you laugh. You think we are funny."

Georgi's mouth opened rather wide at that point and he said nothing for the count of ten. (I know, because I was counting.) Then he dropped down to one knee. He looked me straight in the eye, a very different sort of smile on his face.

"Rashko," he whispered, "I see who you are."

"I'm Rashko, aren't I?" I said. His words had confused me.

"*Ano a nie*," he said. Yes and no. Confusing me even more.

Georgi took my right hand. I thought he meant

to shake it. Instead he turned it so that my palm was facing up. He studied it for a moment and nodded.

"Rashko," he said. "That is what you want me to call you, isn't it?"

I understood that. "*Ano.* I don't like it at all when you or the other servants call me young sir."

Georgi nodded. "Of course you wouldn't." He put his hand on my forehead. "Best for you to forget this conversation for now."

WHICH I DID until this very moment.

"Young sir?" Georgi repeats.

I have several questions that I want to ask. First, though, I step close to Georgi and look deep into his eyes. "Georgi," I say, "have you forgotten that when I was three I told you I didn't like to be called young sir?"

"Rashko," he says, "I've not forgotten. It's good that memory has returned. There's never been a better time to begin remembering."

He holds out his right hand and I put mine in his just as he had placed it when I was a small child. With the tip of his index finger he traces the lines in my palm.

"*Prilezitost,*" Georgi mutters, more to himself than to me. Opportunity? "*Strashne . . .*" He pauses.

Terrible . . . ? Terrible what?

A loud sound, like that of something heavy shattering on hard stones, comes echoing down the hill to us from the castle. It's followed by someone shouting. Screaming, actually.

"Oh my," Georgi says, removing his hand from beneath mine. "Trouble."

Osem

WHAT OLD GREGOR took from his bag surprised Pavol. Not by its appearance, for it looked to be nothing more than a worn brown leather pouch. But when Pavol took it into his hand, its feel was far different than he had expected.

It was heavy and light, thick and thin, smooth and rough, warm as sunlight and cool as ice. More than any of those seemingly contradictory sensations, that strange pouch felt familiar to the young man. Though he knew he had never before held it or seen it, it was as if it had always been his.

"Thank you," he said.

Gregor nodded, but said nothing.

Pavol looked around at his three teachers. They looked back at him with carefully composed faces. Waiting.

"Where did this come from?" he asked.

Gregor's answer was much as Pavol might have expected. "From near and far," the old man replied.

"And what must I do with this?" Pavol asked, sensing that such a question was expected of him.

"It is time for you to find those things that fit within it."

Pavol tied the pouch to his belt. He had another question to ask. He suspected he already knew the answer he would get. But he asked it anyway.

"How will I find those things?"

"By looking," Gregor replied, a small smile on his lips.

"You'll know them when you see them," Uncle Tomas said.

"Or," Baba Marta added with a chuckle, "they will know you."

CHAPTER EIGHT

The Princess's Pet

I RUN UP the hill, leaving Georgi behind.

As soon as I reach the outer courtyard I can see what has happened.

Trouble indeed.

Of course it's been caused by the princess's dear little pet, Laska. That vile feline's disposition is as black as her fur, which is the color of midnight, save for the one white spot in the middle of her forehead.

I'd hoped that Ucta and Odvaha could avoid notice by pretending to be docile dogs. But as soon as Laska spied them, a light had come into her red eyes. First she had walked close to their noses, trying to get them to chase her. But they simply turned their eyes away from her.

Don't react.

We know.

Until now they had managed to avoid her. But not today.

Today, when Laska prowled over and then tried to scratch them, at first they just moved out of the way. Then, when she snarled at them, they trotted out of the courtyard to their favorite place in the shade just inside the entrance gate.

But Laska did not give up. She waited until they were dozing and then leaped to the top of the wall that rose thirty feet above the spot where they lay. A heavy unmortared stone had been placed up there on the wall to mend the gap where an older stone had fallen into the moat. One push and the stone went hurtling down toward my canine brothers. They both had leaped aside at the last second. However, the rock shattered their bowl, spraying them with water and sharp shards of stone.

Ucta's wet muzzle is bleeding and there's a cut over Odvaha's eye. The two are managing to hold themselves back from attacking. But they are standing, shoulders hunched and feet spread wide, showing their formidable teeth as they growl at Laska. The cat, smug as a pike who has just swallowed a duckling, now lolls in the arms of Poteshenie. She's bent a bit under her little pet's weight as she stands in the doorway of our guesthouse. It's the first time today that I've seen her. As yet, Temny has still not appeared.

There's more of a glow of glamour about Poteshenie than there was yesterday. Is it possible that she has become more physically beautiful since her arrival? But her attractiveness is not alluring me. If anything, I feel more repelled. Though her face may mystically radiate loveliness, her personality is poisonous.

"Ayyyy, ayyy, ayyyyy! These monsters want to hurt my precious," she is screaming. Her voice is as harsh as a harpy's. "Someone help me!"

Ah. It's not merely her cat that's behind this little scene. Poteshenie seems as eager for the demise of my friends as is her feline cohort. Is it just part of her nature that she enjoys causing such chaos and longs for the sight of blood? Can she sense the bond between Odvaha and Ucta and me? Is this all part of whatever plan the baron has in mind?

Am I supposed to be part of whatever is about to happen?

I don't have time to ponder that now. Peklo and Smotana have drawn their swords. Two other bullies standing behind them have fitted arrows to their bowstrings.

"*Prosim,*" I say, my voice calm. "Please."

I hold up my hands and step in between the soldiers and my four-legged friends. The archers lower their weapons, the swordsmen take a grudging step back. Peklo glares at me as he does so. Smotana keeps that annoying smirk on his face.

The princess stops shrieking. An accomplished actress, she's recognized that this little scene is not going to go as she directed. Paulek didn't come running at her screams. Probably, he is still snoring in his chair. Neither her dangerous charms nor her theatrics appear to have much effect on me. So why waste her breath?

Smart, I think. And stupid at the same time. Does she believe I'm dull as Paulek? She's not even trying to hide her disappointment at failing to bring about the demise of Ucta and Odvaha.

She is not the most disappointed one, though. Her cat is positively moping. And Ucta and Odvaha furrow their brows at me.

Why stop us? Just getting interesting.

Too dangerous.

We could have taken them.

I know.

I keep from smiling at the mental picture of what my two friends would have done if I'd not held them back. A smile right now might give me away. I have to be a better actor than the princess.

And I do have to protect Ucta and Odvaha from their own reckless bravery. I have no doubt those four men would have regretted aiming their weapons at my two friends. But there are three dozen more men behind them. Though they're still busy drinking my father's wine, they would have risen to their feet and joined in the fight. Even if Ucta and Odvaha would certainly have taken a good many enemies with them, I have no desire to see them give their lives uselessly just to preserve their dignity. And it's not yet the time to confront Temny and his daughter.

Be patient.

For the benefit of those watching, I speak out loud. "*Nie,* bad dogs!"

Ucta makes a huffing sound, but settles back on his haunches and scratches his ear. Odvaha slumps to his belly and begins to lick his paw—which is bleeding slightly from one of those sharp shards of stone. They look, for all the world to see, like nothing more than two unusually large wolfish dogs.

Let them be viewed that way. Especially now that Baron Temny has come on the scene. He's finally emerged from the guesthouse and is standing in front of his daughter. Like her, he seems subtly changed. Stronger. Slightly taller, perhaps. A bit broader of shoulder.

His right hand strokes his mustache, his left caresses the hilt of the curved dagger that hangs from his belt.

"All is well?"

The friendly tone in his voice is so false that it grates like a file.

"*Ano,*" I reply, avoiding his eyes. "All is well."

"*Otec!*" the princess says to the baron, putting special emphasis on that word as she caresses his shoulder. "Father! Those bad dogs wanted to hurt my little pet."

"Ah?" Baron Temny raises his eyebrows. "They must be chained?"

His words are directed at me. Not really a question but a command.

"Of course," I say, still looking down. "I will see to it right away."

My quick answer surprises him. He hasn't expected me to be agreeable. He stops stroking his mustache and slides his right hand down to his chin, narrowing his eyes to consider me.

I grab Ucta and Odvaha by the loose skin at the scruff of their necks.

Pretend to resist, but not too much.

Ucta growls and Odvaha whimpers as I pull at them. But they also trust that I have a plan. Which I do, more or less. Their feet scrabble on the stones of the courtyard as I drag them through the gate, across the drawbridge, and down the hill.

As soon as we are well out of sight, I let go of the scruffs of their necks. They both shake themselves noisily. I understand why. Like me, they want to rid themselves of the taint of the atmosphere that hangs about the baron and his cohorts like greasy smoke.

You chain us?

Nie.

I kneel down and put my arms around their necks. They lick my face.

"Make yourselves very scarce. I will call you if I need you."

As you say.

They trot down the slope. I watch until they disappear into the deep green of the thick brush in the rocky folds of land above the Old Forest.

Then, though I feel like one about to remove his sword and step into a room full of ruffians ready to rob him, I turn and go back up the hill to Hladka Hvorka.

Devat

PAVOL STOOD STARING at the swift-running Hron. Its waters were icy cold, coming as they did from the snows that never left the highest peaks of the Tatras.

He was not alone. Considering what he had just seen, that was unfortunate. He was with the group of young men of his age that he'd known and grown with since taking on his identity as Pavol the wood-cutter's boy.

Both Uncle Tomas and Baba Marta had encouraged him to spend time with others of his own age when he was not busy doing the tasks they set him to. In fact, making friends was one of those needful tasks. Just why, he was not sure, but his guardians told him that a man with no friends is not man at all. Moreover, they added, to know how to work, one must also learn how to play

Although his young comrades had soon bestowed the name Pavol the Foolish upon him, all of them viewed him with affection. Though he was fool-hardy and tended to have more accidents than most, his good nature, his kindness, and his readiness to always help a friend had made him ever welcome in their company. And as far as that nickname went, it was one that Pavol embraced with gratitude and continued to live up—or down—to. For who would ever expect thoughts or acts of treason from a simple, good-natured fool.

None of them knew him by the name that he'd left behind—so long ago that aside from dreams he'd almost forgotten it himself. Like Pavol, some of them had lost their families with the coming of the Dark Lord. When he turned up one day, he was accepted as just another like themselves, an orphaned lad taken in by the woodcutter and his wife.

"Do you think I can leap across?" he said to Janko, the boy standing behind him at a much safer distance from the chilly waters.

Janko's answer was predictable. The most care-ful of their small band, his approach to living was that described by his carpenter grandfather's favorite saying. Measure twice to cut once.

"*Nikdy!* Never."

"*Ano,*" Pavol replied, continuing to eye the water.

If what he saw glinting below its surface was what he thought it was, he knew what he had to do.

"When you see the glitter of iron, you must bring it to your grasp!" So Baba Marta had said in her story of the hero who dared the depth of the Devil's Well to vanquish the monster and bring back a treasure.

Pavol smiled at his friends. "But how do you know for sure if you don't try?"

And with that he made a great leap. It was quite impressive. His lean legs were strong. He sailed much farther than his awed companions expected, a full two-thirds of the way across. So when he landed, it was in the deepest and swiftest section of the headwaters of the Hron River.

"Not even close!" he shouted back as he bobbed up briefly before rapidly disappearing around a bend.

His half-worried, half-amused comrades finally found him, half a league downstream. He'd managed to grasp a branch and drag himself out of the water. Although sodden and shivering, he was sitting on a log staring at something held in his fingers that looked like an iron ring.

"*Ako sa mate?*" Janko called down to him from the high bank.

"*Ako ti je?* How are you?" Peter the baker's nephew shouted.

"*Zhijesh?* Are you alive?" Rudolf the tanner's boy asked.

Pavol quickly slid the object he'd been holding into the pouch that hung from his belt. Then he turned a smiling face up to them.

"*Ano! Dobre,*" he called back. "Now I know for sure."

As, they thought, so did they.

Their friend was surely well named as Pavol the Foolish.

CHAPTER NINE

A Match

THE FIRST PERSON who greets me as I cross back over the drawbridge is Paulek. His face is aglow with pleasure. He's carrying his favorite practice sword.

Nie!

The last thing I need right now is another bone-bruising match with my brother.

But that isn't what he's thinking about.

"Guess what, *Bratcek*," he asks. "They've asked me to have a match with one of their men."

He sweeps his hand behind him. A circle of men has formed in the courtyard. At the head of the circle are the baron and the princess. The two heaviest and most ornate chairs have been dragged out of the guesthouse. Those over-decorated, gilded, ugly, and impractically elevated seats were a gift to my parents from the Duke of the Lichotit, the farthest of the twelve realms from ours. After the duke left, my father had suggested using them as firewood. But my practical mother had decided it would be better to set them aside for guests who might wish to compensate for any feelings of inadequacy by perching in them and pretending to be regal.

Temny and Poteshenie sit atop their makeshift, velvet-draped gaudy thrones with looks of eager expectation on their treacherous faces. The princess sips from one of our silver goblets as Temny holds an apple in his hand.

In the center of that circle, Smotana stands. He is stroking his long spade of a yellow beard with his left hand. His right hand is lazily and expertly twirling a long, slightly curved sword. Smotana's sword is not blunt, but pointed. There's a heavy guard between hilt and shaft meant to protect the hand from an opponent's disarming cut. It's the weapon of a practiced killer. From the way light glints from the edge, it's Damascene steel, razor-honed.

By the head of the dragon!

"Paulek," I say, grabbing his arm, "look at the size of that man!"

He follows my gaze to the blond cutthroat in the middle of the circle. The muscles of Smotana's huge arms ripple as he twirls his blade. Large as he is, he's no taller than my brother, but his shoulders are half again as broad.

Paulek nods seriously. "Good point, little brother. Just as Black Yanosh says, the bigger the target, the easier to hit it. Not so?"

I take a deep breath, grasp the wrist of Paulek's right hand, the hand that is holding his practice sword. "With this?" I ask him. "Look what that man is carrying. He's not using a blunt weapon."

Paulek turns his face so that his eyes are on mine. "Rashko," he says, speaking as slowly as one would to a lack-wit, "the man is a professional soldier. He knows how to use his blade. I am sure that he would not make a mistake in a friendly contest."

"I'm sure of that too. That's what is bothering me."

"*Tu!*" Baron Temny barks. "Here!" He hurls the apple at his man in the center of the circle. Smotana doesn't even turn his head. His sword flashes up, catches the apple in midflight to cleave it in half.

"Ha!" Paulek says. "You see, little brother. Just as I said. The man knows how to use his blade. Nothing to worry about."

Nothing, I think, except your imminent demise.

However, as I think further about it, would the death of my brother fit their plan? Probably not yet. After all, they need a marriage to secure their claim. It's more likely that Smotana's task is to injure Paulek. Perhaps cripple him so Poteshenie can play the part of a nurse and gain further control of him.

Paulek is looking at his sword. "On the other hand," he says slowly, "you are right."

I am? He's not going to do this foolhardy thing?

"It would be an insult to the man to engage in a match with him using something like this."

Paulek hands his practice sword to Georgi, who has just appeared, as if out of nowhere. Behind Georgi is Zelezo, our blacksmith. Zelezo offers what he's been carrying to my brother. It's Paulek's own sword, the one our father gave him when he turned thirteen.

Paulek slides it from the sheath, the sweet steel singing as he does so. Despite the dire circumstance that I, at least, know we are in, the sound of that sword stirs something in my chest like a bird beating its wings.

Paulek's noble blade, twin to the one hanging from my own belt, shines like polished silver. It is long and deceptively thin, not like the palm-wide weapon brandished by Smotana. But I know how supple and strong that sword is, how many hundreds of times the metal was folded and pounded, heated and folded and pounded again at Zelezo's forge. It can bend like a bow without breaking, cut through stone without being dulled.

Paulek swings it once in a wide arc over his head, then brings it down in a whistling cut.

"Ay-yah!" he shouts, stopping his sword so that it points straight at the chest of the blond assassin waiting for him in that circle.

His gesture does not go unnoticed. The rabble of men who'd been talking and joking and swearing is momentarily silenced. Temny lifts an eyebrow. Poteshenie purses her lips in what looks like displeasure. Even Smotana raises his hand to pull at his beard.

Paulek reaches back to punch me in the chest with his free hand.

"*Lepshi, nie?*" he asks, keeping his gaze on his soon-to-be opponent. "Better, no?"

"*Ano,*" I say with what little wind is left in me. It's a bit better.

Temny waves a hand. The circle of men parts to allow Paulek to enter. Every eye in the castle is on him as he strides forward, tall, straight, and confident. But he's not strutting or posturing like Smotana. He's just sure of himself. Even though I feel as if I just swallowed a lead weight, I'm proud of my brother at this moment. Despite his foolish innocence.

"Your Grace," Temny says to my brother. "We

thank you for consenting to this little entertainment. We are honored."

Paulek raises his sword in a salute to Temny. "The honor," he says, "is mine." Then he bows, ever so slightly, to the princess. To her surprise, he doesn't allow himself to be transfixed by the smoldering look she directs at him. If she thinks that her enchantment is going to slow his reflexes or that she may draw his attention away from this martial moment, she is wrong. My brother has never been able to think of more than one thing at a time. His one thought now is this. Combat.

Paulek turns slightly to face Smotana and holds out his sword. Smotana, taking a wide swordsman's stance, his left hand held out behind him, does the same. The two blades ring as they touch.

I scan the upper windows that look down on the courtyard, seeking a familiar profile. Even though he's been no more of a presence than a ghost, Black Yanosh is up there somewhere. The barest flicker of movement from a window four stories above. The gesture of a hand held up with its palm facing down was meant for me. Its meaning is clear enough.

Hold back.

Knowing that our canny weapons master is watching gives me a feeling of relief. That he does not feel it is time yet for him to make his presence known is a reassurance to me. Perilous as this moment may be for my brother, our old teacher is certain of his ability to prevail.

I wish I had that much confidence myself.

"*Hotovo!*" Paulek says. "Ready!"

Smotana does not reply with words but with a sudden half circle push of his blade against my brother's and a lightning-quick forward thrust. A move so sudden it takes my breath away. Big and bulky as Smotana is, his speed is that of a charging bull.

All he hits is empty air. Paulek has simply sidestepped the attack.

"*Dobre!*" Paulek shouts. "Good try!" He taps his sword against the back edge of Smotana's and smiles. "My turn now. *Utok!*"

Smotana is good. He blocks each of Paulek's strikes and lunges. There's no look of concern on the big man's face. He counterattacks. The heavy sword whistles as he spins it, weaves a back-and-forth pattern, thrusts up and down. Their blades clang as Paulek counters each move. There's a big grin on my brother's face. He's pleased that his opponent is using moves that I never attempt against him. Like that backhanded swipe of the blade or the way the blond behemoth starts his swing from far behind him, like a man splitting wood with an ax.

"Good counter."

Clang!

"Fine move."

Ching!

"Never saw that one before."

Paulek keeps up his usual running commentary—almost as if he were the one watching this contest and not me.

As for me, I'm no longer biting my lip with anxiety. Smotana is starting to sweat. He looks as if he's growing winded. The baron appears displeased. The expression on Poteshenie's face is growing sulky. This is not working out as they'd planned.

What none of them know is that, as good as his show of swordsmanship has been thus far, Paulek is only half trying. He's had half a dozen chances to end this fight, either by disarming his opponent—catch the blade, slide up to the crossguard, twist to turn the hilt back against the attacker's wrist—or by taking advantage of one of those foolish fancy spins that leave an excellent opening for a faster bladesman.

Paulek catches Smotana's blade with his. As the two are momentarily locked, I realize that the big man's game is more devious than I thought. He's reaching behind his back with his free hand, pulling out a dagger.

"*Dyka!*" I shout. "Knife."

Perhaps that shout of mine was not necessary. Paulek's left hand intercepts Smotana's wrist. It is hard to say if it is his incredible reflexes or my warning that prevented his being stabbed in the belly. But the smile is gone from Paulek's face. Smotana has just made my easygoing older brother angry.

"*Zle*," he growls, his lips almost touching Smotana's left ear. "Bad move."

What Paulek does next is such a flurry of movement that I doubt anyone other than me catches it. It includes the quick placement of his front foot behind Smotana's leg, a twist of his blade, and a thudding strike of his elbow to the big man's chest. On second thought, since he taught that series of moves to us, I am sure that Black Yanosh watching from behind the drapes of that high window also saw. And nodded his head.

The result, however, is visible to everyone. Smotana is sprawled on his back gasping to regain the wind that's been knocked out of him. His sword is spinning across the stones of the courtyard twenty feet away from him. His razor-edged dagger has flipped through the air and buried its point in the right leg of the heavy chair where Baron Temny sits. That, perhaps, was an accident. It's one that I wish had involved the baron's actual leg—or some higher part of his anatomy.

What's not an accident is that Paulek now holds most of Smotana's yellow beard in his left hand. He'd sliced it off with one sweep of his sword.

Paulek steps forward and puts the point of his blade against Smotana's throat.

"Yield," he says, his word hard as iron.

Smotana takes a gasping breath and nods.

I've never seen my older brother look more like my father. Perhaps there's a chance now that he will see reason. He'll understand these people mean us no good. I'm not sure what we'll do, but at least he'll no longer be enthralled by . . .

The sound of two small hands clapping breaks the moment.

"*Vyborne! Vyborne!*" a seductive voice is crying out. "Wonderful, wonderful."

It's the princess. She is standing up, smiling in such an insincere and theatrical way that I can't imagine anyone being taken in by it. But Paulek is. Though he could stand against their best swordsman, he's no match for this attack.

The angry look vanishes from his face to be replaced by one of moonstruck pleasure. He turns away from his defeated opponent, thrusts his sword back into the sheath that Zelezo holds out to him. I try to say something to him. He walks by me as if I am not there. He only pauses to look down at the handful of beard he is still holding. How did this get here? Then he tosses it back over his shoulder, bows, and takes a final step forward to drop on one knee before the enchantress, his arms held out to his sides.

"I . . . I," my brother stammers, "I am glad I pleased you."

And I think I am going to be sick.

I need advice. There's only one place I can think now to go.

No one pays me any notice as I leave except for Georgi. He catches my eye when I'm halfway to the gate, nods his head.

As soon as I've crossed the drawbridge, I turn left to take the narrow twisting trail that leads to my destination. When Hladka Hvorka is no longer in sight, Ucta and Odvaha come trotting out of the brush to join me.

"We need," I say to them, "to visit Uncle Jozef."

Desat

THE SECOND THING that Pavol found came to his hands when he was alone. A dream spoke to him in the night. A high thin voice called him to wake.

A gift, it cried, as if from high in the sky. *A gift for a gift, a gift for you.*

He sat up and looked around. No sound came from Baba Marta and Uncle Tomas's room. Pavol dressed and walked outside.

The full moon shone down so brightly that his own shadow was visible, though blurred. When he spread his arms, the dark shape that seemed to grow from his feet appeared to have wings.

Wings. He nodded to himself. He knew now where he had to go.

He took the path that led back to the highest hill in the forest, the very place where he had first met

Uncle Tomas. The moon had moved the width of two hands across the sky by the time he got there.

The great pine was still where it had been. It was thicker at the base, but the stubs of broken branches that stuck out all along its trunk made it as easy to climb as a ladder. As he neared the top Pavol saw what he had thought he would see. There, wedged among the top limbs, was a great nest.

Cheeping sounds were coming from within. He knew what it meant. He well understood that even in the night, what he was attempting was perilous. Should the mother eagle seek to defend her new hatchlings from this human invader, his face could be torn by her talons, her wide wings could knock him out of the tree to fall to his death.

He did not hesitate. But he did move slowly as he raised himself up to look into the nest. There, not more than a hand's width from his face, was the mother eagle's beak. Her eyes reflected back the moonlight as she stared at him.

Pavol reached back into the bag hung over his shoulder and then held out his hand. It was not empty. It held the warm body of the rabbit he had taken from one of Uncle Tomas's snares. The mother eagle opened her beak and jerked the rabbit from his grasp. Her wings spread to shelter her young, she shifted to turn away from him. Her tail, its brown feathers fanned out, was now just in front of him, touching the hand that had held the rabbit.

One feather jutted out from the others. Pavol opened his fingers, took hold, and it came away in his grasp.

"Two," Pavol whispered to himself as he slipped it into the pouch that always hung around his waist.

Then he carefully descended the great tree.

CHAPTER TEN

The Same Name

As ALWAYS, WHETHER it is the dead of winter or the heat of summer, the door of Uncle Jozef and Baba Anya's dom is open. A roughly made two-room hut with a roof of thatch, it seems no different from those of any of the other common folk of our valley. A curl of smoke drifts up from their chimney.

Ucta and Odvaha flop down into their usual guard posts on either side of the door. They'll wait there while I'm inside, even if it means spending most of the day in the sun.

Baba Anya's chickens immediately come flocking up to cluck and peck at the earth around them. Ucta lifts up his right front foot so that Uncle Jozef's imperious red-cockaded rooster can pry out a bit of grain beneath it. Unlike the princess's nasty cat, my friends will do no harm to these feather-brained cluckers.

I think they're amused by the foolishness of those strutting, potential snacks.

I sniff the air. There's a lingering scent from one of Baba Anya's mouth-watering stews. But it's from yesterday. Nothing cooking just now. I shouldn't be surprised. It's market day. On market day Uncle Jozef makes do with a cold midday meal while she's off from early morning to mid-afternoon trundling from stall to stall, chatting with friends and bargaining.

"*Ahoj,*" I call as I stand at the threshold of the single-roomed hut. "Uncle Jozef?"

My hello is not to make Uncle Jozef aware of my arrival. I have no doubt that he already knows I am here. But there's a certain amount of ceremony attached to any of my dealings with him. Cesta, again.

"*Vitaj, synovec,*" his deep, gruff voice answers from the shadows beyond the doorway.

It thrilled me the first time he welcomed me with those words. It still affects me like that. To be called *synovec*, nephew, by Uncle Jozef, to be told you are welcome, is like passing a test. Or, to be accurate, being admitted into the examination chamber.

I tried once to explain that to my brother. But Paulek just looked at me blankly. Paulek likes Uncle Jozef. He respects him for his strength. But he has no idea at all what our village wise man knows. He's never been invited into Uncle Jozef's dom.

Nor has he wanted to be. Why would he, the older son of a baron, bow his head to venture into the cramped, smoky hut of some old peasant? Even though he does not know what he is missing.

I shake my head at the wry thought that comes to me. Among the things Paulek is missing from Uncle Jozef are a variety of bruises.

I duck my head and hunch my shoulders as I enter . . . and not just because of the low doorway. I never know what might happen whenever I venture here. I might be crushed in what seems a friendly bear hug but turns into a wrestling lesson. I might have something thrown, swung, or shot at me. Or I might be asked a seemingly simple question that eventually makes my brain start spinning.

Today, it's none of those. Uncle Jozef is just sitting there by the fireplace with his eyes closed, hands held out palms up. There's a benevolent look on his face. This worries me more than having a club hurled at my nose or being asked "Why water?"

"*Sadni si,*" he rumbles.

I sit on the dirt floor. I'm not just being humble. There's little in this room in the way of furniture. Aside from the kitchen area to the left—which is Baba Anya's alone—the main features on this side are Uncle Jozef's massive oak chest to the left of the fireplace, a single chair, and a large writing table strewn with an assortment of quill pens and sheets of parchment. The entire wall behind that table is lined with well-made shelves laden with books and scrolls of all shapes and sizes.

I used to ask why he, a man of such learning, and Baba Anya, an almost magically talented herbalist, have chosen to live in these simple surroundings. With their abilities they could have amassed much wealth and power. Failing that, why hadn't they at least built themselves a finer house?

Uncle Jozef's answers were like those enigmatic sayings like Father loves. Now that I think of it, I wonder if Father learned his proverbs from Uncle Jozef?

"Rashko, no matter how large a salmon grows, it always returns to its own stream."

"My boy, no man can eat more than his belly can hold."

"Nephew, you do not have to climb to the top of a tower to see the stars."

It was maddening. So, finally, I gave up asking why Uncle Jozef is so content with being a mere village sage, Baba Anya with being the midwife and healer for any in our valley needing her help.

But I have not given up inquiring about other

things. And the question I have to ask now is a direct one. What in the name of heaven and earth can I do about the fix in which my family and I have found ourselves?

I can't ask right away. Waiting is part of Cesta. The more impatient you are, the longer your wait will be.

If I were Paulek, I suppose I'd just try commanding Uncle Jozef to give me an answer. Straightforward as an arrow shot at a target—even if that target is a big rock that will shatter your bolt.

Patience, Rashko, patience. Sit. Be calm. Wait. Stop clenching and unclenching your fists.

"You might also stop grinding your teeth, nephew," Uncle Jozef rumbles.

Then he laughs, a huge belly laugh that makes his whole body shake. Uncle Jozef is not fat. There's nothing but muscle on his massive frame. But he is shaped like a barrel, a very big one. That is why his chair in front of that writing desk was made from the heavy limbs of a huge old oak tree. Anyone seeing that monumental seat for the first time might wonder why it was built to bear the weight of a bull. Until they saw Uncle Jozef and said, "Ah-ha."

As Uncle Jozef fills the room with his roaring laughter, I start to chuckle in spite of myself. How foolish my impatience and self-absorption is. It really is funny. I relax into laughter almost as loud as that of my teacher.

Laughter, Uncle Jozef has taught me over the years, is medicine. Even in the midst of pain and confusion, mirth brings healing. It lifts your heart, lightens the load. Without laughter we humans would long ago have been crushed by the weight of the past and its sorrows.

"*Dobre,*" Uncle Jozef growls. He straightens up, suddenly serious. "Good. Now you are ready to ask about what to do about those botflies who have mistaken us and our little land for some herd of cattle they can prey upon. Eh?"

"Unh," I say. "Unh . . . unh." Uncle Jozef does this to me almost every time. He reduces me to the level of a stammering fool.

"*Ano*, yes, it is a big problem. *Pod*. Come."

Uncle Jozef rises. It's an impressive spectacle, as if a hill decided to grow legs and walk. I stand with him, feeling like a badger next to a bear, and we move over to his table. He pulls out his chair, the weighty legs scraping lines in the hard-packed earth of the floor, then he drops his bulk onto the seat. Massive as it is, the chair creaks under his weight.

"That book," he says, pointing with his right thumb. "Bring it to me."

I walk over and reach up to reverently remove the large volume he's indicated from the wall. Holding it with both hands, I carry it back to Uncle Jozef. He takes it with one huge paw and tosses it on the tabletop in almost the way one might throw dice. The book lands lightly and falls open, as if of its own accord. There, on the left-hand page, is a large portrait of a sinister-looking figure. Ornately appareled, the narrow-faced man holds a curved sword in one hand and the head of someone clearly not a friend in the other.

I draw in a quick breath. The woodcut must have been done by a talented artist—one sensitive enough to have been rather nervous while making it. The small sharp teeth, the thick eyebrows. Alive with malevolence, snake-like eyes stare straight up at me from the page. A date is printed beneath the picture.

"Three hundred years ago!" Uncle Jozef's voice is deep as the first warning roll of thunder before a storm strike. "Baron Vladimir Temny."

"The same name? His great-great-grandfather or something like that?"

"*Nie.*" Uncle Jozef tosses his head back in a vigorous shake that makes his great mane of silver hair swish across his face. "Though he has been known by other names, it is he."

One word immediately comes to my mind. I speak it . . . carefully.

"*Vampyr?*"

Uncle Jozef turns and slowly shakes his head. "*Nie.* Your house guest is not one of those."

He turns a page and runs his finger down the words written in Latin. It's a language I recognize but have not yet learned to read, so looking over his shoulder doesn't help. All I can do is wait.

"Ah, here it is. Bitten once by vampire. Vampire died."

I start to laugh, but he gives me a look that shows he is not joking.

"So if he is not one of the Undead, then how has he managed to live for so long?"

Uncle Jozef doesn't answer. He just looks at me in that way he does when I've said something foolish. Is it like the look that I suppose comes over my face when I am trying to explain the obvious to my older brother?

"Care to venture a guess, nephew?"

"Magic," I say.

Uncle Jozef nods. "Drawn from wherever he can find it."

Magic, inexplicable as it is, explains a great many things. As the proverb goes, it is better to believe the truth than investigate why it is so.

"I have another question."

"Of course you do." That pitying look is on his face again.

I ask my question anyway.

"Why has be come to us?"

Uncle Jozef reaches one of his huge hands up, pulls down one of the parchment scrolls and unrolls it. It's a map of our country and the lands around it, those twelve often quarrelsome realms.

"How are we different here?" he asks.

"We're at peace."

"*Ano.* And why is that?"

I think about his question. Is it because we are isolated by our mountains? Because the road that leads here ends at the slopes of the High Tatras? Then it comes to me.

"Prince Pavol," I reply.

"*Ano.*" Uncle Jozef nods, raising one thick eyebrow. "And what did he bring back from his quest?"

Pavol the Good. In the past, small as our realm might be, wars were fought here until my several-times-great-grandfather Pavol gained the dukedom.

I don't know all of my ancestor's story. But what I have been told is that when he was a young man, only a little older than I am now, Pavol set out on a great quest.

Though an orphan, with little to his name other than the clothing on his back, Pavol had an unshakably friendly and positive attitude. He wandered about, his head held high, delighted at the songs of the birds and grateful for whatever good happened to come his way—even if it was a turnip bestowed upon him by some goodwife who took pity on this ragged clown of a man. Even if someone ridiculed him one day, on the next day Pavol would be the first to offer that person help when he needed it. Should a bit of coin come his way, Pavol would invariably give it to the first beggar he saw by the roadside, even if it meant going hungry himself. When things went awry, he would be amused rather than dismayed. If he was so engrossed with watching the clouds that he fell into a ditch and came up muddy and bruised, he would laugh even louder than those who observed his idiocy.

Pavol the Foolish, they called him.

When he went on his quest up into the High Tatra Mountains on the back of an ass everyone assumed that he would perish.

How wrong they were.

I don't know exactly what happened next. I wish I did. But what I have been told is that when Pavol did return, astride a silver stallion with fiery eyes and horseshoes forged of steel, he was a different man. Charismatic and confident, he became Duke Pavol the First. He regained control of our country, which had been held in the iron grip of an evil tyrant, without spilling a drop of blood. He might have even gone further in making our land great. But he stopped when he reached the pass leading into our valley.

"A wise man knows," he said, "when his reach does not exceed his grasp."

It was Duke Pavol the Good who built Castle Hladka Hvorka on top of the hill of the same name, that height where no man had ever dared to venture alone, much less spend the night. In fact, some say— though that does seem to be stretching it a bit—that our great castle rose up complete in a single night, like a stone bud opening in flower.

Then Duke Pavol invited all of the rulers from the human lands around ours to Hladka Hvorka. Amazingly, they all came. They sat together and met in a spirit of truce. However, no one drank the wine that was served to them, and whenever they sat, there was always a bit of a scuffle for the best chairs—the ones with their backs to the wall.

At that great convocation, presided over by Pavol the First, or Pavol the Just, as he began to be called by the surrounding powers, an agreement was forged between us and all the other powers around. We will hold our land in peace. All we ask is that you do one thing. Just leave us alone.

Prosim? Please? Duke Pavol said, lightly fingering the large, bejeweled sword that hung by his side and the pouch that hung at his belt.

The visiting powers eyed that sword. They also took note of the duke's impressive white horse, which was always by his side, even when he was not riding it. Even at meetings inside the castle. Now and then it would lean forward to nuzzle Duke Pavol's ear as if whispering to him.

The assent of all the various barons, dukes, landgrafs, kings, and kinglets came quickly.

Dakujem. Thank you, Duke Pavol said, a wide smile on his face, his great horse nodding its head in seeming agreement.

And that truce, the agreement was still in full force, still watched over by all the powers around us.

Uncle Jozef's voice brings me back from my thoughts of my great ancestor.

"So," he is asking, "in addition to peace, what other legacy did Duke Pavol leave to your family."

I know, immediately, what he means.

"His, ah . . . and the, ah . . ."

Uncle Jozef nods. *"Ano."*

It seems that I must add Uncle Jozef to the short list of those who know about . . .

"Our little secret?"

"*Ano.*" Uncle Jozef raises both eyebrows.

I think I now understand. The baron has been attracted by the rumors that my family has some sort of hidden wealth. That is what has brought this weasel of a man and his despicable daughter to our door. *Kuzlo a bohats.* Magic and wealth. That is what this is about.

A man such as the baron needs material wealth, and not just to purchase the appurtenances of a life of great comfort. Wealth is needed to raise and sustain an army, to bribe officials, to gain and maintain political control. Then, with the land in his grasp, he can do the dark deeds that help ensure unaging life. Of course, in the hands of a dark sorcerer, all wealth, material and magical alike, is quickly used up.

That is how it was long ago in the time of the Dark Lord, according to the stories that Baba Anya told us. Just as a vampire draws the lifeblood from a single human victim, that evil one who longed to live forever sucked the wealth and the life from our unlucky land during the years of his rule. The soil became poorer, the lives of the people shorter and shorter. So, had it not been for Pavol, it would have continued until—like a spider leaving the empty husk of a fly caught in its web—all life would have been sucked away and the Dark Lord would have moved on.

Always seeking out new hunting grounds. That is what those such as Baron Temny must do. Our peaceful realm must have looked like easy prey, especially after he lured my parents away so that he could begin a reign like that of the evil one of long ago. Begin a reign? Or regain it?

I don't have to speak my question to Uncle Jozef. He's already nodding.

"That is also why he has come," Uncle Jozef says. "Here, at Hladka Hvorka, Prince Pavol stripped him of his power. Though it took him centuries to grow enough in strength, he has returned to regain what he lost."

I wish I were older, I wish I were wiser and stronger. I wish I knew what to do.

I wish . . .

"Rashko."

Uncle Jozef's rumbling voice brings me out of my self-pitying trance. He leans down toward me. There's another scroll in his hands. He unrolls the top and holds it out in front of me, I read the first words aloud.

"The True Tale of Pavol."

The air seems to quiver around me as I speak those words.

"Uncle Jozef," I say. My voice is a bit unsteady. "I've wanted to know more of Pavol's story since I was a small child. But I was always told I was not yet ready to hear it. Am I ready now?"

"*Ano,*" Uncle Jozef says. "You have never been more ready. *Citaj.* Read."

I take the scroll in my hands and unroll it. I start to read, as I have done with other documents countless times before. But this is unlike any other reading I've ever done. The scroll vanishes.

And so, in a way, do I!

I'm no longer sitting on the floor of Uncle Jozef's dom. I don't just see the tale in my mind. I'm not just reading the tale of Pavol. I'm with him in his thoughts and deeds.

Jedenast

ALONE IN THE forest, Pavol tossed and turned. He could not sleep. He thought of many things, but most of all about the six objects that now rested in his pouch, each with its own story of how it had come to him. And there was one more thing, one more story yet to be found before he would begin the hardest part of his quest. Not that it would be easy here . . . another reason why sleep would not come.

Pavol had chosen his shelter in Stary Les carefully. It was so deep in the woods and so well concealed that even an experienced tracker would be unlikely to find it. From the outside it looked like nothing more than a pile of brush.

Of course, even an experienced tracker would have avoided and been terrified of the place. Here, close to the lights of the Silver Lands things were . . . unusual. The trees themselves were reputed to be both aware and intolerant of intruders. Ancient oaks, it was said, might creep close and then crush sleeping travelers with their heavy roots.

Pavol, though, who had ventured there at the bidding of his guardians, had no such fears. He felt the magic in the air and found that he rather liked it. However, he did make sure that his camp for the night was well uphill and some distance from the river below, for it was a stream that flowed into or from (some said both at the same time) the Faerie realm.

The waters of that stream, as a result, were quite lively. If one dared to take and eat a fish from its flow, one should not toss its bones back in. Otherwise those bones would come again to life—without their former sheathing of flesh.

Then he heard it. Faintly at first. A cry in the night. He sat up. It was a call for help.

Without a second thought or a torch to guide him he ventured out into the night. The half-moon was bright enough to light his way. He went downhill following the cry that grew louder now.

He soon began to run, drawn by the increasing urgency in that plea for aid. It was surely a stranger's voice but it came, Pavol felt certain, from the throat of someone he might like or even admire.

Though insistent in its need for assistance—help me or I will not survive—it held neither fear nor panic.

He pushed through a curtain of willows. A sparkle like that of a thousand diamonds suddenly was there before him. The moon's light reflecting from the surface of the wide stream that rose in the Silver Lands and continued on along the edge of Stary Les, was broken by the dark-haired, slender figure struggling to reach the shore. Hands held high, that person was being held, pulled by something unseen beneath the surface.

Not mud, thought Pavol. Far worse than that.

Yet that thought did not keep him from taking a deep, deep breath and diving in headfirst. He kicked forward underwater until his outstretched hands grasped the slimy arms that had wrapped around the stranger's ankles. Those arms were powerful, but Pavol was stronger. Dead flesh tore as he pulled them free. Then, as slithery hands reached for him, he switched his grip to the neck. He squeezed hard, digging his fingers in deep enough to feel the bone beneath.

NIE, a voice that knew no breath gasped.

Ano, Pavol thought back. *You go, I let go.*

ANO! ANO! I GO, I GO.

Pavol released his grasp and felt the creature slip

away, back into the mud. His lungs close to bursting, he rose to the surface.

The slender stranger was nowhere to be seen. Pavol shook the stinking mud from his fingers, wiped ooze from his cheek. Had the one he rescued departed without a word?

Not even a simple *Dakujem, pan?*

Was that the way of the Fair Folk, for such he was sure the slender stranger must be, to not show gratitude as mortals do?

The sound of a surprisingly human voice cursing drew his eyes farther downstream. The thin, raven-haired rescuee was there, pulling up onto the shore the small shell of his boat. It must have been the stranger's craft before being tipped over by the eager hands of the creature whose death had not ended its hunger for living flesh.

The stranger turned toward him. The moonlight illuminated a fine, fair face.

Ah, not his boat. Her boat.

"*Dakujem,* Pavol," she said. "I fear that my arrival was less dignified than I planned." She smiled. Quite a nice smile. "It has made it more clear to me why the Folk have observed you with interest. Indeed, the time has arrived for you to have this gift from my cousins."

Cousins, Pavol thought.

He looked at her. Though he had not, to his knowledge, seen any like *her* before, he guessed who she was, a being right out of Baba Marta's tales. It explained why, though her features were Faerie perfect, her hair was dark and not fair.

She was an in-betweener, one whose mother or father was not of the Fair Folk but human. Such half-bloods might remain within the Silver Realm or choose to live as a human.

For some reason, that thought sent a shiver of excitement down his back. And when she smiled at him, his heart quite came up into his throat.

She nodded. "You will need this. And if you complete your quest, we shall meet again. My name," she said, "is Karoline."

Then she placed the bronze bracelet in his hand.

CHAPTER ELEVEN

The Er-ah

I SHAKE MY head as I look up from the scroll at Uncle Jozef.

I'm disoriented. How long have I been here? I feel as if hours have passed. For a moment I panic at the thought of what may have transpired back at our castle while I've been gone.

Then I notice that the sunlight coming in through the door is still slanting at the same angle. I can see Ucta and Odvaha keeping guard on either side. It's the same day, the same hour. It was only a few breaths ago that Uncle Jozef handed me that scroll. In the space of a heartbeat I saw, no, shared an event in Pavol's life that took far longer.

It was not just my imagination. I'm certain of that. I was there, generations ago, watching it happen. And just when it was really getting interesting, I've found myself back again. I'm a bit resentful about that. I'm also feeling a little ill.

"Rashko, *ako ti je?* How are you?" Uncle Jozef asks.

"I just need to sit down," I say. "I feel dizzy."

"You are sitting," Uncle Jozef replies. "On the floor."

I start to stand, but his heavy hand on my shoulder holds me back as effectively as the weight of a fallen tree.

"*Pockaj.* Wait." He studies my face and then nods. "Where were you?"

I feel reticent to share the vision—or experience— I've just been through. Where I really want to be is back watching more of my ancestor's story unfold. I take a deep breath and then let it out through my teeth.

"I was there," I say. "I saw Pavol save someone who gave him a bronze bracelet."

Uncle Jozef touches his thumb to his lips.

"*Ano,*" he says, nodding slowly.

Part of me wants to ask what all that has transpired means. How does this all relate to our problem with the baron? I keep my lips pressed together. Better to let Uncle Jozef talk.

"*Dobre.* Good," he says. "The dragon bracelet."

Uncle Jozef takes a few steps back toward the fire

and then folds down into the cross-legged position he was in before we went over to his books and his desk. It's amazing how one with the weight of so many seasons and so large a frame can be so nimble. I'm no longer dizzy, but when I stand up to go and join him, it is with considerably less grace.

"So," he says. "Let us go slowly now. One who runs too fast may dash past opportunity. Think now about your family's little secret, the first time it was disclosed to you."

I smile as the memory comes to me. It was all so typical of my mother.

THE YEAR PAULEK was eight and I was seven our birthday celebration was memorable. I have not mentioned it before, but we were born exactly a year apart. Our ages differ, but our birth date is the same.

As usual, I had to open my present first so that Paulek could lay claim to it. Then, after opening his gift box, he could, with a show of great magnanimity, announce that he would gladly share both his presents with his beloved brother.

The present partially mine was a small carved horse with a knight bearing a sword and shield on his back. Paulek's was a miniature castle with a dragon perched atop its tower. Both had been expertly crafted, painted with great detail. It seems as if they were alive and about to start breathing—including the little castle!

The birthday feast included all of our favorite foods. *Pierogies* were the appetizer (Paulek and I each ate only seven or so), followed by *zapekane rezne*, huge loaves of bread, a small mountain of pork chops without the bones seasoned with salt and pepper and covered with cheese and a bit of table cream before baking. We consumed no more than a dozen dumplings filled with jelly so that we would not spoil our appetite for the *babovka*, a large, light fluffy cake topped with sugar, raisins, and nuts that waited at the end of our repast.

While we were wiping our plates with heels of bread and searching the serving platters for scraps like two hungry little bears, my father cast a knowing glance at my mother. It was less than subtle, accompanied as it was by a loud "Ah, ahem, eh? Shall we? Now?"

That was Father's way of passing Mother messages he meant to bypass our ears. Shouldn't they be put to bed now? or Can't you save a bit of that cake for me before they eat it all?

As always, Paulek paid no attention. I pretended I didn't notice, even though my parents had become an open book to me by the time I was four.

"What's that, my dear?" Mother said brightly back to Father. She was seldom quick to comprehend his attempts at surreptitiousness.

"I mean, er-ah, you know . . . that we should now show the . . . you know?"

"No, dear."

Father drew Mother aside and whispered in her ear. It was, however, loud enough for my keen ears to hear it clearly.

"Isn't it time, y' know, now that they are old enough, that you showed the boys, that which we do not talk about?"

My father looked around behind him to see if anyone was eavesdropping. Of course Georgi was there, his hands steepled, his eyes looking innocently up at the ceiling—that little smile twitching the corners of his mouth.

Father continued. "Y' know what I mean, in the cellar, the . . . er-ah?"

"Oh," Mother said, understanding coming to her face that was always as lovely as a cloudless sky, "you want me to show them the dra—"

My father's index finger pressed gently to her lips cut off the word she'd begun to speak.

"Exactly," he said. "I'll stay here and guard the door. Make sure no one follows."

"Come along, dears," Mother said, taking us by

our arms. "Put down your knives and spoons. Time for you to see the . . ." My mother paused, noting that my father was making frantic gestures urging her to silence. "Well, you'll soon see."

With that she led us to a hidden passage carefully concealed behind the painted tapestry hung on the castle's west wall whose shifting patterns I always found myself studying.

That day, I recall, I took note of the way the shape of the dragon itself seemed brighter and more prominent than usual. But the overall message of the tapestry was still impossible for me to decipher, unlike the secrets my less-than-clever parents tried to keep from me. Among them was that door my mother revealed by pulling back the tapestry. It was so well hidden that I had not discovered it myself until the day I learned to crawl.

"Look, boys," she said.

Paulek wanted to get back to his new toys.

"Can't you just take Rashko?" he said.

"No, dear," my mother said in a firm voice. "You must do this together."

By now Georgi had produced a ring of keys and handed it to Father.

"Turn your back, Georgi," my father said.

Then, as Georgi stifled the chuckle shaking his shoulders, my father chose the correct key. Not hard to do. It was the only one that had a large wooden tag labeled *"Tajny Prechod,"* Secret Passage, attached to it. Father turned the key in the lock and pulled the metal-bound door open with a loud creak.

Still with his back turned, Georgi handed my mother a torch. Had he not done so, my mother would likely have led us into total darkness and then stood there in confusion wondering why we weren't able to see anything.

"Watch your step on the corners," Father cautioned.

"Yes, dear," Mother replied. "Hold your brother's hand," she said to me.

And we were off to the deep, secret cellars of Hladka Hvorka.

In all the old stories, whenever someone—usually a knight errant—finds his way into a hidden passage that leads mysteriously down into the earth, there are certain things one expects. Among them are the cobwebs, eerie noises, the eldritch markings of twisted magical runes upon slimy walls, and strange cold drafts—to say nothing of the innumerable traps where one steps on a loose trigger stone and is then impaled by sharp spikes or crushed by walls that grind inexorably closer. Then there are the yawning pits that open unexpectedly to send the unwary screaming down into dread depths.

Having heard several such grisly tales from Baba Anya by the time I was seven I was hopeful of adventure after we passed through the hidden doorway. However, none of the aforementioned perils were present in the well-kept passageway that led down below Hladka Hvorka. The walls were dry and freshly whitewashed, the ceiling absent of spiders or webs. All rather a disappointment to me. The prosaic stairs were so neat and free of dust that it looked suspiciously as if they had been quite recently swept in preparation for our little excursion. That impression was strengthened when I noticed the broom closet off to the side on the first landing.

That well-kept "Secret Passage" was further evidence of what I had come to realize, even by the age of seven. Our loyally competent servants were the ones who truly ran Castle Hladka Hvorka. There were no secrets they did not know. At times it made me wonder why they'd never taken advantage of my parents' innocent lack of awareness. Once or twice, I even pondered the possibility that my parents were not quite as unworldly as they seemed, that they actually knew more than they appeared to know.

My final conclusion, though, was that my parents' constant intentions to do good and to treat everyone who worked for them as valued helpers, inspired both loyalty and patience in all our retainers. I also think they all respect my father's great physical strength and my mother's, shall we say, special abilities that I first saw displayed that day when we descended.

On down we went, one neat stairway after another, every step so clean you could have eaten your breakfast on it. How boring, I was thinking. The only strange thing was that, for some inexplicable reason, I felt as if we were climbing rather than descending. It was as if we were ascending a mountainside rather than going down one steep set of stairs after another. But then we rounded the final corner. And there was another door, quite a door!

From that point on, things were quite different. Several things changed for me, including my opinion of my mother. Although little in the realm of intellect was familiar to her, I realized her other talent that day in the deepest cellars of Castle Hladka Hvorka. My, yes.

That door that loomed before us was unlike any I'd ever encountered before. Three times the height of a tall man, it was wide enough to drive a team through. It was made of neither wood nor metal, but a weird black stone that glistened with darkness. It seemed to glow and absorb the light at the same time. I was impressed—and also briefly bemused.

How might it be opened? On its smooth surface there was no lock, no doorknob or handle, not even any visible hinges.

"*Velke dvere.* Big door!" Paulek said in a reverential voice. Even he was awed.

"Give me a bit of space, my dears," Mother said, handing me the torch and pulling up the sleeve of her gown.

There was a commanding note in her voice I'd not heard before. Both Paulek and I were swift to react, taking several steps backward. It wasn't just what she said. She had visibly started to glow. Well, not all of her. Just the right hand that she held up in front of her. It was already twice as bright as the torch she'd passed to me.

As she took a step toward the massive door, her hand became as difficult to look at as the midday sun. The look on her illuminated face was more determined than I'd ever seen it, even more than when she was trying (with little success) to thread a needle. Sewing was my mother's favorite hobby, even though nothing she stitched together would have ever proved wearable, but for the patient assistance of Grace, Grace, Grace, and Charity.

Now, though, there was power and certainty in every step she took. She spoke again.

"*Teraz!* Now!"

The voice that came from her mouth was hers but different. It rumbled and rolled, echoed around us and through us, out beyond the edge of the world and back again. We were more than awed.

That is sooo loud, I thought. *I hope Mother never yells at me with that voice. As soon as I get back upstairs, I am going straight up to her bedchamber to remove that frog I put into her sewing box.*

Then she spoke again in that voice of thunder.

"VELKE DVERE! OTVORTE SA!"

Yes, that's what she said.

Big door! Open!

Unexpectedly potent as my mother revealed herself to be at that moment, she also proved she was still predictably unimaginative.

As commanded, the door began to move. It lifted up a little—it had, I could now see, lots of little feet on the bottom—then waltzed backward and slightly sideways, leaving the immense portal open for our entrance.

"Dakujem, dvere," my mother said. "Thank you, door."

Then to us, "Come along, dears."

We came along. Neither of us uttered a peep. What could we say? Other than "Oh my!" or "Gah!"

The room we tiptoed into was vast. It seemed, rather troublingly, much too big to fit into the space below our castle. It didn't feel as much like a cavern in the depths of the earth as a cave that belonged high atop the Tatras. Its size, however, was only part of what we noticed.

All around us was the "er-ah," my father had mentioned.

There were great heaps of rough nuggets. Innumerable coins spilled out of wooden trunks. There were finely worked goblets and statues, diadems and coronets, even chairs and thrones—some bearing scratches in their soft metal surfaces, as if they'd been at one time or another snatched up by sharp-clawed feet. Even though we were young boys, Paulek and I knew enough to be vastly impressed.

"Oh my," I said, finally regaining my breath.

"Gah!" my openmouthed brother added.

"*Ano,*" my mother agreed. "It is rather quite a lot of gold."

THE DRAGON'S GOLD.

Note that I did not say "our gold." No one in our family would ever dream of saying or thinking that. None of us are greedy. Not even Paulek. True, my brother did enjoy confiscating my childhood possessions and we still have been known to scuffle over the last turkey leg. But food and mutually owned toys are one thing. Mountains of precious metal and stacks of jewels are quite another.

Paulek and I understand certain lessons that Mother taught us. If you become possessive about wealth, it does strange things to you. Especially gold that is cursed. The best thing to do is to keep it hidden away.

A second lesson was equally simple. Don't attract too much attention. That's been the motto of our family since the time of Pavol the Good. Admittedly, when my ancestor caused a hill to rise and a sizeable castle to appear overnight, he did create a bit of a stir. However, mystically appearing buildings do not attract the avaricious the way that the glow of that soft heavy metal does.

Also, it was explained to Paulek and me, if one tried to remove too much of the er-ah from that cavern, even though it is, technically, under our control now—it might awaken the gold's unseen guardian. Not to say what it is, but it is big, scaly, toothy, and breathes fire, don't you know?

However, my family does not hoard that gold like jealous misers—or the dog in the stable that keeps the horses from the hay it can't eat itself. What my parents have always done with that treasure is to share it, a little bit at a time. The thing about cursed wealth is that those who are generous of spirit may actually use it, as long as it is for the needy and not themselves.

Thus Mother makes her twice-yearly foray down to that cave to fill a few picnic baskets with coins. Then, masked and hooded so that no one can ever guess who they are—unless that person takes note of the fact that beneath their masks and hoods my mother and father wear their usual monogrammed clothing and travel in our castle's ducal coach—she and Father distribute that wealth. Despite his rather limited grasp of economics (or history or geography or mathematics or virtually any subject, for that matter), Father can sniff out a swindler or thief from miles away. Thus only the truly needy ever benefit from my parents' largesse. Homes for orphans, food and clothing for those in need, and so on.

The help that my parents bestow is always accepted with gratitude. I know that firsthand. Paulek and I have accompanied them ever since our first visit to the cave. When we were little, it was a bit difficult for us to assist. Imagine yourself a seven-year-old boy lugging a large and suspiciously sagging picnic basket, while pretending that its contents are nothing more than a roasted pheasant, some bread and wine and cheese. Even a small handful of gold is heavy.

"Might I help with that, young master?"

"No, Georgi, unnnhhh, it . . . isn't . . . unnnhh, at all heavy."

Naturally, there are rumors about our fortune.

"Oh, that old story," my father always chuckles whenever some visiting outsider brings it up. "Rather exaggerated. Dragon's gold and all. Quite amusing. Wouldn't believe that if I were you."

Within our dukedom, those favored by our family's subtle philanthropy always say thanks—rather amusingly at times.

Such as last summer when my father dropped sufficient gold coins into a famer's hands to enable him to rebuild his barn and house burned down by lightning.

"Dakujem, dakujem," the man sobbed, tears filling his eyes. "Thank you, thank you." He grasped my father's hand and kissed it—something that always embarrasses my father, though he graciously did not attempt to pull his hand from the farmer's grasp. "Thanks to you and your wife, Duke—ooof!"

The "ooof" was a result of the farmer's wife elbowing the man firmly in his stomach before he could finish his sentence.

"Mysterious strangers," she said, "we will always be grateful for your kindness."

"Ano," said the farmer, having recovered his breath, "my wife is right. We thank you . . . ah,

unknown people who have probably come from far away and not from any castle that we can see from our front door."

He looked over at his wife, who had raised an eyebrow, but nothing more. "May you live a thousand years," he continued.

"And," he added, emboldened by her lack of response, turning his glance toward Paulek and me, both of us as mysteriously and ineffectually masked as our happy parents, "may good fortune always attend your two sons, Pau—ooof!"

The woman was amazingly adept with an elbow.

IT HAS TAKEN only a few heartbeats to revisit my memory. I look up at Uncle Jozef.

"I've thought about it," I say. "About the dragon's treasure."

"And?" he asks

What else was I supposed to remember?

He remains maddeningly silent. I wait. So does he. Despite my understandable impatience with my family, I actually can be patient when I need to be. But this is like having a contest with a boulder to see who can sit still the longest. I give up.

"What?" I ask with a sigh.

"Ah," Uncle Jozef rumbles. "Don't you know?"

Do I? Perhaps I do. It's another of the mysteries that hang about the tale of Duke Pavol. Such as his building Hladka Hvorka in a single night. Or his marriage to the mysterious Karoline, who was acknowledged by all as the cleverest and most beautiful woman in the land. And where did she come from? Or the way neither he nor his wife nor even his horse ever seemed to grow older despite the fact that Pavol's blessed rule lasted four decades and a day? Then Pavol and his wife rode off toward the west, never to be seen again.

Of course, as is true in so many old stories about great heroes, the saying in our realm is that when he is truly needed, Pavol the Good will return again.

This mystery, though, is something other than Pavol's disappearance. It's something I have often seen—more or less. It's the object pictured in the center of the vivid tapestry that always most powerfully draws my eye.

It's surrounded by a nimbus of light. Rays of gold radiate from it with such energy that it seems as if it is going to burst into flame. More than once I've been drawn to it, felt impelled to touch it—rather hesitantly. I always half expect it to be as hot to the touch as a kettle heated over a fire.

I look down at my hands, remembering all the times I've tried to grasp that pouch in the tapestry and felt disappointed when it has turned out to be no more than embroidered threads and cloth.

"Prince Pavol's missing pouch?" I ask without looking up.

"*Ano,*" Uncle Jozef rumbles, his voice pleased. "*Pozri.* Look."

I raise my head and see what he is holding toward me. Another scroll. I read the first words:

Pavol was climbing the mountain.

Dvanast

HE'D BEEN CLIMBING for a long time. It wasn't bad enough that he had set himself a goal that might quite logically lead to his death. True, he'd had better training with a sword than most. But that was against a more or less human opponent. As fine a teacher and as worthy an opponent as Gregor had been, he was not a fire-breathing reptile reputed to be the size of a hill. Confronting a dragon was not something an inexperienced young man such as himself should hope to survive.

In addition to his probably imminent mortality, he also had to deal with discomfort along the way. First there was the merciless heat of the sun on his head. Then there was the difficulty of making his way back and forth along a narrow mountain track that seemed to wend ever upward to the point where his journey now felt as if it had begun when the trees around him were no more than mere seeds in the stony earth.

His disquiet was added to by the small incessant insects, of some species he'd never seen before and thus could not identify when they appeared in great sociable swarms to demonstrate their fondness for humanity. Actually he now did have names for those little blood-suckers, none of which might be repeated in the presence of polite company.

He looked up at the golden eagle that had just come to circle overhead, its head cocked to watch him. How much easier it would be to undertake this quest if he had wings.

Pavol sighed and looked over at what had become his greatest trial, that which made his journey seem totally interminable—his steed. He had set out not astride a horse—which his purse would not have been able to afford even if he had been given a choice— but atop a slow, stunted donkey named Jedovaty.

Jedovaty. Poisonous. A well-named mount.

Jedovaty's lack of a saddle (which Pavol had been too impoverished to lease or purchase) was compensated for by the innumerable bony ridges of his spine. The uncomfortable young man had shifted his weight first from one side and then to the other to no avail. He even tried a sideways stance, both long legs dangling and scraping the ground, in a vain attempt to find a comfortable seat. Finally he had slid off to walk beside the bony beast.

That, however, had not made things easier. Although Jedovaty might have been uncomfortable as a mount, the delightful creature was just as unpleasant as a walking companion.

Indolent, bad-tempered, uncooperative, vicious, stubborn.

Those were some of the many words that Pavol had catalogued to describe Jedovaty's unendearing traits—each vying for first position. If his back was turned, Pavol now knew, the donkey would attempt to sink his yellowed teeth into any nearby portion of the young man's flesh.

The only good things about his current situation were two. First, it was slightly faster to drag his unwilling steed uphill by his halter than to use him as a means of transportation. Second, with his saddlebags on Jedovaty's back, Pavol was still able to use his recalcitrant (another word to add to the list) companion as a burden carrier.

Not that Pavol's burden was heavy. It consisted of a small bag of provisions, a rusted sword, and a much dented shield. The age of each of the latter two well outweighed any ability they had for attack or defense. Pavol had chosen this weaponry with care. No traveler ever went unwatched in their small kingdom since the Dark Lord's reign began. Thus he knew that his departure would be observed by suspicious eyes. But he had learned—been well taught—that to appear ridiculous remained his best defense. A callow lad with laughable armaments might be the target of jests and insults, but not seen as any sort of threat.

"They will say let the fool go seek his doom," Uncle Tomas had chuckled.

In fact, quite similar words had been spoken by two of the Dark Lord's men when they stopped him on the road that led past the blackened ruins of what had been his family's small but proud castle.

"Where are you going?" they asked, disappointed when a quick search of his pack proved he had nothing worth looting.

"Up the mountain," Pavol replied with a bright, slightly loony grin. "To meet and defeat the dragon and take its treasure."

They looked him up and down, sneering at the ignoble steed old Uncle Tomas had helped him choose.

"What's in the pouch?"

"Treasures of great worth," Pavol replied, opening it and spreading the contents on the ground before him.

The two shook their heads in disbelief. Only a fool would call such things treasures. A shiny stone, a broken bear's tooth, a bent eagle feather, a goose bone, an old iron ring, a worthless necklace, and a tarnished bracelet? They waved him past.

"Let the fool wander off to his doom." The first of the men, a great straw-haired brute with a scar down his cheek, chuckled.

"If he even finds the great worm," the second soldier scoffed.

"Fool today, dragon dung tomorrow," laughed the first.

As PAVOL RODE on he thought of how quickly they had dismissed him. The fact that he cut such a silly figure had worked well. If the eyes of the Dark Lord ever recognized him for who he really was, he would give the command that would end the line of Pavol's family forever.

Of course, his current quest might do just that too.

Pavol smiled and shook his head. At the very least, he had accomplished one thing. He was not being prevented from going to risk his life by scaling the dread slopes that even the Dark Lord avoided.

"Intrepid traveler," Pavol said to himself as he paused to wipe his forehead, positioning a bush between his bruised hips and Jedovaty's bared incisors, "where fareth ye? Questeth thee for adventure, for fair fortune and fine fame?" Then he laughed. "Or, more likely, to prove yourself a fool indeed by taking on this fool's errand."

Amazingly, despite his nearly complete discomfort, Pavol was not feeling sorry for himself. His ironic laughter at the seeming stupidity of his quest and the likelihood of it proving to be a complete failure, was amused, not bitter.

"Pavol the Foolish." Pavol grinned to himself once again. He rubbed the bruise on his shin and edged a bit farther upslope from Jedovaty's back legs that were taking aim. The donkey had now come up with another way of demonstrating his total devotion to Pavol's discomfort by employing not only his teeth but also his hooves.

Pavol looked at the clear blue sky above him and grinned even wider. A little breeze had come up and actually blown away all but the most stubborn of the gnats that had been billowing about him in a jovial cloud. The broad-winged eagle that had become their constant observer cried shrilly from above. Pavol brushed away the remaining bugs, then closed his eyes, enjoying the warmth of the sun on his face.

"What a wonderful day," he said.

Then, for he was not totally heedless of his own

well-being, he opened his eyes and turned in the direction where he had heard a hoof scrape against a stone.

It was loyal Jedovaty, stealthily extending his lanky neck uphill in the hopes of sinking his yellow teeth into Pavol's arm.

Pavol quickly drew his limb out of biting range. He had to admire the little donkey's persistence. He went down on one knee and looked straight at his recalcitrant beast.

"*Kamarat,*" Pavol said. "What better thing could we be doing than this?"

Jedovaty drew his head back and stared at Pavol. "Hunnh-ah? You must be joking," the donkey said. "How about resting hunnhh-in a nice warm stable and eating oats? And since when have hunnhh-I been your comrade?"

Pavol lifted his right hand to his chin in mild astonishment. "You can speak?" he said. "I'm surprised."

"Hunnnhhh," Jedovaty replied. "No more surprised than hunnhh-I am that you can listen."

Despite his transformation from mute beast of burden to conversationalist, Jedovaty's personality had not changed. As soon as he finished that second statement he made a determined lunge toward Pavol's left hand, which had come to rest on a nearby rock. Pavol pulled back just in time to avoid losing a finger or two.

"Are you enchanted?" Pavol asked once he'd slid upslope to a more discreet distance.

"Hunnhh-ah, not that hunnhh-I have noticed," Jedovaty brayed, slapping his tail at a new swarm of flies that had not yet discovered Pavol's more tasty flesh.

"Then how can you talk?" Pavol said.

"Hunnhh-I might ask the same of you," the donkey replied. "Perhaps," he added with what could only be described as a sneer, "hunnhh-I do so by opening my mouth and forming words."

Pavol was not quite sure what to say next. He'd heard many a tale from Baba Marta of talking animals. However, he had never heard of one being as fluent in sarcasm as speech.

I could ask why he is talking, Pavol thought. *No, then he will likely just answer that he is talking because he wants to talk. There has to be some way to approach this. But what? This is giving me a headache!*

Pavol closed his eyes and lifted both hands to massage his temples with his fingertips.

"Would you like to know why hunnh-I am talking to you?" Jedovaty asked. His less than friendly voice was a little too close to Pavol. Pavol scrambled quickly out of range of what might have been the loss of his left ear.

Even if he starts reciting poetry, Pavol vowed to himself, *I am not closing my eyes around this donkey again unless he is safely tethered a stone's throw away.*

Then he realized that the question asked by his four-footed fellow traveler had been straightforward.

"*Ano*, I would," Pavol replied, looking the donkey straight in the judgmental eye that was turned toward him.

In point of fact the animal's attitude at that moment brought back to Pavol the memory of one of his childhood tutors, back before the death of his parents in the days when he'd been known as a prince. Magister Utchtel had been the man's name. He was a stork-like scholar who'd viewed his daydreaming pupil with an air of disappointment. Yes, Jedovaty and old beak-faced Magister Utchtel made a fine pair.

The thought of the two of them—donkey and teacher alike—staring down their long noses at him in disapproval brought a broader smile to Pavol's face. Then he realized Jedovaty had not yet responded. Was the beast waiting for something?

Ah, Pavol thought. *Be polite.*

"*Prosim*," he added. "Please. Would you be so kind as to tell me why you have now decided to converse with me?"

The change in approach worked. A somewhat mollified look came over the creature's face.

"Hunnhh-ah," Jedovaty brayed, "you do have some manners? In that case hunnhh-I will tell you. Hunnhh-I have spoken to you because hunnhh-I do not want to be eaten by the dragon."

"The dragon!" Pavol said. "How do you know about the dragon? No. *Prepac!* Pardon me. Please continue."

"I know about the dragon," the donkey replied, "because my nose, like my brain, is far superior to that of any pitiable two-legs. I can smell it."

Further, Jedovaty added, that dragon was both hungry and waiting for them. He knew that because— as any intelligent four-legged beast knows—a hungry dragon's smell when it is lying in wait is quite different from that of a dragon when it is unaware of any potential prey, or when it is sleeping, or when it is just sitting for days and weeks at a time and contemplating the shapes of clouds and stones as dragons frequently do.

That drooling dragon was now just ahead of them. Its excellent hearing had picked up their approach and it was now lurking in ambush in its cave next to the trail.

"The very same trail you have, hunnhh, been hauling me up to our, hunnhh, eventual mutual doom. A fine fate for a donkey in the prime of his life, dragged to his doom by an idiot human," Jedovaty concluded.

Pavol sat in silence for a long time. He had no doubts at all about what he'd just been told. But, as he sat, he was not contemplating either stones or clouds.

Finally Pavol nodded and sighed. He had put off this moment long enough. Jedovaty's words, biting as they were, had just saved not only his own life but Pavol's skin as well. He stood up and walked the few paces downslope to where the donkey stood. He reached into the left-hand pack and took out the largest of the three pathetic pears it held.

"Thank you," Pavol said to Jedovaty, giving him the pear. "You are the best companion fate could have ever chosen to accompany me on this quest."

The donkey widened his eyes as he chewed, turning his head to look at him. He was surprised by the new tone in Pavol's voice.

"Do you like being a donkey?" Pavol asked.

"As compared to what?" Jedovaty replied. "Being dinner for a great lizard?"

The sarcasm, Pavol noted, was still there, but at least not squarely directed at him. Further, the annoying braying that had accompanied all of his previous comments had vanished. Jedovaty was looking at him with what appeared to be real interest.

"I mean," Pavol said to Jedovaty, "would you like to be something better than you are now?"

The little donkey looked hard at Pavol, whose face was so close to his that he could easily have bitten off his nose.

"Yes," Jedovaty replied with absolute sincerity.

"I thought so." Pavol smiled.

CHAPTER TWELVE

Seven of Them

ONCE AGAIN I am back in Uncle Jozef and Baba Anya's dom blinking my eyes. I look toward the door of their hut. From the slant of the light, I know that once again little time has passed. I'm not ready to be back here yet. I want to see what happens next with Pavol and Jedovaty. But that doesn't matter to my old teacher.

"*Dost cas!*" he rumbles. He takes the scroll from my hands, holds out his wide paw, pulls me up to my feet, thumps me on my back, and guides me to the door with his tree-trunk arm around my shoulder.

I know enough not to protest. My sessions with him always end this way. Just when it seems as if I am about to understand something, he speaks those words. *Dost cas.* Enough time. And I am on my feet and out the door.

To my surprise, though, Uncle Jozef—who always before has just stood watching in silence as I depart—adds a parting word.

"Rashko," he growls. "*Davaj pozor*. Be careful. The wise man is watchful even in his own backyard."

There's no point in my asking Uncle Jozef about it. Just as it would make no sense right now for me to ask him for further guidance about my problem. The fact that I have gotten no clear answer from him about what I can do to save my family is no surprise. Cesta is not always easy to understand when you start on The Way.

Yet, and this is a bit of a surprise to me, I'm actually feeling less worried now than I was before I visited Uncle Jozef. Experiencing part of my fabled ancestor's quest seems to have helped me. Even though I am aching to know what happened next, I've seen that even a hero can feel unsure of himself. I feel a deeper connection to Prince Pavol than I ever did before. It's as if a part of him is in me.

It's hard to explain, but I feel as if I have taken a step forward.

But how far have I actually gone? And is the direction in which I'm going the right one?

What am I supposed to do next?

What will I find awaiting me when I get back home?

My smile vanishes, trampled under the feet of the endless questions that crowd into my mind like uninvited guests pushing their way into a banquet hall.

WE'VE ALMOST REACHED the uphill path that will wind its way back up to our castle. Ucta and Odvaha walk on either side of me, so close that their shoulders brush my hips.

It is good to have two such loyal, large, and sharp-toothed companions by my side. Especially just now. When I ducked my head out from Uncle Jozef's dom, they were no longer just standing guard. They were sniffing the wind. Not a good sign.

Their heads are up, ears pricked as if hearing something in the underbrush that might prove interesting to chase. No, that's not it. It's more as if they hear something that might chase us.

I reach down to lift up a branch that has just fallen with a thump at my feet from one of the old oak trees whose limbs spread above us. Unlike the usual rough dead branch, it's solid, shaped as if designed to fit my hand. I heft its weight. It's as well-balanced as a sword.

"*Dakujem ti,*" I say in a soft voice as I lift this stout club. I nod toward the oak. "Thank you."

We leave the forest. The trail uphill starts here.

Ucta leans against my hip, growls, and then look into the bushes to my left.

Be ready. Something dangerous.

To my right Odvaha has moved a stone's throw away. He curls up his lip and glares into the underbrush on his side.

Something here too.

The path we are on is visible from the towers of our castle high on the great hill. But there's a dip in the trail ahead where one is concealed from view and the bushes are even thicker to each side. As we enter that little glen there's one thought in my mind.

Good place for an ambush.

I stop. Ucta and Odvaha stop with me.

"*Ukashte sa!*" I say in a loud voice. "Show yourselves."

And they do. They lazily stalk out of their places of concealment from behind trees, brush, and piles of rocks. They are large, long-clawed, and sharp-toothed. They appear pleased at having us not only surrounded but outnumbered.

Three of us. Seven of them.

At first I think that they may be lions. Unusual, for there have seldom been lions in our valley, but not impossible.

My judgment as to their species is only at first glance. As they began to circle, gradually getting closer, I note that they're not at all leonine. The long, narrow shape of their heads shows that they are a different sort of cat altogether. Their long tails are thick-furred, not sleek, with a tuft of fur at the end. Their bodies are not the royal gold of those kingly beasts but the black of a night without moon or stars.

Whatever they are, they're no less formidable or smaller than an average lion, a beast that weighs as much as four grown men with enough power to kill an ox with a blow of its paw. The huge muscles under their skin ripple as they edge toward us, drooling mouths gaping.

I'm impressed by the dagger-like fangs they're displaying. I understand what is meant by their purring throaty growls.

We have you. You cannot escape us.

As they slowly circle, I hold my club tightly in both hands. There's something unnatural about these beasts. Something malevolent. A dark aura of evil about them. They're exactly identical one to the other, including the white spot in the middle of each of their foreheads. Why do they look familiar?

The closest of the seven cats suddenly crouches. Its shoulder blades move back and forth. Then it hurls its huge body through the air at me—front paws spread wide, deadly claws extended.

I react without pausing to think. All those sessions of being drilled and battered by my brother and Black Yanosh have made quick reflexes as much a part of me as breath. I don't freeze in panic at the sight of a huge beast descending on me. I step to the side and swing my club around and down with all my strength. It connects solidly with the center of the white star on the huge cat's skull.

The resultant bone-cracking thunk is quite satisfying. To me, at least. The big black beast is now past caring, sprawled limply on the earth.

One down.

"Grrooowr-urgggh!"

I glance quickly over my shoulder at that sound of a roar cut short.

Make that two.

Ucta and Odvaha back away from the carcass of the second monster that attempted to attack me from behind as I dealt with its companion. Their jaws are red with blood from Ucta holding the cat's flank as Odvaha ripped out its throat.

The five remaining creatures circle us more warily now. They seem somewhat smaller than before. I'd think that strange were it not for the fact that strange has lately become commonplace.

Which of them looks to be boldest?

Ucta and Odvaha have that same thought.

That one there crouching down in front of a lime-stone outcrop.

Now.

We move as one. Ucta clamps his great jaws on the surprised creature's left hind leg, Odvaha digs his teeth into the loose flesh of its neck, my club crunches down on its backbone. It sprawls dead.

Three down.

When we leap back, no more than a few heart-beats have elapsed. We're not untouched. The flail of the black cat's claws caught each of us, but our cuts are shallow.

The three of us stand back to back, keeping in clear sight the four dark beasts that still stand.

No doubt about it. They're all . . . diminished. Before, each was massive as a lion. Now they're only two-thirds that size. The fierce glow in their eyes has dimmed. Not only have they shrunk in size and ferocity, they're even more familiar now to my eye.

Ah! Of course.

"Bezhte!" I stomp my foot on the ground and lift my club. "Run!"

As one, the four surviving ambushers do just that. They flee as one, side by side. Like a single panicked being they disappear back up the path.

In the direction of Hladka Hvorka.

My two companions by my side, I jog up to the next hilltop. I can see the open hillside in front of our castle. No sign yet of four black panthers.

But I do see Princess Poteshenie. She's standing at the end of the lowered drawbridge. Her arms are raised high and spread wide, her head lifted and her mouth open. It's too far away for me to hear what she is shouting, but I'm certain who she's calling back to her side.

Sure enough, out of the low scrub brush, a single black creature comes limping, looking back fearfully over its shoulder. The princess bends down to lift it up. She kisses the white mark on her black cat's forehead and glares down in our direction.

It is just as well that we are not close enough to hear her. From the gesture she makes—quite impolite—I doubt that we'd enjoy the words she's spitting our way. If my infatuated brother could see her now, his opinion of her beauty would change.

Or perhaps not. Love is doubly blind when the besotted one is as dense as a block of wood. Infatuation and blindness reinforced by sorcery.

Still, I cannot help but smile as Princess Poteshenie turns and stalks back into the castle bearing her diminished pet, minus three of its seven selves, in her arms.

I turn and descend back into the dell where our

dangerous encounter occurred. The three bodies of our attackers are gone. The grass where they lay is seared as if by fire.

I lift up the club given me by the Old Forest and feel its reassuring weight. I may have a sharp sword stored in our armory, but I'll hold on to this battle-tested gift.

"*Dakujem,*" I say again. A wind stirs the trees at the edge of Stary Les. A graceful bow of acknowledgment.

An angry cut sliced down the length of my right forearm begins to sting, then throb. Blood is dripping from the two gouges on Ucta's muzzle and the four long slashes along Odvaha's side.

I'm worried about the time we've been away from the castle—even more so now that I know the princess no longer believes I have been fooled by her. I need to get back there soon. But not wounded and bleeding as all three of us are. I look up at the sun in the sky. From its position, Baba Anya should be back by now from the market. She'll take care of our injuries, using her herbal salves to make certain that our injuries are neither poisoned nor infected. Perhaps too Uncle Jozef will let me experience more of my ancestor's story.

* * * * *

"How many times have I stitched you back together, child? You have more of my thread in you than my quilts."

Baba Anya's voice may be teasing, but there is no disapproval in it. She's never said anything harsh or critical to me, even when I've been ruining one of her rag rugs by bleeding excessively upon it. Rather often, now that I think about it.

A loving word is better than sweets, according to the proverb.

But there is nothing wrong with enjoying both at the same time.

As she sews together the long slice down my forearm, I am using my other arm to reach out for another one of her warm, luscious pastries.

Buchty are lovely steamed dumplings that Baba Anya fills with plum jam made from the trees that Uncle Jozef planted behind their dom. Though I love her cooking, I am showing remarkable self-control as I eat them. I've only had a few. Well, actually eight thus far. I have to admit that *buchty* stand little chance of survival when I'm within arm's reach.

"*Dobre*," I say as I down that doomed dumpling in two bites, hand cupped to catch any jam rolling down my chin. No need for fine dining manners here. That's another reason, apart from the fact that she is an excellent cook, that I love coming to her and Uncle Jozef's humble table.

I have always made certain that I've honored their hospitality with equal gifts of my own. Baba Anya and Uncle Jozef firmly refuse payment in any form other than whatever physical tasks I may undertake to show my appreciation. Though a prince, I am also a young strong man who—thanks to Uncle Jozef and Georgi—is good with his hands and unashamed to use them. I helped craft the table at which we are sitting and all four of the kitchen chairs. I've been Uncle Jozef's main helper when it comes to re-thatching their roof or carrying in firewood. I've also hung numerous strings of trout from the hook by their door.

I look over at Baba Anya. I'm almost embarrassed by my gluttony. But not quite. I take a ninth plum *buchta*.

Baba Anya beams approvingly at my appreciation for her food. When she smiles like that she seems younger—barely old enough to be a grandmother. However, if one believes the rumors about her longevity, her only seniors are the ancient oaks of Stary Les. Of course she denies that.

"*Nie,* such stories may be confusing me with my great-grandmother Baba Marta, who lived here before me," Baba Anya said.

One undeniable thing about Baba Anya is that no one ever remembers her as anything other than an old woman. But a kind one, which may explain such a lack of curiosity among the *sedliak,* the common folk, as to the way she and Uncle Jozef always seems to have been here. Peasant wisdom, like not seeking an explanation for the blessings of fair weather and fine harvests, is to never question a benevolent presence.

That's not at all my way. I always want to find the answers to so many things that there's such a swirl of questions in my head it's as if a trio of birds have taken up residence between my ears. Their names are How, Why, and What. They constantly twitter, wings fluttering, as they roost on the overburdened branches of my mind.

I look up from my plate at Baba Anya. She's nodding her head in approval. There's a gentle smile on her face . . . and also a twinkle in her eye as if she knows exactly what I am thinking and is amused by it.

Though Baba Anya is said to be the oldest woman in our little land, there's nothing feeble about her. She may stoop over and move slowly whenever she is out in the public eye, walking down the road to the market. However, I've noted, she stands quite straight and moves with ease and grace when she thinks no one's watching.

Sometimes when I am sitting with old Uncle Jozef and Baba Anya, there is this little signal they exchange. Each of them places their right thumb to the left side of their nose, accompanied by a quick look in my direction and a small knowing nod. They always do that when they think I'm looking the other way. By the head of the dragon! Why is it that I am the only one who ever seems to notice that? Aside from Georgi, that is. Who, now that I think of it, sometimes makes that same gesture to each of them. I wonder . . .

"Yipe!"

Baba Anya has just jabbed the threaded needle into the edge of the worst of my wounds. It takes my thoughts away from wherever path they were about to follow. She holds the edges of the cut together with the fingers of her left hand, deftly stabs and tugs with the needle held in her right. One stitch, two, three, four . . . a strong tug to that final stitch. Then she ties the thread, bends her head to bite it off. Only a little blood is still welling up from the sutured gash, which was deeper than I'd realized.

By the time I reached Baba Anya's house my cuts and the gashes in the flesh of Ucta and Odvaha had looked much worse. Despite the bandages I'd made by tearing my already ripped tunic into strips, blood had soaked through and was dripping from all three of us.

Uncle Jozef was splitting wood by the door. To my

surprise he seemed to expect us. He examined our injuries and nodded.

"Lot of blood, nothing too bad," he said. "Baba Anya will take care of you. She's waiting out back."

Not only was she waiting, she had set up a wooden tub, a bowl of water, washcloths, and a pile of clean bandages. How had she known?

"Come here, grandson," she said, holding out her hands.

I shook my head. "Please," I protested. "Ucta, Odvaha. Could you care for them first?"

Knowing my stubborn nature as well as she did, Baba Anya did just that. She swiftly cleaned, sewed, and bound their wounds, her hands a blur of movement as my two friends sat patiently on their haunches.

Then she turned to me.

"Here."

She held my arm over the small wooden tub. Taking a ladle, she dipped out the gold-colored liquid and poured it over my wound. It felt cold at first and then just the opposite! It produced so sudden and searing a sensation that it seemed as if thrusting that same arm into a fire would have been a relief. But the burning was brief and my bleeding stopped.

Then she'd led me inside, plumped me down at

the table, and produced a bowl of goulash. The scent that rose up to fill my nostrils was intoxicating, made just a bit sharper by the rings of raw onions arrayed on top of that delightful dish. It's hard to believe that her goulash is nothing but a mix of flour and table cream, cubes of pork meat, onion, sauerkraut, salt, and paprika with a bit of sugar added to sweeten the taste. It's a mystery how she makes everything she cooks taste so marvelous.

That big bowl of hot goulash was a mystery in another way. It takes at least two hours to make something this good. Yet I smelled nothing cooking when Ucta, Odvaha, and I arrived. I don't think there had even been a fire in the stove. And she just returned within the hour from the market. Another of Baba Anya's mysteries that she left me no time to ponder.

"*Yedz!*" she'd commanded, putting a spoon in my hand and poking me in the ribs. "Good for blood."

I did as she said quite willingly. I emptied that ample goulash bowl, not even sparing the raw onion rings!

Then she produced that wonderful platter of plum dumplings—as if from midair—and repeated the word that has always been one of her favorites.

"*Yedz!*" Eat.

* * * * *

THE TWELFTH AND last of the plum dumplings sits forlornly on the wooden plate. Poor pastry. It misses its comrades.

I look over at Baba Anya again. She nods.

I pick up the last lonely dumpling.

Come, no longer be alone. Join your friends.

As I chew, Baba Anya's grin grows broader. Watching me eat appears to nourish her more than putting food into her own mouth.

Another thought comes to me. Why does her smile appear snaggly and gap-toothed when she is out in public? Yet the wide grin she just favored me shows that she has all of her teeth, not a one of them yellowed with age.

"The eye sees what it wants to see, child," Baba Anya says.

Of course. Just like Georgi and Uncle Jozef, she's able to read my mind. And just like them, she offers me an explanation that explains nothing. I sigh. It's like everything else happening around me. No answers. Just more uncertainty.

The questions flutter back to their accustomed roosts in my brain. How will I bring back my parents? What can I do to rescue my brother from wedlock with a witch? Why am I the one who has to figure out how to rid us of our malevolent guests? Will I live to see another sunrise? What next?

As if in response to my unspoken questions, Baba Anya nods and looks over my shoulder.

"You are ready for more of the story, child."

Uncle Jozef's voice comes from behind me. He's entered so quietly I haven't heard even the creak of a floorboard. He leans over and places a third scroll before me.

I unroll it and look down on the mountain.

Trinast

PAVOL LOOKED AROUND. There was no one to observe what he was about to do save himself and the donkey, unless one counted the eagle overhead. He tossed the pouch from one hand to the other.

He undid the leather that was wrapped seven times about its neck with slow deliberation and opened it. One by one, he reverently removed the items from within and arranged them in a circle on top of a flat granite boulder. When he was done, the empty pouch placed in the middle, the flecks of quartz and feldspar within the big stone seemed to reflect the mountain light with more intensity.

The lanky young man and the scrawny donkey studied the strange assemblage: a rough brown river stone, the canine tooth of a bear, a goose's wing bone, a small eagle's feather, an iron finger ring, a bronze bracelet, a silver necklace. Seven in all.

Pavol took hold of the hilt of the rusted sword that hung in the battered sheath on Jedovaty's back. He carefully selected the rough brown stone, picked it up between thumb and forefinger as if holding an egg, and held it in front of his face. Then, with surprisingly swift competence, he drew the rust-flaked blade from its sad sheath.

"Stone to sharpen steel," Pavol intoned.

Then, holding the dull sword high by its cracked hilt, the slender youth drew the stone along the time-worn blade, once, twice, three times.

The first draw of the whetstone produced a sound like that of a metal gate being forced open after years of disuse. With that stroke all of the rust fell away. The second draw of the whetstone made the steel cry as shrill as an eagle and a sharpness keener than any razor came to the no longer nicked blade. The third produced a high, long note as sweet as an anthem of victory. The sword now shone more brightly than a mirror. From tip to hilt, it glowed, fine and finished as the best blade fashioned by a master smith. Strangely, though untouched by that transformative stone, the sheath too had been transmuted. No longer patched and shabby, it was now a worthy receptacle for a noble weapon, shining silver subtly inlaid with red and green precious stones. The threadbare rope from which it had hung was now a wide four-buckled belt of tooled leather interwoven with steel threads.

"*Ano!*" Pavol shouted in delight, holding high his sword as sunlight glinted from it.

Jedovaty stared but briefly at the transmogrified sword.

"Now me?" the donkey asked. His voice was remarkably like that of a child taken to the market by parents who promised him sweets.

"Not yet," Pavol said.

He returned the stone to his pouch and picked up the white fluffy feather. It quivered in his grasp as if seeking to take flight. Turning to the battered shield, so pathetically thin and cracked that it seemed an eggshell might offer more protection, he stroked the feather across the dented metal.

"Wind against fire," he cried.

The shield throbbed like a beating heart in response to each touch of the eagle's plume. The first throb sounded like the dull thud of a hammer against wood. The second was the martial clang of steel against steel. The third was the deep roar of the storm wind that overthrows all before it. And with each note the shield grew in size until it was twice its original circumference. It did not shine like the spear. It was as whole and solid as bedrock and dark as the heart of the night. Upon its surface a single word became visible in raised golden letters.

Skala. Bigger.

"What next?" Jedovaty asked. He was impressed, but not enough to shed his impatience. "Will that bear tooth turn you into a ten-foot tall warrior?"

Pavol patted the donkey on his shoulder. *"Nie,"* he said with a grin. "Pavol stays Pavol. A man must do the best he can with what he is. However"—he lifted the silver necklace with his thumb and little finger—"it is your turn, my friend."

Pavol tossed the necklace up and shouted a single word.

"Dospej! Grow up."

The silver strand began to spin in the air, twinkling like a flight of fireflies. As it spun it increased in size before settling about the neck of the little donkey, who stood up straighter at its touch. Then that necklace began to melt and blend into the donkey's dark coat. A wash of color flowed as a river's color alters where a stream carrying clay enters dark water. A sudden cloud of dust rose. When it cleared, the donkey Jedovaty was gone. A white horse eighteen hands tall stood there, looking back along its body appraisingly.

"Dost dobre?" Pavol asked, an amused smile on his lips. "Good enough?"

"Ano!" Jedovaty, the warhorse, replied in a deeply satisfied voice. "More than good . . . *kamarat.*"

Pavol took the four remaining items from the flat stone. The bear's tooth, the wing bone, the iron ring, and the bronze bracelet were placed back into the pouch, the leather string wrapped about its neck four times and tightly tied.

"No more miracles this afternoon?" Jedovaty asked.

Though his voice was now deeper and no longer carried a bitter overtone, it was still as ironic as it had been when he was a mere donkey. Pavol felt grateful for that. He had not liked the thought of traveling with a companion who was deadly serious or overawed by wonders.

"Not for now," Pavol said. "Let us see what happens when we reach the Cave of the Worm."

"Of course," Jedovaty said. "I can hardly wait."

Irony still, Pavol thought, *but eagerness too.*

"Ano," Pavol said.

He vaulted up into the fine saddle that had previously been nothing more than a loosely fastened moth-eaten blanket and some mostly empty and nondescript saddlebags. Those saddlebags were now much larger, well-made and happily bulging. Pavol patted them once, wondering if their contents had also been made into better fare than the previous few handfuls of grain and dried beans. But there would be time for eating later—provided they were not first themselves the main course.

"And we are off," Pavol said.

"In more ways than one," Jedovaty agreed.

But despite his sarcasm, there was nothing but determination in the way he charged up the steep slope, his steel horseshoes ringing against the stones and shooting off sparks.

On up the mountain they continued. But a bit slower now.

Jedovaty's first eager charge up the slopes had been brief. When they reached the top of the pass, what they saw was not the top, but yet another, even steeper ridge ahead. And beyond that was yet another. So it went through much of the morning, which grew hotter and hotter.

"Oh my," the mighty charger sighed, not winded, but a bit discouraged.

"Ah well," Pavol said, leaning forward to pat Jedovaty on his neck, "as the proverb says, one does not reach the end of the day any faster by running. Up we go."

"Up indeed," Jedovaty replied. But he did not hesitate to move forward.

And so, at that considerably less brisk but steady pace, they continued on. The sun rose higher and their shadows shortened. It was a long, slow journey.

Plenty of time for Pavol to think even more about this quest. Perhaps too much time. In the heat of action, one has little opportunity to ponder over whether or not one's nickname of Pavol the Foolish will, indeed, turn out to be unfortunately appropriate. He reached down to touch the sheath of his sword, reassuring himself that it was truly there, lifted up and hefted his impressive shield. Just the sort of weapons that a true hero would carry into battle.

Real enough, he thought. *Proof of something.*

He looked toward his waist. The pouch still hung there, securely fastened to his belt. And the wide, thickly muscled back of his sturdy steed beneath him was further reassurance that at least one or two things had gone quite well thus far.

I have been trained for this, he thought. *Wise words and strong hands have guided me. This is my true destiny.* But still the doubts remained.

Finally, the merciless sun directly overhead, they crested one more ridge and saw it half a league above them—a blotch of darkness on the mountainside. The large mouth of a cave.

What if there is no dragon at all up there and that cave is empty? Pavol thought. *What then? Go back home in disgrace or stay on top of the mountain and live as a hermit?*

His doubts, though daunting, were fleeting. They were all too quickly replaced by musings about . . . technique. What exactly should one do when actually confronted by an immense fire-breathing lizard? Though Pavol had heard much mention of dragons in the stirring stories of Baba Marta, and read in Uncle Tomas's books numerous lengthy tales of heroes defeating such baleful beasts, all those accounts had been unsatisfyingly inexact about the precise tactics to be employed. As far as he could recollect, all that was ever said or written was along the lines of *With one swift swipe of his sharp singing sword, the hero sliced off the dragon's head.*

Pavol swabbed his sweating brow with a kerchief. Though the other peaks around them were topped with ice and snow, this part of the mountain range was quite dry and bare. The higher they had gone, the warmer it had become. Pavol thought he knew the reason for that, but did not voice his conjecture until Jedovaty spoke up.

"Hot dragon breath," the former donkey sneered, no lack of his previous irony in his tone. "Delightful, isn't it?"

Indeed it was not. Imagine the stench of rancid meat mixed with peppery smoke.

They were now no more than a spear's cast from the cave mouth. So much larger than it had appeared from far below.

Three times the height of a tall man, Pavol thought as they moved slowly forward. *Wide enough to drive a wagon through.*

His eyes were beginning to water from the sulfurous air streaming out of the ominous dark opening. He blinked, trying to peer within its obsidian depths. Almost anything could be hidden in there.

Pavol did not feel afraid at that moment. However, strangely enough, it came to him that he had never checked the contents of his transmuted saddlebags to see what his meager meal of beans had been transformed into. Breast of pheasant? A leg of lamb? Some stuffed pierogies? A roll of poppy seed cake? He'd been so excited when he set out that morning that he had failed to eat anything at all. His stomach rumbled and his mouth watered.

Then there was his steed to think about. Poor Jedovaty was probably half-starved too. Being metamorphosed from a donkey into a warhorse had to work up a bit of an appetite. Might it not be a good idea to turn back and pause for a late breakfast somewhere a bit farther and cooler down the slope—say back down in the valley they had started out from?

No, it was too late now for that. He could not

abandon his quest, having come so far. Even though perhaps the only one consuming anything edible that day might be a large reptile.

And is that why I am feeling interested in eating just now? Pavol thought. *Because there is an almost palpable atmosphere of hunger all about me, the sort that might emanate from a huge ravenous monster?*

Like that one.

A singularly large, one-horned head, its mouth over-supplied with fangs, poked out of the cave at the end of a long neck.

"*Ja som* Jedna," it growled, leaning so close that its nose was an arm's length away. "I am Jedna. Prepare to meet doom!"

"*Dobre den*, Jedna," Pavol said, "Good day. Prepare to meet my blade." Then, unsheathing his singing sword, he sheared off the dragon's head with one swift swipe.

"*Do videnia*, Jedna," Jedovaty said, turning to watch the dragon's head roll down the slope like a large green boulder. "Bye-bye."

The blood-spurting neck of Jedna swung back and forth a few times in apparent confusion before being jerked back into the cave. Almost immediately another larger head on an even thicker neck thrust itself out from the cave mouth. This head was two-horned. Its eyes glowed red as the fires of Hades.

"*Ja som* Dva!" it roared, its mouth gaped to display at least twice as many fangs as Jedna. "Your fate is sealed!"

"Oh my," Jedovaty sighed. "Here we go again."

CHAPTER THIRTEEN

Still Watching

I'M NO LONGER watching from far above, no longer sharing Pavol's thoughts. A great mist as white as a sheet of parchment has swept in, obscuring Pavol and Jedovaty and the dragon from view. I'm back in Uncle Jozef and Baba Anya's dom, sitting at the table staring at the blank space at the end of a parchment.

"What happened next?" I ask.

Uncle Jozef holds up another roll of parchment with a ribbon wrapped about it.

"Here," he says. "You read it later. Now go back."

Baba Anya nods.

They're both right. I've been away too long. But I have the distinct feeling, the foresight, that if I were to try to enter the way I always do, across the drawbridge and through the front gate, another ambush will be waiting for me.

"What shall I do?" I ask. I don't expect a direct answer and I don't get one. Just another question, this time from Baba Anya.

"What do you hear?" She taps her forehead with her little finger.

However, it's a question I understand. I need to search my mind.

I close my eyes. And as soon as I do so I hear a voice. It sounds like the voice of Pavol that I've heard in my visions.

"Our tapestry," it says. "Look."

I look. In my mind's eye I see the huge wall hanging that depicts our ancestor's tale.

I hold that image in my mind, study it. There's the dragon and Hladka Hvorka. Strangely, our castle is not portrayed as the usual front view at the bottom of the hill where the road begins that leads up to the gate. Instead, it is shown from the back. Ah! The back way. Of course.

And there, glowing in the midst of the tapestry, brighter than ever before, is Pavol's pouch. And as I look at it, I realize that I've seen it in three places. Once in the tapestry, once with my great ancestor as I have been watching his tale unfold . . . and one other time.

The first day when my mother took us down into the cavern I had felt something. A pull toward an object as plain and simple as a piece of homespun cloth. I had not known then what that power was, how that power felt. But now, after watching Pavol's tale unfold, I do. I recognize its pull on me—and how it might draw one like Baron Temny, who would seek such power in the hopes of turning it to evil use.

I know where Pavol's pouch is! It's the key to everything. Of course it's what Temny has come to find. But if it still holds any of the objects of power that Pavol gathered, I may be able to turn them to our defense.

I start to open my eyes, but then Pavol's voice speaks again.

"Look further."

Something else in my mental image of the tapestry begins to glow, to stand out. It catches my attention so strongly that I cannot look away. It's the figures that have always seemed out of place in the tales, the shapes of those two agile jugglers.

As soon as I take note of them, the tapestry vanishes and I find myself remembering something else. I remember the market day just last week.

Paulek and I had gone there because we'd heard there were going to be jugglers. I suppose our initial interest in that deft art had been piqued by growing up playing next to that great wall tapestry. By the time I was nine and Paulek was ten, the jugglers in the great cloth hanging had so fascinated us that we began to try tossing balls back and forth between us.

Then, and this may surprise you, juggling actually did become one of our shared skills.

How did the sons of a king learn the skills of itinerant, minor entertainers? Blame Black Yanosh for that. Hired by our father to teach us martial ways, he arrived at our castle and entered our lives not long after Paulek and I had begun enjoying some success at tossing three balls back and forth. We were doing just that when someone suddenly was there between us. It was an elegant old man, all dressed in black, with a beard trimmed so precisely that its edges appeared sharp as a knife. But it was not just that neither of us had seen him approach that made our mouths gape open. It was also the way, without looking, that he snagged the balls we had just thrown out of the air with one hand. It made me think of a hawk catching pigeons on the wing.

"So," he said, "you like this game? I am Yanosh, I also juggle. Shall I show you?"

I nodded for both of us.

But balls were not what Black Yanosh used to demonstrate his ability. The grizzled old weapons master yanked our daggers out of their sheaths. Then, hurling them high up into the air with his own larger blade, he proceeded to catch and toss, catch and toss, catch and toss each in turn. The light that reflected from their razor edges was hypnotic, the exactitude of each catch and toss, the calm look on Black Yanosh's face as he did it, natural as breathing.

"I want to do that," Paulek whispered.

"Can you teach us?" I asked.

"Can you learn?" Black Yanosh replied, turning his hooded eyes toward us. Then he caught each dagger in turn and flipped it—again without even looking—spinning through the air. Chunk! Chunk! Chunk! All three embedded themselves in the center of the wooden target thirty feet away.

"We can try," Paulek and I answered as one, something we did as children until my vocabulary outpaced his.

"Good answer." Black Yanosh nodded.

We were good students. The best he'd ever had, he admitted in an unguarded moment.

Juggling, our old weapons master believes, is not just an amusement. It tunes the senses, quickens the reflexes, makes more precise the movements of limbs that might bend a bow, swing a staff, thrust with a sword, block or evade a killing strike.

The gymnastics that went with it were part of that same philosophy. Within a year the two of us could leap, cartwheel, and flip as well as any acrobats.

Juggling is perhaps the only time when Paulek and

I can do anything together that is neither competitive nor limited by his lack of comprehension. My brother may be a disaster as a classroom student, but he's a brilliant juggler. The quick flurry of his hands as he passes back to me one, two, three, four clubs, from the front, from behind his back, between his legs, even blindfolded, is inspirational to watch. I can barely keep up with him. And when he handles a dozen balls and they blur into one continuous circle, the look on his face is so intense, so knowing, that I can hardly believe he is the same person who always seems to be amazed in the classroom that two and two never fail to make four.

So Paulek and I have always tried to never miss a market fair—when such entertainers might appear. Jugglers and tumblers who visit our kingdom more than once learn to expect the eager faces of two tall, well-clad lads at the front of the crowd. Some know us well enough to bring us into their acts by hurling their clubs or balls our way, knowing we'll catch and return them as easily as another man lifts a hand to greet a friend.

The two jugglers we saw that day were new to us. Their faces were masked, their hair unusually long, their clothing loose and flowing. They raised their arms, spun around a few times, then backed off to face each other from a distance of a dozen paces.

"Now," cried the bald, black-mustached leader of the little caravan of painted wagons that had brought the Gypsy entertainers into our midst, "my two talented offspring will amaze you!"

"*Zacni!*" said the first slender youth, producing a handful of knives. "Begin!"

"*Teraz,*" cried the second, pulling out a similar number of blades. "Now!"

Then, their hands moving as quickly as any I'd ever seen, they began hurling those knives back and forth. In most such acts, the blades are shiny but dull, their weight light. But these knives were different. For one they looked to be quite sharp and weighty. For another, each bore a wide twin, double-edged blade with a single hilt. That made catching them as they spun a more complicated feat.

I was fascinated—as was Paulek. Their skill and grace were impressive. My brother and I might match them, but it would take some practice. I found myself liking the way the two lads moved as they juggled. Soon I was hardly noticing their blades, but focusing more on the dance of their bodies. I was especially fascinated by the slender one who spoke second. I mentally identified him by the word he'd called out in a husky voice. *Teraz. What would Teraz look like if he raised his mask? What would he . . . ?*

Nie. By the head of the dragon! Not he, she! A strange feeling came to the pit of my stomach.

I opened my eyes and found myself back with Uncle Jozef and Baba Anya.

"Rashko," a gentle voice says. "You liked?"

Baba Anya's hand is on my shoulder. She looks amused. She's not just talking about the food.

"*Ano,*" I admit.

I liked very much. So much so that when their performance was done and those two jugglers had disappeared into the nearest wagon, Paulek and I sat outside waiting for them to re-emerge. Paulek wanted to talk with them about juggling. So, more or less, did I. Paulek seemed less aware than I that the two we'd watched so intently were young women.

To our mutual disappointment, the girls failed to re-emerge. Paulek finally dared to knock on the wall of that wagon. No answer. He peered tentatively inside, turned back to me crestfallen. "No one there."

Baba Anya and Uncle Jozef are still looking at me, knowing smiles on both their faces.

I hold up my arm and study the long cut. It's rapidly healing—as my wounds always do when I come for help to Baba Anya. Soon all that will remain of the deep slash will be a faint scar down my forearm. Eventually, that wound may be forgotten.

I don't think I am going to forget the memory of those two sisters. In fact, now that I think of it, they exactly matched the jugglers pictured in Pavol's tapestry!

How do they fit into Pavol's story? Or is it that the tapestry portrays not just his tale but some part of my own?

I stand and tuck the parchment into my shirt. Uncle Jozef holds out something to me. It's a large, well-honed butcher knife.

"You need," he says, slapping the heavy knife into my palm. "Cuts good."

THAT KNIFE IS now in my belt as my two companions and I approach the rear of Hladka Hvorka castle through the forest. As we cautiously make our way up the hill I wonder what threat will next rear its head. Sentient stones rising up to crush us? Flying demons from the sky? The worst thing that happens is that a squirrel hurls down some twigs, accompanied by curses in rodent talk. We've passed a bit too closely under the two oak trees he considers his private fiefdom. We reach the wood's edge and look out at the back of the castle without having had a single new misadventure.

On the other side of the thirty-foot-wide moat

rises the blank lower back wall of the castle. Eighty feet up are the first embrasures—recessed, well-reinforced windows from which an archer might shoot down at enemies attempting a rear assault. Those barred portholes are not manned. They never have been. Ours has been a realm at peace since Pavol assumed rule.

Hardly anyone, except for Paulek and me, ever mounts the steep stairs to peer out at the pleasant view of the nearby forest and distant fields below.

The back wall is indeed formidable. Any enemy would be foolish to attempt to breach Hladka Hvorka from this direction. Scale a blank wall seven stories high? Try to break through the thirty feet of solid stone at its base?

But every castle has its ways for those within to slip out surreptitiously. When Hladka Hvorka rose, mystically shaped, it was provided with another egress. (An egress is an exit. Not, as my brother believes, a large sort of bird.) Only our family and our trusted retainers know the other secret way.

Baron Temny and his band do not. I am certain of that. Spellbound though he might be by the princess, my brother would never reveal the hidden passage to any outsider. Of course, that might be because he's forgotten all about it.

I walk back down to the twin oaks and sit beneath

the one unoccupied by a chattering furry-tail seeking to repel invaders.

Ucta and Odvaha come to lay themselves down on either side of me, placing their large heads in my lap.

Impatient as I am, I'm again hearing Pavol's silent voice.

Wait, he is saying. Gather strength.

Whether his voice is real or merely in my imagination, it's good council. It's been a very long day. The sun, now close to the top of the hills, will soon set. I'm exhausted. The fighting, the healing, the worrying, have all taken a greater toll on me. Also—minus the worrying, which is more of a human trait—on my two faithful friends. We need all our strength to take the next step. If we hurry too much, we may make some fatal misstep. As Father says, the mouse that rushes out of its hole without looking is the best friend of the cat.

Rest.

Ucta and Odvaha close their eyes. Just like that they are fast asleep.

I wish I could sleep. But I can't, not with all these uncertainties. What will we find inside the walls of Hladka Hvorka now? I sigh heavily. But only once before taking a deeper, more determined breath and straightening my shoulders. I can no longer allow myself the luxury of either uncertainty or self-pity. Pavol himself was not always certain that he was up to being a hero. That was an important lesson for me. Still he pressed on. It has to be the same for me. I need to find what is hidden there in the darkness beneath our castle. I need to find more of Pavol in me. I'll need it.

Though Paulek and I have used this secret way to sneak out of our home, we've never used it to enter. From what my parents told me, one who tries to come in this way from the outside will find the way is quite well and dangerously guarded.

I'm not sure I want to think about that right now. I shift my position and something under my shirt digs into my side. The scroll! I'd forgotten all about it. There's still light enough for me to read it. What better way to pass this time?

Strnast

DESPITE THE FACT that Dva's head was larger and fangier, it loomed no farther above Pavol than had its brother Jedna.

Bigger does not mean smarter, Pavol thought.

This time he ventured no reply. Instead he stood high in his stirrups to swing his sword in a second strong stroke.

Chonk!

Dva's head went bounding down the mountain slope after Jedna's.

The snake-like neck of Dva waved back and forth a few times much as Jedna's had done. It appeared, if it is possible for a headless neck to do so, not only confused, but also disappointed and even a bit betrayed. Then it too was yanked back into the darkness of the cave mouth.

"Jedna," Pavol said musingly, repeating the name that meant "one," and raising his sword at the ready.

"Dva, two" Jedovaty added, with yet another sigh. "Do you suppose that means the next one will be . . ."

"*Ja som* Tri!" roared the titanic three-horned head shot toward them, fangs dripping poison. "You perish here on this . . ."

Chonk!

Tri's head, rounder than its two predecessors, rolled a bit farther down the mountainside before lodging against a boulder.

"How high can dragons count?" Jedovaty said as Tri's resentful neck dragged itself unceremoniously back into the stygian depths.

Pavol studied the ominous glow beginning to emanate from the cave.

"At least up to four," he said, raising his shield. "And four is for . . ."

Fire came shooting out of the cave mouth, a great searing wave meant to reduce them to cinders. It surely would have done so, had it not been for Pavol's shield. Somehow its surface caught those flames, sucking them in, absorbing them as thoroughly as if the shield had been a lake and the dragon's deadly breath no more than a burning brand dropped into its waters.

As it was, the ends of Jedovaty's mane and tail were singed and Pavol's right eyebrow quite burned off.

"*Ja som* Shtyri!" howled the triumphant four-horned head that fast followed the flames. "Burned to ashes your bones!"

It looked down, a smile on its befanged countenance, expecting to see nothing more than charred flesh. Then it paused, quite taken aback by the sight of horse and rider still standing. A bit blackened, but nonetheless intact.

Shtyri lowered its grim head toward them. "Hunh," it growled, "how . . ."

Chonk!

Peht was next, a five-horned horror just as dense—and speedily dispatched—as the dragon heads before it.

Silently and somewhat more tentatively, six-horned Sest came snaking out to make its quick acquaintance with the edge of Pavol's sword—Chonk!—and the force of gravity.

Jedovaty peered down the slope. "Plenty of room down there for more," he observed.

"Let's hope that one was the last," Pavol replied. "Or that any remaining ones are as stupid and slow to learn as were those first six."

"*Ahoj,*" a high voice came trilling out of the cave.

"Hello. *Prepacte?* Excuse me, human with long, sharp sword."

"What now?" Jedovaty said.

"*Csakaj,*" said Pavol, raising both sword and shield. "Wait."

"*Ahoj!*" the high voice repeated, breaking just a bit into roughness. "I lovely young human woman who was prisoner of bad monster. Is safe now to put down sword and shield and come rescue me. I not dragon trying to trick you."

Jedovaty looked up at Pavol with one eye. "Seven heads," the former donkey observed, "and not a working brain in any one of them?"

Pavol nodded. "Sedem," he shouted. "Come out."

A moment of silence followed. Then the high trilling voice spoke again, "How you know my name Sedem?"

"Because we can count," Jedovaty said. "Because you are stupider than the stones of this mountain. Because one wise man is better than a thousand morons. Because—"

"Shh," Pavol said, trying not to smile. "Sedem," he shouted again. "Come out. If you do not try to harm us, we will not hurt you."

There was a longer pause and then the dragon answered, its voice no longer a falsetto.

"*Ano.* I come out. I no try harm you."

The voice was followed by the sound of heavy scales rasping along the rough stones deep within the cave. As that sound came closer and closer, Pavol chucked Jedovaty in the side with his heels, quietly urging him farther back from the cave mouth and behind a very large boulder as the dragon began to emerge.

But not headfirst. First slid out a sharp ridged tail, as long and stout as the main beam of a great hall. As soon as it emerged, that mighty tail swished back and forth, crushing rocks and sending sprays of dust into the air as it scraped the surface of the ledge where the young man and his steed had stood. The tail's intention might have been lethal, but it was ineffectual. Pavol and Jedovaty were safely sheltered by the cottage-size stone.

"Oh no," said Sedem as he turned around, raising up a crested head that was surprisingly small and deficient in dentition compared to its deceased brothers, whose snaky necks were even now being absorbed back into the dragon's massive body. Sedem looked left and then right, slanted yellow eyes hooded in a clever expression. "What my stupid tail do by accident? I no try harm poor human and horse." His voice was tinged with theatrical regret.

"No harm done," Pavol said as he and his steed stepped out from behind the stone.

"Not yet," Jedovaty added.

It would be an understatement to say that Sedem the dragon was abashed by his lack of success in accidentally dispatching his enemies with his tail. Rather like saying that the razor-edged sword Pavol swung high in his strong right hand was slightly sharp.

The dragon closed his eyes and cowered, certain that the last sounds he would remember would be the quick snick of a brilliant blade through scale, muscle and bone.

Instead, Sedem heard no more than his own rather labored breathing. Dragons are prone to asthmatic attacks when upset, a not uncommon ailment among those whose throats must intermittently bear the force of fire.

Sedem cagily opened one eye. There was his armor-clad adversary and his magnificent, albeit sarcastic, steed. Both a good double tail's length beyond the dragon's reach. The man was actually smiling. An equally amused expression was on the horse's face as well.

Sedem ventured a cautious intake of breath.

Prince Pavol's smile grew grim. "*Nie,*" he warned, tapping the hilt of his sword against his blackened but no less strong shield. "Fireproof. Remember?"

The dragon attempted an ingratiating grin, managing only to look even more evil and untrustworthy than before.

"Why you think I shoot fire at you?" the dragon said, swallowing down a sizeable gout of flame and then burping a conspicuous smoke ring out of the corner of his mouth that he tried to fan away with his foot. "*Nie, nie.* I no do that. That my bad brother Shtyri. He hotheaded. Ho ho ho? Now he gone."

The dragon lifted his head to look down the slope where the impressive array of decapitated reptile noggins lay scattered among the stones. A shudder ran down the length of his scaly backbone.

"Me good," Sedem added, an assertion that seemed at least half plea.

"Hmmm," Pavol said, tapping a fingertip against the pouch that hung at his waist. "So, you will surrender to me and do as I say?"

"*Ano, ano.* You say, I do." The dragon nodded his last remaining head with great enthusiasm. "I promise."

Jedovaty stomped his right front hoof against the ground and whinnied. "Hah! The only promise likely to be kept by a dragon is from a beast that is deceased."

Pavol nodded. "Based upon our experience thus far, my friend, I would tend to agree. However," he added, untying the pouch with one hand while still holding his sword firmly in the other and keeping his eyes on Sedem, "I do have these."

He took two objects of metal from the pouch. The first was a bronze bracelet that Pavol slipped over his wrist. He held up the second item he'd removed from the pouch—a small iron ring.

"*Kruh!*" he commanded. "Circle!"

The ring lifted from Pavol's palm, spun in the air, and grew until it was a great glowing hoop. Pavol pointed his finger. The ring began to circle the dragon. Once, twice, three times it spun as Sedem stood, transfixed by the glitter of the shimmering ring. Pavol closed his fist. The iron ring dropped like a diving hawk to slide over Sedem's huge head, slip halfway down his snaky neck, then shrink in size to an exact fit.

Sedem coughed once. "Ring tight," the dragon said.

"Tight enough to prevent any, shall we say, inadvertent discharge of flame." Pavol smiled. "But nowhere near as tight as it will become if you attempt anything, intentional or accidental, that might bring harm to me or mine now and in all the years to come."

"Well-worded," Jedovaty observed.

"*Dakujem,*" Pavol replied with a bow.

Pavol gestured toward one side with his sword. Sedem nodded and shifted his great bulk away from the mouth of the cave. Now Pavol could view what was within. The cave was large, but it was not its size that led to his low whistle. A great store of treasure filled it from side to side, from floor to ceiling. Only a few narrow corridors of dragon's-width lent access to the stacks of gold and silver and precious stones.

Also, just inside the cave mouth, in what was clearly Sedem's dining room, were the skeletal remains of numerous dragon-sized meals. Most were the bones of cattle, save those that had been encased in armor—piled neatly off to one side, peeled away like the husks of chestnuts.

"Pretty," Sedem said, peering over Pavol's shoulder into the cave.

Does he mean the treasure or the piles of bones and armor? Pavol thought. *Probably both.*

"You defeat dragon, treasure yours," Sedem growled, his voice markedly resentful. Then his tone brightened. "Dragon gold bring much bad luck."

Pavol reached out to place his palm on the necklace that encircled Sedem's neck. "I have thought of that," he said. "So I have a proposition. The treasure may remain yours if you share a bit of it with me—and mine—every now and then. Gold given for good, never gotten by greed. Thus reversing the curse."

"*Nerozumiem,*" the dragon rumbled, shaking his head. "I no understand."

"You will," Pavol replied, turning his head to peer up at the eagle that was still circling.

CHAPTER FOURTEEN

Onward and Downward

I LOOK UP from the scroll. I'm back under the oak tree, again released from Pavols's quest—perhaps because it is too dark now to read. No moon or stars shine in the sky. All round, nature seems to sleep. Not even the hunting call of an owl comes from the fair forest far below. I am wide awake. I stand and so do Ucta and Odvaha. After their refreshing slumber, they are ready.

Fortunately, someone has left a light burning in the highest room of the castle. It shines down brightly, illuminating the very tree I'd been sitting beneath. The way that beam strikes, it seems that it might have been aligned for just such a purpose. Who climbed up to that high room while I slept? Who lit that lantern and left it there?

A smile crosses my lips. Georgi, of course. Who

else but our family's most faithful retainer would be so aware of my need? How, though? How much does he really know about not just the present, but also the past? Well, when things quiet down a bit—if they ever do and if I am still breathing when such calm finally arrives—I must have a talk with our omniscient majordomo.

Time now to try what I was taught by my mother when I was seven. She tried to give it to both Paulek and me, but I was the only one who learned it. My brother was already paying little attention to anything unless it had to do with horses, hawks, weapons, or military tactics.

"You're the one who will remember things, brother," Paulek said to me. As if I didn't know that already.

As Mother explained, there are certain magical formulas that one can learn to find and open hidden entrances. Those charms are like verbal keys. However, unlike a metal key, just remembering such a formula does not mean one can use it. One must remember it for seven full days after it is taught or it will never allow itself to be learned. Further, there are precise gestures, marks, or signs that must also be employed. Plus, one must have a certain affinity for such things for them to stick in one's mind. As you may have gathered by now, I have an unusually sticky mind. It's rather like facts are iron filings and my mind is a magnet. Sometimes it feels like I remember far too much.

Paulek, of course, promptly forgot everything Mother tried to teach about the finding and opening of hidden ways. But not me. On the morning of the seventh day after Mother gave it to us, I went straight to her and repeated it back to her exactly as I'd been told.

"*Ano,*" she said, then went back to her knitting.

And with that word of agreement the door-opening spell was mine to use in whatever way I needed it. Such as to enter our castle through this hidden way. As I now plan to do.

Ready? I ask my two companions.

They nudge their heads against my side.

Born ready.

I take out the dagger given me by Uncle Jozef. Starting from my right and moving toward my left, I lightly scratch the outline of a door on the wide trunk of the second oak tree. Then, holding the knife blade up in front of my face, I place the palm of my left hand against the exact center of what I hope will transform itself into an entrance.

"*Strom dvere, otvorte sa!*" I command, moving my fingers in a certain way. "Tree door, open."

Predictable and unpoetic as those words are—

having come, after all, from my mother—they're effective. A door shapes itself in the bark and then swings open smoothly. The light from the high window shines on the hewn stone steps leading down through a passageway narrower than I remember. Much narrower.

Did I mention how much I dislike dark, tight spaces?

Once I've gone past the limit of that lantern's glow, how will I be able to see my way? When Paulek and I last negotiated it from the other end, four full years ago, it was with the aid of torches. I little like the idea of feeling my way blind down along a winding passageway.

But I don't have to—at least not without light. Though my mother may not be the best person in the world with words, she is thorough. She thought of this and gave me the word.

"Svetlo," I say. "Light."

In answer the walls of the passageway immediately emanate a silvery glow.

No excuse now not to do this. I swallow hard and take the first step. Then another. At least I'm not alone. Ucta is in front me, Odvaha close behind. Three steps, four.

Thwomp!

I should have expected it, but it makes me jump. The door in the tree has just closed solidly behind me. I don't bother to look back. It will just make the lump in my throat larger. No way to go but onward. And also downward.

Why is it that I am not overly fond of being squeezed into lightless places where my chest feels as if it is being stepped on by a giant? Perhaps it comes from Paulek's game of "Lock Rashko in the Wardrobe" from when we were small.

Breathe, Rashko. You are not in the closet now.

We continue down the tunnel. The lustrous light flows along the walls with us. It's bright enough to drive away the near dark, but all is unsettlingly black but a few arm's-lengths before and in back. I reach my hands out to measure the distance between the walls. No, the tunnel is not getting narrower. Despite the sweat that now beads my brow, it is not getting hotter in here.

Ucta looks back over his shoulder at me and growls, sensing my discomfort.

"Cesta," I whisper to myself. Follow the path. Stay on the Way.

"Esta, sta, sta, sta . . ." an echo answers me.

One trick that Uncle Jozef taught me—after the day I spent locked in the closet—was how to make time pass more quickly. It's a technique to use when stuck in some seemingly interminable situation. It might be listening to a boring speech from a visiting dignitary. Or it might be while trying to keep going and not freeze to death as your foolhardy brother tries to lead you back home after luring you out into the midst of the blizzard.

It is done thusly. Count to yourself slowly, one, two, three, and so on, while drawing in a single deep breath. At the count of thirty, pause briefly and then begin to breathe out and count again. A single breath in and then out—and a minute will have passed. Do it sixty times and an hour will be gone.

I wipe the sweat from my forehead with the back of my hand, the one not gripping the dagger that I'm holding out in front of me as if it is a candle. I keep counting.

One, two, three, four, five . . .

By the time I reach ten breaths, I reassure myself, I will reach the other side.

And I will not think right now about what may be waiting for me there.

THIRTY BREATHS COUNTED. And still counting. This tunnel is longer than I remember or I'm breathing much faster than I intended or it is somehow, against all logic, farther going in than getting out. Perhaps it is all three.

But even if this heaven-forsaken burrow is curled

like a snake around its prey (and why did that image have to come to me just now?) should I not have already reached the end of its tight, stuffy, unpleasant length?

I stop walking and drop down to one knee. With the ceiling of the tunnel no longer brushing the top of my head I feel a little less confined. I reach out my arms to Ucta and Odvaha.

Come here.

We're with you.

The feel of their thick fur against my fingers is comforting. I press one side of my face against Ucta's neck as Odvaha licks my other cheek. How much harder it would be to do this alone!

I have to think logically. As Baba Anya says, every journey, no matter how long, must always have an end.

So how much longer must we be trapped in here?

No, be logical. I am not trapped. I'm free to move forward.

Forward toward whatever peril may await at the other end.

An encouraging thought. Crouched here, though, I take note of something I missed. The long flight of downward steps ended when I reached the count of twenty. I'd been walking along a level floor since then. But now, from this perspective I can see that the floor before me is slanting upward and just ahead are stone steps leading upward. I stop counting and start climbing the stairs that spiral up like a corkscrew through the living stone. I'm so eager to reach the end that both Ucta and Odvaha fall behind me now as I climb. Up we go, up and up. My legs are strong from years of training. So, though the way is steep, I am not tiring but going faster. The ceiling is high, so there's no chance of my hitting my head . . .

Thonk!

But I did just run into a solid wooden door around the last turn of the stairs. I bounce off it and am saved from tumbling back down the stairs by my two canine companions close behind me. They slow my backward sprawl and Odvaha grabs the end of my tunic firmly with his teeth.

As I stand again and brush myself off, I notice their mouths are open and their tongues are hanging out. Wolfish grins. They love me, stand ready to defend me with their very lives, but they also allow themselves to be amused whenever I do something foolish.

I grin back at them.

Dakujem. Thank you.

Za nitch. It is nothing.

I turn back to study the oak door, and study what is before me. What must I do to pass through this portal? Will the opening charm serve me here? I lift one hand up to cup my chin in careful contemplation.

Ucta whines and then lifts up a large paw to the right side of the center of the door. One of his claws catches the simple latch that I'd not noticed. It clicks and the door swings open. The silver light that had accompanied us is replaced by the golden glow that gleams from the great room beyond.

Ucta turns his head to look back over his shoulder at me. He even raises one eyebrow.

Tu je to. Here it is.

I have to chuckle at my own foolishness. Nothing seems to stand in our way. I step through with Ucta and Odvaha on either side. My laughter is cut short by the warning growls of both my four-legged comrades and the sudden whirlwind of dust that rises up before us.

"Password?" intones a slow voice, cold as a dark winter night.

A chill wind whips over us. That black breeze emanates from the breath of the tall skeletal warrior clad in iron armor who has now manifested himself from the swirling cloud. He seems as solid as what he holds in his bony hands—two long, sharp swords.

"Password?" the colossus repeats in a grim voice that echoes through the cavern.

Password? Think, Rashko. Password?

"Alebo smrt," the skeletal warrior adds with an eager, toothy grin. "Or death."

He spins his lethal blades and moves toward us.

The armored skeleton's singing swords are now only a double arm's length away. Ucta and Odvaha are moving farther out to my left and my right. They are ready to attack from either side should I give the signal.

But will their strong jaws and sharp teeth pierce the iron greaves strapped to the skeleton's stout shanks? And even if they did, they'd meet naught but bone. No flesh remains on the dread figure before me.

I have no sword, only a short knife and a wooden club. But even with my favorite blade in hand, could I hope to stand against a being with no mortal parts to wound?

What is the password? I was never told it. What might my mother, with her deceptive lack of cleverness, have chosen?

Wait? Could it be as simple as . . .

"Prejdi!" I shout. "Pass."

A friendly grin comes to the gaunt giant's jaws. The spinning of his weapons halts. He tosses both blades aside.

"Prejdi," Pavol, he replies, bowing deeply. He ges-

tures past himself with one arm as gracefully as a host inviting a welcomed guest into his home. Then, in a swirl of dust, he disintegrates.

Ruffs on their necks still raised, Ucta and Odvaha cautiously sniff the spot where the specter stood.

We are safe.

For now.

I look around me. It has been two seasons since I've been here within this cavern to gather our usual basket of coins from the great piles of gold left to our care by our ancestor Prince Pavol.

Pavol? Did I hear the skeletal warrior call me by that name before he fell back into dust?

No time to ponder that. I now have to figure out exactly where in this measureless cavern I've emerged. Then I see the direction that I must go. It's the widest tunnel in front of me. I can feel it.

I take the dagger from my belt and leave it on top of a pile of gold coins. A dagger will do little good against the one I might run into here. And it is best to have no weapon on my person now to show that I come not as an enemy, but as . . . an old acquaintance. I just have to find something else first.

I gesture toward the floor with the palm of my left hand. Both Ucta and Odvaha drop to their bellies and rest their heads on their paws.

Wait.

Why?

Trust me. I'll be back.

I half expect them to question me further, but they don't.

We wait.

I'll be back soon.

I hope.

I walk into the tunnel. I'd feel better with them by my side. But it's better for them to wait here. I must do this alone. Their scent might upset him before . . . Before what? Before I end up as dinner? I stop and take a deep breath. Thus far my intuition has not failed me. Each step I've taken has, it seems, been the right one. Even if I don't know exactly what lies ahead. It might be the path that leads to my family's salvation.

Or it might be the step that takes me over the edge of a high cliff!

I continue down the dragon-wide corridor that glitters to either side with the gleam of precious stones, the moon shimmer of silver, and the sun gleam of gold. It's interesting and pretty to behold, but I feel no lust for this wealth. It's that way with Mother too. Each time we come here, she just matter-of-factly leads us to one of the smaller piles where the gold coins are less ostentatious, fills our baskets, and marches us out again.

Paulek too is always unaffected by the dragon's hoard. There's no greed for gold in his honest heart. In fact, whenever we come down here his mind is on more practical things—such as how long it may be before we can return upstairs for a meal and a bit of juggling or weapons practice followed by a nice ride.

As I near the end of this corridor I see the stack of coins from which we last filled our baskets. It is easy enough to identify it. It's not just that the pile looks exactly as it did last time we finished taking our small portion. It's also what is left, or should I say left over, next to it. A much larger pile that is not gold or silver.

It is a pile of bones, surmounted by two large white leg bones that are all that remains of the offering that Mother, as always, had Paulek and me carry down with us. The bones are gleaming white—as if licked clean by a serpentine tongue before being added neatly to the stack of similar bovine remains.

"Fair exchange," Mother explained the first time we lugged down the two halves of a bull's freshly butchered hindquarters.

I walk past the pile of bones and look into a small niche cut into the wall. There it is. It is humbly placed on an old wooden stool much like the ones in Baba Anya's dom, the ones made for her by Uncle Jozef. Exactly like the ones in their hut, now that I think of it. It's not glowing with a silver light as it does in the tapestry, but this time when I look at it my eyes don't quickly pass it by. I see it for what it is and feel the emanation of power from it.

Pavol's pouch.

But there is something else on that stool as well, something I had not noticed before. It's a scroll like the ones I've been reading Pavol's story from.

First read the ending, Pavol's silent voice bids me.

I pick up the scroll and unroll it.

PAVOL'S LEGEND

Patnast

THAT NIGHT WAS one that would long be remembered by good and bad alike. It was a night whose power and strangeness would be memorialized in story and song.

As soon as the darkness fell over the mountains, it began. First there was a rumble like that of distant thunder. But soon it began to resemble something more like the beat of a drum. But no ordinary drum, one as big as the distance from one horizon to the next. Then it changed further.

Footsteps, people thought. But not the feet of humans or animals or even giants. It was the sound one might imagine a mountain would make if it grew legs and decided to go for a stride.

No one ventured outside, some out of fear and a few out of respect for what they knew was happening. *Magic,* some whispered.

Dragon magic, three others quietly said, smiles on their faces. The change they had hoped for had begun.

When the dawn came, and people dared to step outside, they saw marvelous things. The small hill near the edge of Stary Les was no longer so small but twice the size it had been before. Atop it rose a castle that had not been there before. Hladka Hvorka. Strange as it was and obviously the product of magic, those whose hearts were good did not find it fearful. They had long lived in fear but now, this sight, for reasons they could not logically explain, gave them hope. It drew them to climb the hill, to cross the drawbridge.

A noble-looking figure clad all in white stood by the open gate, welcoming each new arrival. Hard as it was for most to believe, that handsome, finely dressed one was none other than Pavol the Foolish.

While most had questions, all were too awed to speak. Some were men and women of minor nobility, some were well-off merchants, others no more than humble peasants. But Pavol's smile and his words to each were the same.

"Come, eat."

When they entered the great keep they saw that a feast had been prepared, food of all kinds placed on great tables—goulash and meats and good bread, plum dumplings, *buchty,* apples, and pears. So they sat and ate, better than most of them had in years, for in their small kingdom all the best food went to the tables of the Dark Lord's henchmen.

Some remarked at the fact that none of those henchmen were present at the feast. Others mentioned that they had been seen, all of them together, riding fast toward the north as if something had frightened them. And that, still others observed, was not good. Surely they were going to summon their master. The Dark Lord would return bringing doom and destruction.

That realization should have frightened the people. But for some reason fear did not come to any of those gathered in the presence of this new Pavol. Something about him made people feel at ease and reassured. Illogical as it was, it seemed as if nothing bad could happen while he was there with them.

When the meal was done, their eyes turned toward Pavol. He sat at the front of the hall at a table that was no higher, no different than any of those the assembled crowds sat at. Yet it seemed finer—perhaps for his shining presence. Strangely, he was joined there by five figures.

The first, the one everyone noticed immediately after taking in the splendid figure of Pavol, was the slender woman seated to his right side. Her silver garments seemed to mark her as one of the Fair Folk—those who were no realer than myth to most. Yet her hair was as dark as night and she seemed to lack the calm disinterest expected from one of the Fair Folk. Her face was animated, her gestures, the way she sometimes actually poked Pavol in his side and the laughter they shared at their private jokes, showed that she was of another kind.

Perhaps a princess from some other distant land. Might a wedding be in the offing?

The other four were, to say the least, odd and far from anyone's idea of nobility. The first two were not much of a surprise. After all, they were the ones who had raised Pavol—old Uncle Tomas and his wife, Baba Marta.

The third figure at Pavol's table was almost the least likely of all. It was none other than the old bald Gypsy who came from time to time to their land.

However, the most surprising figure at that table was not a human at all. It was a horse. A large, gallant steed, to be sure, an impressive beast. But a horse at the table? And why did Pavol keep leaning over and talking to it?

Still, the food was good and free and the atmosphere in this new castle so warm and welcoming that no one, though they might wonder at the weirdness of it all, cared to question any aspect of it all.

Then Pavol stood up to speak.

"My friends, though you thought me a fool, you see me now as I truly am. I am the child of those who were the true rulers of this land. That day when the Dark Lord came, I escaped. I am sorry for the pain all of you have suffered under his rule. Now that is ended. Karoline, my wife-to-be, and I will do all we can to serve you and this land," he said. And that was all.

Then Pavol climbed on the back of his white horse and rode from the hall. As people watched him go down the hill, they saw where he was heading— toward the gathering dark clouds to the north that signaled the imminent arrival of the Dark Lord.

"Ah," some said sadly, "our new Prince Pavol may be riding toward his doom."

"Can anyone defeat the Dark Lord?" others wondered.

"Surely there will be a great battle."

On that everyone agreed.

PAVOL REACHED THE narrow mountain pass just before the great host of men heading for his land arrived there. He watched them approach. Save for their leader, every man in that dire army was heavily armored and armed with many weapons. All Pavol held in his hands was a worn leather pouch, but there was a small smile on his face.

He looked up at the great cloud that rode above the host of grim men who confronted him. He turned his gaze to the arrogant face of the huge caped, black-clad rider who led them and had spurred up to loom over him.

The black rider hauled hard on the reins. His huge ebony war stallion reared up on its hind legs, striking with its front hooves at the white horse and rider. Its blows, however, struck nothing but air. With nonchalant ease, the objects of its attack had simply stepped calmly to the side. As a result the black stallion came down so awkwardly that its rider was nearly unhorsed—to the accompaniment of what sounded much like a horse laughing.

The Dark Lord angrily regained his seat and turned his horse back to face Pavol and his mount. His displeasure increased as the large white horse raised its lip in what looked like a sneer.

"Greetings," Pavol said, staring straight into the man's jet-black eyes. "You may not pass. You are not welcome here."

"Fool!" the Dark Lord growled. "Bow down to me or die!"

"I think not," Pavol replied, that maddening smile still on his lips.

The tall Dark Lord raised his right hand, his index finger pointing at the cloud above them.

"*Blyskat!*" he shouted. "Lightning!"

The jagged bolt that came crackling down straight at Pavol's chest would surely have killed him had it not been for what he had taken from his pouch. Instead of striking him, the lightning was extinguished by the bear tooth as easily as a man's breath might blow out a candle. Not only that, the whole of that great black cloud disintegrated at that self-same moment.

Still holding the bear tooth, Pavol lifted his right hand, displaying the bronze bracelet about his wrist.

"Your magic is no use to you against me," Pavol said in a soft voice. "Would that it had been the same for my innocent parents."

He pointed at the Dark Lord with the tip of the bear tooth.

"By the head of the dragon who now guards this land, I take from you all that gives you strength."

At those words a wind came up, as if rising from the earth itself. It swept over the Dark Lord and his host of men, hurling those who were mounted from their horses, knocking those who stood off their feet. Strong as that wind was, it did not even stir the hair of Pavol or the mane of his mount as they stood there, unmoved. That wind blew and blew, blew as the sweet spring wind does that comes from the south to melt the last of the winter snow. And when it ceased at last, all of the Dark Lord's army were no longer there, swept away like soot by a chimney sweep's broom, not destroyed, but scattered to the four directions with no memory of who they were or what they had done.

Only the one who had been the Dark Lord remained, much diminished now in size, bent and stooped over, his right hand that had wielded such power shriveled to the size of a monkey's paw.

He looked up at Pavol with an equal mixture of anger and fear, cringing as he waited for the word or stroke of a weapon that would end his existence.

Pavol calmly put the bear tooth back into the pouch, tied it, and then studied the shrunken being who had once been a figure of dread.

Pavol shook his head. "I will not begin my reign with a death, even yours."

"Too bad," Pavol's horse said.

Pavol leaned forward and patted its neck.

"*Nie,*" he continued, pointing at the one who had been the Dark Lord. "Instead, I send you off to wander and think of all that you have done. If your dark heart can find kindness, it may heal."

"Not likely," Jedovaty added.

Pavol nodded, a firm look on his face.

"If not, then your evil will fester within you, eating at you like a worm in a fruit. Go now, and know that if you ever return, one who guards this land will be waiting. And with your second coming there may be no mercy. Now go."

And with those words, the shriveled figure that had been the Dark Lord was gone.

And Pavol's long and blessed reign of justice and peace was begun.

CHAPTER FIFTEEN

One Who Guards

I PUT DOWN the scroll, thinking of all that it has shown me.

One who guards. I have to be that one.

I reach for Pavol's pouch. As my fingertips touch it, I hear what sounds like a heavy exhalation of breath from somewhere behind me in the deepest shadows of the cavern. I do not turn to look. I expected that sound. I pick up the pouch. Its weight is not great. However, as I lift it and put the cord around my neck so that is hangs down against my chest, I feel something settle upon me and within me.

My whole body feels the tingling power still held within it. And I understand, accept who I am. I am Rashko, but I have always also carried someone else within me. And now that consciousness is waking. Am I ready or worthy to be this generation's . . .

PAVOL?

The thought that touches my mind is not from either Ucta or Odvaha. It is a bigger, breathless voice. It's deeper, colder, infinitely older. I do not turn to face the direction from which it comes

My answer must be honest. I don't hesitate to give it.

Ano. Ja som Pavol. Yes, I am Pavol.

A shadow looms over me. I feel a gaze that does not just stop at my skin. It goes deeper, into the place where Prince Pavol lives within me.

ME KNOW YOU. ANO! PREJDI. PASS.

"*Dakujem,*" I say out loud.

I feel as much as hear that great voice harshly hiss a reply.

"*VITAJ.*"

The dragon's presence slowly recedes. But another voice speaks.

Wait.

I stand and wait. I have this unexplainable feeling that something else is about to come to me. I'm not sure what it is, but I know that I must continue to wait. I remain like a tree rooted into the living stone.

I'm not alone.

We're here.

Ucta and Odvaha have ignored my request. They're on either side of me, leaning into me, steadying me.

It is a good thing that they do. Though it comes slowly, when it does arrive it is with such force that it almost knocks me off my feet. It's a great wave of awareness.

Hladka Hvorka is no longer just above me and around me. It is within me. All of it, all of them. The hill, the great cave, the castle, Pavol the Good, and every generation of my family that followed in here.

I sigh deeply. *Ano.* I accept it.

I am too young for this. I still don't know if I have the strength and the knowledge to accomplish what I must now. But I accept who I am. I am the one who must thwart the Dark Lord this time.

But I cannot do it alone. I need all the help I can get.

As that thought comes to me, a window seems to open before me. I look through it and see, once again, the silver ballroom, the elegant figures of the Fair Folk, the solid shapes of Father and Mother among them. My parents turn their heads. They see me. They smile, and then those smiles widen as their eyes drop to the pouch that hangs around my neck.

"Rashko," my mother remarks, "how nice to see you this way!"

"Well done, son." Father beams.

Then they both nod and wait. The looks on their faces seem much the same as the expectant expression that comes to Uncle Jozef whenever he believes I'm about to solve some hard problem he's posed for me.

Or is Father just getting ready to quote one of his meaningless proverbs? Perhaps the one about the salmon always knowing the way to its own brook?

"*Otec, Matka,*" I say. "Hear me. Come home now. We need you."

"We'll be there soon," Father says, without even a hint of a proverb. "In the meantime, trust yourself."

"And trust your brother," Mother adds.

And that is all that I have time to say. The window vanishes. There's only the wall of the cave before me. I only hope they've understood. I look down at Ucta and Odvaha.

Now?

Now, I agree.

We turn and start walking. It takes a long time, but when we come at last to the great door it seems too soon. I'm not ready. However, it's too late to turn back. I take a deep breath and shout the words.

"*VELKE DVERE! OTVORTE SA!*"

The big door opens. We pass through. It closes behind us.

Now to go upstairs and see what will happen next. Shall I take the narrow, winding passage that leads to the door concealed behind the tapestry?

Or shall I just walk over to this smaller door to my right? It opens onto a straight set of stairs up the great hall. My mother never uses this simpler, more direct route whenever we descend to our secret treasure cave. But she sees nothing wrong about going back up the easier way, weighed down as we usually are by soon-to-be distributed wealth.

The most obvious approach to your enemy may be the one he least expects.

We pass through the right-hand door. As the three of us climb the wide, straight stairs, I see through the embrasures that the sun has moved far across the sky. Much of this new day has passed. Once again, the clock has played tricks on me. It must be close to the evening meal. There's been more than enough time for Baron Temny and Princess Poteshenie to consider any number of imaginative ways to deal with me—all of them fatal.

To my considerable surprise, when I reach the top and open the heavy door to our great hall, I am confronted by neither spells nor daggers. A grand party is in full swing.

A party?

A party, indeed. It is nothing less than a wedding party with my besotted brother as the groom—or should I say victim?

"Isn't it marvelous, Rashko?" Paulek says to

me. "I'm to be married tonight! They made all the arrangements for me! Come." He yanks my arm. "Take your place by my side."

"Paulek," I say, Ucta and Odvaha by my side, "this is not a good idea."

I'm talking about his impending wedlock, but he misunderstands me. He looks down at our two faithful friends and pats their heads.

"You are right, little brother. Bringing Ucta and Odvaha into the hall just now would not be good. The princess has her little pet with her."

Rather than argue, I decide to agree with him. I need to spend my energy convincing him he's making a terrible mistake.

Wait, I tell them.

So my two allies step back and allow the door to be closed, shutting them outside.

Paulek leads me toward the raised platform that has been erected at the back of our hall and has been garishly decorated with streamers of silk and lit by tall iron braziers topped with candles. The baron is waiting there, seated in his raised chair. To his right and slightly behind him is the bride-to-be. Her poisonous pet in her lap, the princess wears a falsely demure self-satisfied smirk. Paulek sits down on her other side, a delighted and innocent smile on his face.

"Ah," the baron says, his voice oily. "The brother

of the groom at last." His sardonic smile shows just how certain he is that I've been checkmated. Temny lazily gestures to the chair at his left. "Do take your place, my lad."

If I sit there, he'll be between me and Paulek. So I do as he says. I take my place, picking up the heavy chair and carrying it over to thump it down in the space to my brother's right.

Temny is not pleased, but he makes a small gesture with his left hand. Immediately his two captains, Peklo and Smotana, move over to stand behind me. They're well armed and both grinning like jackals.

I look out at our hall that is filled with more people than I've ever seen here before. Many of them are among the better-off in our valley. Tradesmen and women, merchants, farmers who own large plots of land. There are equally as many faces that I do not recognize. They must have arrived from outside our kingdom during my absence. They're easy to distinguish from our people by their avaricious expressions. The eager expectation on the fat countenances of Temny's friends and supporters is like a gathering of cats surveying a meadow full of mice. They've come to join him in sucking the life from our land.

Among them are two dozen or more of Temny's other men who seem just as happy. Well and conspicuously armed, they lounge about with cups of wine in their paws, delighted to be present for my brother's imminent marriage. Too imminent. Paulek has just whispered to me that the ceremony is to take place at the end of this very hour.

I look around the crowd again. One face is conspicuously missing—Georgi's. As majordomo he should be here, there, and everywhere making certain that all goes well. Has something been done to him? Have they recognized that he too cannot be fooled or misled by magic? Did they discover him lighting that lantern in the high room of Hladka Hvorka? Is he somewhere in chains? Is he even still breathing?

Paulek's face is glowing. He still hasn't asked where I've been all this time. Perhaps he's been so bespelled by the princess that he never noticed I'd been gone. He gestures at the garish way our hall is decorated.

"Wonderful, no?"

"*Nie,*" I reply. "No."

He turns to look at me. Is there a different look in his eye, almost one of agreement with me? He opens his mouth as if to reply—then his attention is caught by the sound of music entering our hall.

"Look, Rashko!"

A group of male and female dancers, dressed in the traditional wear of our valley, swirl in front of us. Usually, like Paulek, I'd be enjoying this. The red and gold embroidery of the women's skirts and aprons, bright, fine-stitched designs that represent flowers and trees and the arch of the rainbow, would usually delight my eyes. I'd be admiring the fur-trimmed vests of the men, the broad, tooled-leather belts, the tilt of their wide-brimmed hats topped with eagle feathers.

Under normal circumstances, my feet would be tapping with the beat of the men's black-booted feet. My heart would be lifted by the rhythms of the drum, the skirl of the long-horned bagpipe. I'd be joining in the song. It's one of my favorites, about the small cold streams that come down the mountains, to join the rivers and dance to the sea.

But not today. Not for this party!

"*Ano*, Rashko!" Paulek exclaims. "*Dobre! Dobre!*"

The dancers make one more circle, one final turn, then stomp and shout to signal the dance's end. They wear the smiles of practiced performers, but I suddenly realize how much those smiles are for show. There's uncertainty on the dancers' honest faces. As they try to make their way out of the hall, one or two of them catch my eye with looks that seem to be pleas for help.

They're attempting to exit as far as possible from Temny's men. Several of his mercenaries move to stop the youngest women in the troupe. It's not innocent flirtation on their minds as they grab at the women's dresses. Captain Peklo steps forward to watch the little drama. One of his armed men looks up toward the platform. Peklo nods and makes a small hand signal of assent.

My brother seems oblivious to all of this. He's too busy right now looking over his shoulder at the princess, who's drawn his gaze to her with a little movement of her hand, like a puppeteer pulling strings.

I reach down to touch the back of Ucta, who normally would be resting to the right of my legs. I don't find the reassuring thickness of his fur and his warm heavy-muscled shoulders. The space is empty where he normally lies. Nor is faithful Odvaha there to my left.

Nails and bones! I forgot. They're shut outside. I curse under my breath.

They sense me looking for them

We come now?

The door behind which they wait is on the far left side of the hall. The bulk of the tightly packed crowd is between them and me. There's no way for them to reach me soon enough if those soldiers do more than just threaten our dancers near the back of the hall.

Not yet. Keep waiting.

My hand moves up to my left side, but finds no weapon. I left the dagger Baba Anya gave me on top of that pile of coins. If only I'd thought to visit the armory. I could have retrieved my sword. But would it do any good against so many of the baron's men?

Ah! Do I see? Yes. There's a familiar figure at the back of the room. He's just entered the hall, so quietly that he's gone unnoticed by everyone but me. A hood is pulled over his head, but it doesn't conceal the small, elegant white beard. Black Yanosh. At last! He feels my eyes upon him, subtly raises a hand. I touch my chin with my right index finger, a sign of readiness that he taught me.

He repeats his signal, this time looking toward Paulek. To my surprise Paulek also touches his chin. No, wait, he's just scratching himself. It was too much to hope.

But at least Black Yanosh is here. I'll trust his signal and bide my time. At least I'll have one competent ally by my side if things should go from bad to worse.

Unfortunately, Yanosh and I are not the only ones considering whether or not to take action. The bagpiper is fingering the ceremonial dagger at his waist. The drummer is starting to unsling the stout walking stick hung over his back. They're readying themselves to try to protect the women . . . and end up badly hurt or killed by Temny's soldiers.

"*Zastav!* Stop!" The baron's loud command rings through the room.

He lifts his silver-mailed right hand.

His soldiers release the women dancers. Nearly all of them turn as one to look toward their master. As the dancers and musicians seize this chance to quickly leave the hall, an old hooded man hobbles forward, then stumbles clumsily between them and the two soldiers who've ignored Temny's command and are attempting to follow the women. The two soldiers stumble over him.

"Take pity on a small, helpless old man," Black Yanosh begs in a high, weak voice. He lifts a trembling hand in supplication toward the nearest soldier, who's rising to his feet and pulling out a cudgel.

"*Nie!*" The baron's voice, hard and cold as deep winter ice, freezes his soldier in mid-strike. The mercenary cringes like a cur. Black Yanosh slides back into the shadows.

The baron shakes his head—a patient father whose overeager child has reached for the sweets before the end of dinner. A cruel smile crosses his lips. Then he nods.

He extends his bare left hand toward the other large entryway that leads into the great hall.

"More entertainment," he shouts.

In through that doorway enter six figures. The first

two come cartwheeling, doing the fancy flips of professional acrobats. The other four, similarly masked
and appareled in Gypsy garb, follow. They're playing
tambourines and drums and carrying jugglers' bags.
Filled, no doubt, with the items soon to be brought
into play by the duo of main performers who each
do a final spinning backflip to land and bow deeply
before us.

"*Vyborne!* Excellent!" Paulek says, clapping his
hands together. "It's them! Remember how much we
liked them, Rashko? Isn't this nice?"

Strange as the circumstances are, I have to agree
with my brother. There below us, looking up into
our eyes over the masks that cover the lower halves
of their faces are the graceful jugglers Zatchni and
Teraz.

One good thing about the arrival of the twin jugglers is that for the moment my befuddled brother
is not staring in adoration at Princess Poteshenie's
overly rouged face. His attention is riveted on the
two slender performers as they reach into their
sleeves in readiness. Even a subtle sorceress's charms
are no match for Paulek's lifelong love of action.

"Begin!" Teraz cries, pulling out a handful of
bright-colored balls and hurling them.

"Now," Zatchni answers, instantly producing and
tossing back an equal number of rainbow-hued orbs.

Soon they have a dozen in play. Every ball is expertly caught and arced back. Not only are they nonchalantly juggling, the two supple entertainers are now performing spins and flips with near-boneless ease. It's being done so spectacularly that the tambourines and drums of the musicians accompanying them are almost drowned out by applause and shouts.

The two suddenly swing to face the bald, mustached man who declared himself their father that day in the market. He's not at all showy like his children—but was probably their teacher. With his right hand he plucks the balls that fly toward him out of midair, depositing them into the open basket grasped loosely in his left. He drops the basket, lifts his hands.

"*Nozhe!*" he cries. "Knives!"

The tambourine players and drummers put aside their instruments and begin to remove double daggers from their bags, placing them in the mustached man's hands. One, two, three, four. As each knife is slapped into his right or left palm, he hurls it spinning, to be caught effortlessly by either Teraz or Zatchni. In no time at all the sharp, singing edges cut the air between the two of them as they hurl the lethal blades back and forth. Why only four knives this time? They did far more in the market.

Deadly as those double dirks might be if mis-handled, my own juggler's eye notes that Teraz and Zatchni are dividing their attention. Their focus is not just on the whirling blades that they handle as if they were no more dangerous than eggs. They're edging closer in our direction, watching our podium out of the corner of their eyes. I recognize that look. It is not that of performers seeking approval. They're gauging distance. Are they actually assassins? Hired by the baron to kill a meddling younger sibling?

Paulek elbows me. For once, it is neither heedless nor accidental.

There's a serious look on my brother's face. Though he may be painfully unable to grasp when he is being manipulated by glamour, one thing that he does understand is a direct threat. He's also seen the way Teraz and Zatchni have been eyeing the podium.

"Look out!" Paulek shouts.

Four double-edged blades fly toward our podium.

My brother's reaction is no less quick than my own. As one, we leap over the table, land on our feet with our hands raised.

Catching a knife lobbed to you by a partner whose plan is that you catch it is one thing. It's quite another when whistling weapons wing toward you, hurled by adversaries who hope their blades will find beating hearts as sheaths.

But Paulek and I were trained to catch arrows. Our reflexes serve us well. Though the force of the throws make us spin halfway around, when we turn and straighten we're both unharmed and armed. Paulek and I hold up all four blades, one in each of our hands.

Zatchni and Teraz stare in disbelief at us. The masks that covered the lower parts of their faces have fallen down. It's clear now to everyone that these two, far from being the sons of anyone, are pretty girls.

It's also clear to me now, too late, that those daggers were not aimed at me or my brother. That's why we had to reach to the side to catch them! Their intended targets still sit in shocked silence behind us on the podium. Our ill-considered intervention has just saved the baron and the princess.

The heads of most of those in the crowd are going back and forth. First at the jugglers, then at us, then back at them again. There's no longer any music. The other Gypsies are gone. The drummer, the tambourine player, and the mustached man ran for the doors as soon as Teraz and Zatchni made their move. The silence in the room is like that between a distant flash of lightning and the eventual rumble of thunder.

A few people, locals who know the heirs of Hladka Hvorka love to juggle, begin to applaud. They think this was planned. My brother and I are just part of the act. My mind is moving faster than those blades that flew through the air.

Can I get Paulek to see it this way? With a little effort I can usually lead Paulek to believe almost anything—such as when we were children and I convinced him that if he planted an egg he could grow a chicken tree.

Yes, it might be possible. Then I might manage somehow to get these two young women out of the hall before the baron does something to them.

I've not taken into account the passionate feelings unleashed in those whose plans go awry.

Teraz points a trembling finger at me. *"Blbec!"* she says, her voice indignant. "Idiot!"

Zatchni is making an even more insulting hand gesture at my brother. *"Nepotrebny blbec!"* she snarls. "Useless idiot."

Their gazes turn from us to Temny. They step forward, hands clenched.

"Beast," Zatchni hisses, staring up into the baron's snaky eyes. "You murdered our parents."

"Impostor," Teraz says, her voice cold as steel on a December day. "You are no more noble than the pig sty that gave you birth."

"Our vengeful blades should have pierced your heart."

"Your soul and that"—Zatchni's ringing voice

rises as she shakes her fists at Poteshenie—"of your bony misbegotten wife there, should now be shrieking on their way to the Pit."

Wife? Oh my!

I wonder if Paulek heard that?

Others have taken note of Zatchni's words. A collective gasp goes up from the local tradesman and merchants who'd maneuvered themselves closest to the front of the crowded hall.

"She's his wife, not his daughter?" a cloth seller just below me says to his nervous-looking wife, who is trying to shush him.

"Not really a nobleman?" asks one fat merchant, looking toward the door.

"Vile monsters!" Zatchni screams.

"Dung heaps!" Teraz shouts.

So much for any hope of making it all seem part of the act.

The baron stares at the two young ladies confronting him. His heavy-lidded eyes are as unblinking as those of an adder. There is a tight-lipped smile on his face as he scans the disquieted crowd. He tilts his head toward Poteshenie.

Who is not his offspring but his spouse?

She nods and some of the bloom vanishes from her cheeks. Little lines appear at the edge of her eyes, and the luster of her hair lessens. She's still glamorous, but her beauty is no longer that of a seeming innocent. She's aged at least twenty years in less than a heartbeat by letting go of whatever enchantment she was using. There's no longer any need to hide her true self.

There's also been enough of hiding the sword in its sheath. Temny gives his men the signal—a stab of two steel-clad fingers toward the defiant sisters. A dozen of his burly mercenaries immediately begin to shove roughly through the still-stunned throng of confused celebrants. The soldiers' naked swords and drawn dirks indicate that their design is bloodthirsty rather than taking the two girls captive. By the head of the dragon!

Though armed only with the knives I caught, I'm not about to stand for a slaughter in my family's hall. There's not enough time for me to untie the pouch and reach into it. Slipping the left-hand blade under my belt, I leap from the podium, grasp Teraz by her arm, and turn so that I'm between her and the onrushing troopers.

"Good idea, brother," says a voice to my right.

It's Paulek, who leaped at the same moment I did. His right hand brandishes the blades, his left is holding Zatchni just as I am holding Teraz.

"Even when I didn't realize she was old enough to be our great-grandmother I knew she was too old for me."

His expression is clear-eyed. The moony look returns for a moment to his face. Then he crosses his eyes, grins, and elbows me so hard in the ribs it will probably leave a bruise.

The old Paulek is back.

But was he ever gone? Is my brother cagier than I thought? Was he merely pretending to be entranced? Just playing along with the baron until our parents returned or it reached the point where our only choice was to fight? Tactics?

Was that why he invited them into our castle after seeing how much greater their force was than ours—just to stall for time and avoid any of our people being injured in a siege? Has he been counting on me to find a way to save the day all along?

One thing is certain. No matter what, I can count on my brother to stand firmly by me in any time of obvious peril. Even though a well-armed phalanx of grim-eyed guards is plowing toward us, I feel strangely happy.

Part of the reason for my feeling of well-being is that Teraz is so pretty and so close to me. How could I ever have mistaken her for a boy?

"*Je mi luto,*" I say to her. "I am sorry."

Her response is to elbow me in the stomach with almost as much strength as one of my brother's bone-bruising blows.

"*Blbec,*" she says again, "Idiot!" But this time her voice is almost comradely. "Don't be sorry. *Bojus!* Fight!"

Then she turns so her back is against mine and she can see what is coming from behind.

Right. I bend my knees slightly, roll my shoulders to loosen the muscles. Out of the corner of my eye I see Paulek do the same. As has happened during times of mock combat, my mind is racing ahead so quickly that the attackers, who've now broken through the throng, seem to be moving slowly. The first cut will come from that mercenary at the front of their phalanx. Heavily armored like the rest, he's broad-shouldered, sure of himself. He's missing an upper front tooth, his nose appears to have been broken more than once, and there's a large mole with two black hairs protruding from it on his right cheek. Shorter than me by a head, he plans to remove mine with his cocked sword. The look of anticipation in Gaptooth's eyes tells me he's done this sort of thing before and enjoyed it.

What to do? Receive and parry? His greater bulk

and the speed of his attack might carry him into me. Try to disarm him with a cut at his wrist? Slash at his legs?

Thirty feet before he reaches us, something comes sliding across the smooth wooden floor. Twice the length and three times the thickness of a spear, it's one of the tall iron torch holders from the side of the room. Thrown with perfect aim and timing, it cracks into Gaptooth's ankles. His head-thudding descent to the hardwood floor knocks loose not only his shield and sword but also an additional incisor. The mass of men behind him, unable to stop in time, trip over his body. Weighed down, made clumsy by their armor, they crash to the floor.

Conveniently, Gaptooth's sword and shield both come bouncing toward my feet.

I drop the dagger. Well, not exactly. Actually, I hurl it at one still-standing soldier who, farther to the side, avoided falling into the groaning mass of prostrate men. My aim with the unfamiliar knife is good. The double blade pierces his left boot—and foot— collapsing him onto the pile of disabled attackers.

The shield rolls past me like a wheel, but I manage to snatch up the sword. It's not the best. Its blade is notched, its handle wrapped with wire. But the dark stains near its hilt are not from rust. It's done the work of death in the past. It balances well in my hand. It will do to defend our front—though I'd feel better if I had managed to also grab that shield.

To my surprise, the shield appears beside me. I turn slightly, catch the eyes of Teraz as she braces that buckler to cover our left. Her large eyes, brown as those of a doe, have a fine, fighting glow in them right now. She's no helpless maiden in distress. Fiercely ready to fight, the fire in her eyes is quite striking.

"*Zobud sa!* Wake up!" she says.

A knife comes hurtling at us from somewhere in the crowd. Teraz hardly looks at it as she quickly raises the shield to deflect it.

"*Tam!*" she says. "There!"

What a melodic voice!

She raises her hand, grasps me by the chin, and turns my head toward the front.

A second group of somewhat more tentative mercenaries is advancing. Having seen that torch holder come flying out of nowhere, they're looking over their shoulders.

Who did that?

I know, of course. But as I scan the hall, I see no sign of our old teacher.

Paulek leans his head back toward me again. I take note out of the corner of my eyes that he is still armed with one of the captured blades. The other knife is not in his belt. He's placed it into the competent hand of Zatchni.

"Black Yanosh never taught us that move," he says.

"*Ano*," I agree. "Good one to remember."

Zatchni punches my brother in the chest. "No time for jokes," she says.

Paulek responds by grinning at her.

"What is wrong with you two?" Teraz asks, her eyes on our adversaries. Her tone is that of a mother trying to get the attention of two slow-witted children.

How can I explain to her and her sister just how happy I am to have my brother by my side again and, even in this potentially fatal situation, how much I'm enjoying her company?

That enjoyment may be short-lived. A third, larger group of armed men has entered the hall. They're advancing, one slow step at a time, from our right.

Paulek and I stay shoulder to shoulder as we start to move. Zatchni and Teraz retreat with us as we shuffle back and to the side toward the door that leads down to the treasure cave.

More of the baron's men, five of them, are heading that same way to flank us. However, they do not see the two large, furry shapes creeping up behind them.

"Aghhh! *Pozri!* Look out! *Nie!*"

The shouts and gurgling screams are followed by silence, then two satisfied growls.

Got them all.

Ucta and Odvaha come to stand at our sides.

"Our little doggies," Paulek explains to Zatchni.

"Our two sweet puppies, who would not harm a fly," I say.

"However, armed men are not flies," Paulek concludes with a straight face.

We can't help it.

Zatchni rolls her eyes, then reaches out her hand to pat Ucta and Odvaha on their huge heads.

Teraz mouths the word "fools" and shakes her head again. But the side of her mouth curls up a little bit.

Not surprisingly, the crowd of celebrants has thinned out. The ordinary citizens have all exited hastily and ungracefully out the back doors. Now we can see not only the whole of our great hall but also the dais where Temny stands, his pose that of an emperor. Only Temny's allies have not seized this chance to depart from the fray.

"Poor manners," I say to Teraz. "Not one of those who left stopped to thank us for a good time."

This time Teraz laughs out loud. *"Prestan,"* she quickly adds. "Stop it."

I'm ready to make another quick quip. But the baron beats me to it.

"Hold!" Temny's command is hard as iron. It halts his men in their tracks.

He turns to us, stretches out his arms.

"My young friends," he intones, his gaze falsely benevolent. "My soon-to-be-relatives."

His deep, reassuring voice is hypnotic. I feel his magic seeking a foothold. It's like the strands of a spiderweb that stick to your face as you pass through a dark hallway.

Poteshenie stands slightly behind her lord, mouthing something under her breath. Her hands move as if weaving on an invisible loom. Once again, she seems a perfectly lovely girl in her teens, not a mature woman with hints of gray in her hair.

"Poor young mad girls." Temny gestures toward Teraz and Zatchni. His voice oozes pity. "From my small kingdom. Their parents died in a plague. Grief deranged them. They imagine themselves princesses, bereft of a throne they never owned."

He pauses, sketches a shape in the air.

"Poor young mad girls. They imagine me and my . . . daughter as the agents of their woes. Poor young mad girls." He throws out both hands as if tossing a ball.

I feel the force of the incantation. It's meant to

catch Paulek and me like a net. I raise my hand as one might guard against a strike from a more solid and visible weapon. The failed enchantment scatters around us in tatters.

From the raised eyebrows of Temny and the disgruntled grimace on Poteshenie's face, they didn't expect this. Temny opens his mouth to say something further.

"Liar!" Teraz shouts. Her mouth is so close to my ear that she almost deafens me. However, her warm breath washing over my cheek is pleasant.

"Conjuring beast!" Zatchni adds.

I raise my captured sword. As I do so, my wrist grazes the object hidden beneath my doublet. It sends a fiery tingle up my arm, an expanding wave of heat that flows to the center of my being. I open my hand. The battered blade clanks down on the boards as I reach into my shirt.

Teraz gasps. Temny's smile intensifies. He thinks his words have disarmed me.

"*Nie,*" my brother shouts. He grabs up the sword and points it at Temny. "You'll not fool my brother again."

Regardless of the fact that I was not fooled before, I am proud of Paulek right now. He looks every inch a hero: tall, strong, and determined. From the expression on her face, Zatchni is just as impressed.

As my fingers find the pouch, I can see from Temny's scowl that he knows his attempts at deception have failed. What follows now will be force.

No more than a few heartbeats have passed since Teraz and Zatchni's unsuccessful attack on the false pair who loom there above us. But it has been long enough for the word to reach Temny's ranks outside.

Even more men than I expected are pouring in through the courtyard doors to our beleaguered hall. Mercenaries are often men of low or no character, ready to do anything for a fistful of coins. Our false baron appears to have gathered every one of that ilk from the twelve kingdoms. A hundred or more swordsmen stand shoulder to shoulder before us. Behind those bladesmen are at least twenty archers. Razor-tipped arrows are fitted to the strings of their longbows.

Temny points at the archers, then back at us. He raises his mailed fist. When he drops it, they'll let those deadly missiles fly.

A hooded figure bursts out from behind the wall hanging. Metal flashes as he darts through the startled ranks of enemy bowmen. Some are so surprised that they let go their arrows before Temny can give the command meant to turn us into pincushions.

However, the released arrows do not fly through the air, but fall to the ground at the feet of the archers. With his two sharp steels, long blade in right hand, short blade in left, Black Yanosh has severed their bowstrings. Some of those bowmen are now bent over and crying out in pain. Not only did Black Yanosh effectively disarm them, they were also defingered as he spun like a white-mustached whirlwind through their midst.

Three leaping steps, precise as a dancing master, and our loyal old weapons teacher is with us, adding further protection to our left flank.

"*Dakujem,*" I say.

Black Yanosh raises one perfectly shaped white eyebrow at me, then strokes his mustache.

"Did I not teach you to never give up your weapon?" he asks, eyeing my empty right hand.

"Unless, sir," I reply, looking down at what I'm holding in my left, "I can exchange it for a better one."

My fingers have finally untied and loosened the mouth of the brown leather pouch. As I start to reach my hand inside I note that the hundred hardened grim-faced swordsmen are about to attack us.

The odds are terribly uneven. How sad. For them.

"We defy you," Zatchni cries, pointing her blade at Temny.

"You and that ugly hag at your side," Teraz shouts. Then, clearly knowing another woman's most mortal weakness, she adds, "How could anyone ever mistake her for a princess? Look at that ugly dress she's wearing. I've seen finer frocks on a fishwife."

Poteshenie snarls and thrusts forward past her husband. Her pinched face is twisted as she raises both her hands above her head and balls them into fists.

"*Smrt,*" she shrieks. "Death! We kill you all now." Her voice is indeed hag- and fishwife-like.

"*Nie.*" Temny's chill voice is like the rasp of serpent's scales against stone. He grasps his wife's shoulder and draws her back. "Capitan Mral, Capitan Burka, take them alive," he commands. "I want their death to be slow, wracked with exquisite pain."

Those words bring a happy smile back to his spouse's features.

Two cold-eyed, black-armored men step forward. I've not seen them before. They must have arrived with further reinforcements for the baron while I was gone. Mral and Burka. Cloud and Thunderstorm. They're both built like bears, but are likely less civilized.

Mral lifts his large right hand from the hilt of his sword. He makes a half circle in the air that ends pointing at his own lower legs.

A dozen new bowmen edge to the fore, step in front of the ranks of soldiers. They nock their arrows, raise their bows, move until they are only twenty feet from us. They aim low. The plan is to disable us. Easier to take an adversary alive once brought down by a shaft in thigh or calf.

My hand is now well inside the leather pouch. It is deeper than it looks. But my fingers are touching something solid. Before I can get hold of it, Paulek surprises me again. He pushes me to the side and lunges forward with the speed of a diving hawk. Each swift stomp of his forward foot is accompanied by not only a great heroic shout but an effective slash or thrust of his blade.

"Raz! Dva! Tri!"

His quick attack is as tactical as it is effective. Most of that line of bowmen have been felled or had their weapons cut in two before he retreats back to us as quickly as he advanced. Zatchni and Teraz look thrilled.

In truth, I'm not as pleased as are they. Paulek's lightning attack has not just wounded, but fatally felled some of those who stood before us just a few breaths ago. The edge of his blade is stained from tip to hilt with the lifeblood of men who will never rise again. I know my brother well. I've seen him climb trees to return small fallen birds to their nests. If we survive, the realization will come to him that his actions meant some mothers will never see their sons again—even if the dark deeds of those men earned them such a fate. Seven of those he attacked look to be dead or gravely wounded.

Two others also fell, but not at my brother's blade. The knife I'd thrust into my belt is gone. That's another reason Zatchni and Teraz are exultant. They contributed to the tally of fallen foes.

Mral was one of them. So surprised—or contemptuous of one young woman daring to confront a man in full armor—he stood unmoving as Zatchni ran at him. His armor did not stop her swift stroke to the side of his throat.

Burka had swung at Teraz with his sword. But the buckler she carried absorbed the blow.

"*Svina!*" she'd shouted, "Pig," as the quick thrust of her double blade slid into the narrow chink in the side of his armor and her narrow knife reached his heart.

"That was the one who killed Mother," Teraz says, tears in her eyes.

Zatchni squeezes her sister's shoulder. "Neither will ever murder another child as they did our little cousin."

Black Yanosh's back bumps against mine. "The back stairs," he says in a low voice only I can hear as he turns to face the raised podium. "Now."

I know what's in his mind. It was one of his first lessons to us.

When fighting a snake, strike at its head.

My hands are occupied again with the pouch as I fish around trying to find that elusive circular shape again. I can't stop Yanosh as he turns and leaps like a leopard toward the dais where the authors of all this evil stand.

His long steel is aimed at Temny's black heart. His short blade is raised like a dagger to stab down into that vulnerable space between neck and collarbone where a killing strike may sink deep. So sudden, so beautifully lethal is his attack, that it seems for an instant as if it might succeed.

"*Cierny vietor!* Black wind!" Those two words explode from Temny's mouth in a harsh cough of breath that expands into a dark-tendrilled cloud. It ensnares Black Yanosh in mid-leap.

Our old weapons master tries to escape, but cannot. The thick dark wraps itself about him, pinning his arms to his sides. He's still holding his blades, but his struggles are to no avail. The inky mass squeezes its charcoal coils tighter, an endless headless serpent.

Temny laughs. Our old teacher's ribs are as stout as oak staves, but under such pressure even strong bones will crack.

Poteshenie holds up her hands, curled as if grasping an invisible ball. Small sparks flicker between her fingertips. She's also about to release something sorcerous.

Something finally comes—as if of its own accord—to my grasp. I yank my right hand from Prince Pavol's pouch and lift the eagle feather that found its way to my questing fingertips. As I raise that plume, it seems too large and perfect to have been in so small a sack.

Pavol's silent voice speaks two words to me.

Jasny vietor!

I repeat them aloud.

"*Jasny vietor!* Clear wind!"

The feather bends in my hand. A buffeting gust bursts forth as if from the wing-stroke of a great bird. It peels the suffocating mass from Black Yanosh, tears it into thin strands of smoke that dissipate and disappear. That same blast, filled with the cleansing scent of a spring breeze, strikes the baron and his wife.

Temny takes a step backward, but braces himself and barely manages to stay upright. Poteshenie, though, is bowled over. She tumbles back, rolls head over heels, and ends up under the great table in an ungraceful heap.

Rather than assist his partner in treachery, Temny ignores her and her inventive string of curses as she struggles to her feet, trying to comb back with her fingers the rat's nest of disarranged hair that has fallen across her face.

Temny's thin-lipped smile seems almost pleased. His hooded eyes focus upon what I'm holding.

"Sooo," he hisses. "Finally! You've brought me just what I seek. *Dobre!* I knew you would do so, fool. All I had to do was apply the right pressure, no?"

His words send a chill down my back. His plan? He expected me to retrieve the pouch for him? Instead of a hero, have I been the world's biggest fool?

Temny holds out his mailed left palm. "And now I shall recover what was taken from me. Give the pouch to me. Now!" He slowly curls his iron fingers in a beckoning gesture.

His voice had seemed hypnotic before. However, I now realize he was barely trying then. It's as if that steely hand of his has grasped me by the throat, cutting off my breath and pulling me forward at the same time.

And as my traitorous feet twitch and begin to move, I suddenly see it all clearly. Too clearly. Rather than the wise one of our family, I'm the opposite. I have been so proud of being undeceived that I've fooled myself. I've fallen into Temny's trap. He and his wife have experienced setbacks, but not to his larger plan. Unable to enter the cave beneath our castle because the one power he fears is there, he has used me to do it.

If he holds the pouch he can regain all that was stripped from him by Pavol, become the great Dark Lord once again.

I've failed to understand my parents, underestimated everyone else around me. I've imagined myself to be the hero of a story in which I am actually the dupe. Not a knight, but a pawn who has failed his teachers, his family, his great ancestor Pavol, himself. By the head of the dragon!

Temny's stare locks my eyes to his, which are now as red as twin pools of blood.

No one else around me moves. My brother with his raised blade, Teraz and Zatchni in their postures of defiance, Black Yanosh, who fell to the floor after the dark cloud released him, but bounced back to his feet, twin blades at the ready—all of them are frozen in place. They've been paralyzed by the false baron's forceful spell. Even the hosts of Temny's mercenaries seem unable to twitch. It's unnaturally quiet. I can't even hear anyone breathing.

All I hear are my own feet shuffling slowly across the floor, closer and closer to Temny, whose hand is held out in an imperious gesture, whose fingers are about to grasp Pavol's pouch.

"*Pod!*" the baron demands. His voice is as certain and harsh as blood and steel. "Come."

I feel as if I am leaning over the edge of a precipice. I'm struggling against not only gravity, but also a great weight around my neck. It would be easy to overbalance and fall. But I do not.

Powerful as his pull may be, I cannot allow him to drag me forward as much as a hair's breadth. If I do, I'll be lost. I grit my teeth, shift my weight onto my back leg.

Yes, I have been foolish, but not selfish. Temny's evil is strong, but it stands alone, even though he has allies who obey and fear him. He does not have what I have. My brother, who stands by me; my parents, whose love is always with us; my teachers, my new friends, my loyal dogs, and this very place itself, this castle that is rooted in the blood of my family like a tree in deep fertile soil. And Pavol himself.

"*Pod,*" Temny commands again. This time his voice sounds strained.

Then, from that place within me, another word comes.

Nie! No!

I take a breath and feel my lips move, no longer paralyzed by the spell.

"*Zosilni,*" I whisper to the eagle feather. "Strengthen."

The feather grows heavier. It increases in size, becomes more solid and substantial in my hand. I feel a wave of power flow from it into me.

Sweat is appearing on the baron's brow. Even the

blood red of his eyes is not as bright. He shakes his head infinitesimally.

Temny relaxes his hand. His spell dissipates around us. Life and motion return to the hall and I hear the intakes of breath, the creak of leather, the soft clank of weapons brushing against armor. Temny's men are moving to attack from behind.

I turn quickly, sweeping the feathery wand like a sword delivering a crossing blow.

"*Rychly vietor!* Quick wind!"

The swift wave of wind strikes Temny's men with such force that it hurls them staggering back, losing their footing and their weapons as they go rolling out through the back doorways.

My two faithful dogs and my other four companions were untouched by the gale from my feathery sword. Recovered from their spellbound paralysis, my brother, our two warrior maidens, and Black Yanosh stand with me. They're all looking at me.

For some reason, they seem to be waiting for me to take the lead.

What we do now?

Ucta and Odvaha too.

What we do now, indeed.

I'm not that sure their trust in me is well-founded. That last gust of wind did not affect either Temny or his two bodyguards, who remain above us on the raised platform. Having regained her feet, Poteshenie is again standing beside her hateful husband. Her lips are moving in a silent spell to call up something else. Heaven knows what.

Further, that was my third request of the powerful object from Pavol's pouch. Magic often runs in threes and then runs out. It seems this feather is no exception. It is shrinking in my hand. Rather than a large feathery wand, it is now something I can hold between my thumb and forefinger. It's no bigger or more threatening than the limp tail feather of a half-grown chicken.

Think, Rashko! What else was in Pavol's pouch?

I place the depleted feather in the pocket of my tunic and slide my hand into the pouch a second time. This time something long and smooth finds my fingertips.

Black Yanosh lets out a shout and raises both blades. A dark shape has just appeared to stand before him. No, not one black shape. Three more, materializing as if out of the air itself. They are twice the size they were before. Each one is as big as a draft horse. Razor-clawed, sharp-fanged, and hungry for our blood, they're the remaining incarnations of Laska, Poteshenie's little pet.

CHAPTER SIXTEEN

The Goose Bone Sword

THE FOUR MONSTER cats spread out around us slowly. They don't seem at all wary of us—even after losing three of their number against just Odvaha, Ucta, and myself. I'm a bit surprised by that. After all, Paulek and Black Yanosh and the two skilled sisters have been added to our side. Perhaps their increased size has made them more sure of themselves.

Then again, their mistress is here, as is the baron—as are his soldiers, who have begun to regather themselves after that wind sent them tumbling. Peklo has left the podium to rally one group of them at the far left of the hall. To the right Smotana is doing the same. No sign of Truba, their herald. Probably hiding safely behind something.

One of the giant cats crouches in front of me. There's a lazy, self-satisfied look in its eyes. Its front paws move up and down as it flexes out its scimitar claws. Its black tail flicks back and forth.

We are ready, Ucta tells me.

Very ready, Odvaha adds.

Neither of them seems worried. I wish I could say the same for myself.

Paulek elbows me in the ribs. "I have the one to the left, Rashko."

"Get ready, Teraz," I say.

"*Nie* Teraz!" she answers. "Appollina!"

She's not taking her eyes off the second of the crouching monster beasts that is staring at her. If it thinks it has singled out a weak adversary, it's in for a surprise. She's holding up not one but two double-edged daggers. I'm not sure where that additional blade appeared from. Perhaps it was concealed in her boot.

"Appollina," she repeats, more forcefully this time.

"Appollina?" Is she calling the beast by that name? "What do you mean?"

"*Moje meno je* Appollina," she says in the sort of voice one uses with the slow-witted. "My name is Appollina."

Lovely name! Enchanting, in fact. Appollina. Much better than Teraz. Should I introduce myself now? Hello, I'm Rashko? No, she already knows my name. After all, it is our castle and Paulek just said my name and . . .

Stop! I'm smiling and mentally babbling like an idiot. There's no time for that now. I need to act.

I pull out the object that just slid into my palm in Pavol's pouch. It's the white polished wingbone of a goose. Words come to my lips.

"Velke dyka!"

The goose bone throbs as if it has a heartbeat. Then it lengthens, grows heavier, shines. A goose bone no longer, it's now a long, silver-bladed sword with a bone handle. I lift it, make a double crossing cut in the air. Perfect!

"Napred!" I shout. "Forward!"

Odvaha and Paulek leap at the one farthest to our left. Teraz, I mean Appollina, and Zatchni take the one next to it. Black Yanosh and Ucta attack the monster farthest to our right.

I'm alone as I take on the one directly in front. But when one has a long, sharp, swift magical sword, that is a bit of an advantage—even attacking a creature the size of a small house. When a monster is that large, its heart is an equally sizable target. My sword thrust drives deep into the middle of its chest. The giant cat melts away into gray mist.

I turn just in time to watch the conclusions of the other three contests. Ucta has the second great cat by its flank. Black Yanosh's twin blades cross in midair to slash out its throat. A second cloud of mist takes the creature's place. Odvaha's leap has carried him onto the third creature's back. His teeth dig into the back of its neck as Paulek drives his blade so hard into the black horror's side that he breaks the worn blade off. Gray mist again.

Thonk! Thonk! Appollina's dagger sinks into the fourth black cat's right eye as her sister's knife, hurled with equally deadly accuracy, dives just as deeply into its left, piercing its brain. And yet more mist.

Those four gray clouds coalesce, then dart like a frightened bat back to the podium, where the visibly aged Poteshenie opens her mouth and sucks that mist down her throat.

Appollina's sister turns to my brother and directs a wide smile in his direction.

"My name," she says, "is Valentina." Her voice, though less lovely than her sister's, is quite pleasant. She then does a little curtsey.

Appollina rolls her eyes toward the ceiling as if to say this is no time for courtly gestures. I wonder if her relationship with her sister is like mine with my brother.

Paulek sketches a bow in Valentina's direction. "I am most pleased to meet you, Valentina, even under these difficult circumstances."

My brother turns to me, holding up his broken sword. "Rashko, it appears I need a new weapon. Do you have one for me in that magic pouch of yours?"

"Use this one," a commanding voice intones from behind us.

Paulek turns as Baron Temny steps down from the podium. He's holding a sword in his left hand. Its hilt is bejeweled. Its blade glows with strange markings, runes that spell out some message I cannot read.

Before I can react, Temny tosses his weapon toward my brother.

"*Nie!*" I shout.

But Paulek does not seem able to hear me. His right hand thrusts out to catch the glowing sword that spins in midair and settles its hilt firmly in my brother's grasp. The glow flows like water from the hilt into his hand.

Paulek turns slowly to face me. There's a look I've never seen on his face before. His eyes are as red as blood. Behind him, Temny's lids are closed, his right hand held out as if grasping an invisible blade.

"Now," Temny says. "Kill your brother."

Black Yanosh leaps between Paulek and me as my brother turns the enchanted sword toward me. I know what our old weapons master has in mind. I've seen him do it a dozen times. Block up with the left blade to lift the opposing sword as his other blade slides across to twist the weapon from his adversary's grasp. It's an effective tactic to harmlessly disarm an opponent.

Paulek's never been able to counter that move before. Until now. Paulek spins, steps sideways, and strikes down at the first blade. The baron's glowing-runed blade sends a pulse of power down the length of the old man's sword. Black Yanosh's left hand convulses and lets go of the sword. Our old teacher is stunned by that surge of magic, frozen in place, open for a killing blow. Paulek simply shoves him out of the way.

Paulek takes a step toward me, the glowing blade held low. It's a position he's never used in any of our countless sparring sessions. Behind him, eyes still closed, Temny is in a similar stance. Red, unblinking eyes glare at me from Paulek's face. It's my brother's body, but not my brother about to attack.

Temny must have done this sort of thing before. Smotana and Peklo have come to stand, weapons drawn, on either side of the baron. Guarding him from attack.

There's something else in Pavol's pouch that might help me. I felt it when I first reached in. But I can't reach in now.

The blade held by my brother's unconscious hand stabs toward me swift as the strike of an adder . . .

and just as silent. No shout of *Utok!* or *Stavka!* or *Udriet!*

My reflexes can move faster than my thoughts. I avoid that deadly thrust at my heart with a quick leap back. There's an opening for me to counter, but a slash of my weapon would cleave through arteries and tendons and would cripple him for life. He might even bleed to death. I can't do that, not to my brother.

"Paulek," I shout. "*Prestan!* Stop."

No response. Temny's unblinking, crimson eyes still stare at me from my brother's strangely calm face. Paulek himself is no more aware than a wooden marionette whose arms and legs are being manipulated by a puppeteer.

Led by Temny's blood red eyes, Paulek's body attacks with a quick pair of cuts. The first is aimed to remove my head, the second to take my legs off at the knees. The rune-edged blade itself sings as it slices the air. Yet I duck under the first strike and leap over the second.

Again, I see an opening. There's one after each attack. It's almost on purpose. Does the baron have less control over my brother than he thinks? Is part of Paulek fighting back by leaving himself just vulnerable to counterblows? Sacrificing his body to save me is just the sort of thing my brother would do. But

I am not ready to badly injure my brother to save my own life.

"*Hyb sa!*" Black Yanosh shouts. "Move!"

I dive and roll to my left, barely escaping a whirlwind of strikes, one after another, that my brother's strong body is delivering. I'm thinking too much now. If not for my old teacher's warning, one of those blows might have connected.

I come up in a corner, my back against the wall. Paulek's last blow intersected with the edge of the dais. The rune sword sheared through the heavy oak planking as easily as a knife cuts through fat. I shudder at the thought of being caught by even a glancing blow from that deadly blade.

My brother turns, raises the sword above his head in both hands. Behind him on the podium, Temny has taken that same stance. Oh no! I can see what is coming. It is a rush straight at me. Here in the corner I can't leap to the side. He'll be open for a lethal strike from my sword, but that awful rune blade will come down from above onto me at the same time. There's a satisfied smile on Temny's face. His intent is to kill us both with this move.

Somewhere, behind those reddened eyes, is my brother. Both he and I are descendants of Pavol. Is it possible that we both have Pavol the Good within us?

I lower my bone-handled sword so that its tip

touches the floor of our hall, the hall that is part of Hladka Hvorka, part of all that Pavol made.

"*Bratcek,*" I say in a soft voice meant for Paulek's ears alone. "Brother."

A ripple of light dances across the floor from my sword toward his feet. And as soon as it touches him, his eyes close. When he opens them again, the blood color is gone. He shakes his head, then his whole body the way a dog does when it comes out of the water. He lowers the sword that was held high overhead.

A look of deep regret comes over his face. I was right. Part of him remained aware of how he was being used.

It's all right, I mouth to him.

Thank you, brother, he replies just as silently.

He holds up the rune sword and looks at it in distaste. "Too fancy. Not my sort of blade."

I know what he is about to do.

"*Nie!*"

Too late. Paulek turns and hurls the enchanted blade point first, back at Baron Temny. If Temny was a target dummy or another man, it would have pierced him to the heart. But he's neither. Temny opens his eyes and extends his mailed right hand. The glowing weapon slows in midair, turns, and settles its hilt into his palm.

"If one wants something done right," Temny says in a disappointed voice, "it seems that one must always do it himself."

He leaps, twice as far as a normal man unaided by sorcery might jump. His red eyes are as predatory as a leopard attempting to ambush an unsuspecting deer.

Not being a deer, however, I do not wait for him to fall on me. I hop back and the downward stroke of his sword misses me by a foot.

Temny immediately attempts another move. It's one I've seen before—the same first blow that Paulek never completed—a low rising slash that turns in midair into a thrust toward my throat. I parry it to the left.

Ka-ching!

Sparks fly as his sword clashes against mine.

But there's no paralyzing surge of power from his blade to my hand. The silver sword in my hand quivers as it absorbs the force of Temny's magic.

I riposte with a quick return thrust toward the chest that almost skewers the surprised baron. He is forced to briefly retreat, but then plants his back foot and renews his attack.

Magic or not, he's a more than capable swordsman, perhaps almost as good as Black Yanosh. But I have an advantage. I've already fought a trial match with him when his eyes looked out of my brother's face. I know his style of attack. His arms are strong, his reach a bit more than mine, but I keep his blade from connecting—first to my thigh, then my shoulder. Down toward my forearm, then a quick thrust to my eyes.

Strike, parry, back and forth we go. Beads of sweat form on his brow. His lips move as he mumbles one spell after another. None of them work. The power of my own enchanted sword and my years of training are protecting me from both the seen and the unseen.

There's a moment that may come in any fight, whether practice or mortal combat, when you know exactly what your opponent is going to do before he does it. At just such a moment I parry Temny's blade across his body, take half a step back, and then thrust straight toward his heart. Instead of piercing his chest, the point of my blade skitters to the side. Through the rip in his velvet blouse I see that the baron is wearing a mail vest of ornate gold and black.

Still, my blow knocks the wind out of him. He stumbles to one side with a curse, raising his sword as he does so. Good thing for him. Otherwise my sideways slash might have removed his head.

Not completely good for the baron, however. The

keen edge of my blade cuts through the metal of his mailed glove just below the pommel. It severs his index finger and sends the rune sword spinning.

"*Nie!*" Baron Temny screams, his voice higher than usual. He steps back, clutching his wounded hand.

"*Ano.*" I lift my sword up in a mocking salute.

I'm not sure what to do next. Ask him to surrender? Make a quick thrust at some part of his anatomy that is unmailed? His throat, perhaps?

Temny scuttles sideways like a crab, his bleeding hand held tight to his chest.

"*Pomoc!*" he shrieks. "Help!"

Two huge shapes block my path. They've appeared so quickly that I suspect the baron's magic assisted their arrival. It's Peklo and Smotana, of course.

"Now you die," Peklo growls, starting to swing his sword down at me.

"You will . . ." Smotana begins to snarl.

I don't have time for boring threats. I knock Peklo's sword to the side with a backhand parry and then kick him so hard in the belly that he folds like a creased sheet of parchment. Smotana's unfinished fulmination is punctuated in mid-sentence by my elbow, which removes his front teeth. As he falls, a knife skitters out of the sheath at his waist. Appollina darts forward to pick it up and add it to the several she has already thrust under her belt. She does like knives.

I turn toward the dais where the baron has retreated. Poteshenie has retrieved her husband's rune sword. Temny is wrapping a cloth about his injured hand. He's not looking at me, but behind me.

"Rashko," Paulek's voice comes from my left.

I glance quickly in his direction. The wide back doorway on that side of our hall is filled with armored figures.

"*Tam,*" another voice says from my right. "There too."

My eyes follow the jerk of Black Yanosh's chin to our far right, where the other big entryway is disgorging even more uninvited arrivals.

More than the original remnants of the false baron's little army are thrusting their way into our great hall. It's not just those forty or more who were bruised and bloodied by the blast of wind from the eagle's feather. Twice as many more dark-armored mercenaries are with them, as well as a score of bowmen.

"It appears," Appollina says from behind me, "that I need more knives."

I turn. Yet another large group of mailed men has appeared in front of the platform where Temny and his wife stand. I swallow hard, but the lump in my throat remains.

Temny raises his hand and lets it fall.

The dark-armored men encircling us begin sliding forward, one slow step at a time. They tap their spears together in time on the hard metal edges of their high-held shields. The sound of their heavy boots scraping against the floor is counterpoint to the thunk of wood against steel and the accompanying exhalation in unison of breath from the soldiers.

Shhhhh-thunk-hunh! Shhhhh-thunk-hunh! Shhhhh-thunk-hunh!

Black Yanosh readies himself, as do Paulek, Appollina, and her sister. All of them are now armed with weapons dropped by Temny's troops when the wind bowled them over. Ucta and Odvaha stand to either side of me. Everyone is ready to sell their lives dearly.

Nie. I cannot let that happen. Think, Rashko! What can I do?

I hand the silver sword to Paulek, fumble the pouch open, and thrust my right hand in. The round object I'd almost grasped before comes to me. Its cool metal draws itself like a magnet to my fingers.

As I pull it out and lift it, it slides down over my knuckles and around my wrist. I hold it up before me. It's a simple unornamented bronze bracelet. The dull metal does not glitter like silver. No bolts of lightning burst forth from it. Yet I feel its connection and hear a breathless voice whisper to me.

Speak my name. I come.

"Sedem!"

The entire castle thrums like the plucked string of an enormous lute. Now that is dramatic! But not as dramatic as the hissing roar that comes from everywhere and nowhere at one and the same time.

The warriors crouch behind their shields. Temny and Poteshenie lift their hands as if to ward off a blow.

WHOM! WHOM! WHOM! WHOM! WHOM!

A series of heavy thuds follows next. They might be mistaken for the sound of a huge hammer striking the bedrock of the hill below us. But I recognize what it is—massive feet thudding up stone stairs.

KER-WHOMP!

The wall tapestry is thrust to the side as the hidden doorway behind it bursts open, bolt bent, hinges ripped free, thick planks splintered. A head as large as an entire draft horse rams through. Two floor-shaking steps and the rest of Sedem, Pavol's dragon, enters our hall, along with quite a bit of broken lumber, dislodged stone, and mortar. Our secret doorway is secret—and intact—no longer.

Appollina grasps my shoulder. Paulek wraps his free arm protectively around Valentina to draw her to the side. He points the silver sword I just handed him at Sedem's nose. Black Yanosh steps behind me and leans his back against mine. Even a dragon cannot distract him from guarding our rear.

Armored men are bumping into each other. Weapons are falling to the floor as they attempt a quick exit. They are shouting such various things as *"Dratchie! Dratchie!"* *"Nie!"* *"Pomoc!"* "Help!" "Agghhhh!" "Get out of my way!" "Nails and blood!" and so on. Strangely enough, none of them are making use of my own favorite oath—even though the head of the dragon is staring down at them.

The wide back doors of the hall clog with panicked mercenaries, tripping over each other and becoming entangled. Heavy armor provides protection against human weapons, but does not make it easy to retreat rapidly. Nor is it of much avail against a huge fire-breathing beast.

The dragon lifts his long neck. His head rises up until it almost scrapes the high ceiling. Ucta and Odvaha growl deep in their throats.

Big.

We attack?

No. Wait.

I reach down to pat their loyal heads, but keep my focus on the huge emerald green eyes that peer down quizzically from high above.

Paulek is readying himself to use the silver sword I handed him.

"*STOV!*" I cry, loud enough to be heard over the echoing din of clanging armor and panicking soldiers. "Stand!"

Paulek lowers the sword, though his knuckles remain white from the tightness of his grasp on its hilt.

The long neck, the massive scaled body, the impressive, twitching tail—which I am also keeping one eye on—are all quite familiar. Sedem is just as I saw him when I looked down on his mountain through an eagle's eyes. There around his neck is the ring my ancestor placed there. The bracelet on my wrist throbs as I look at that silver neck ring and I feel the connection. As does Sedem, who gracefully lowers his head closer to study my bracelet. I note the bright rainbow sheen of the great dragon's scales.

He is actually rather beautiful!

What might be a smile curves up the monster's jaws. Did the creature hear my thought. Was he pleased by such praise?

Fine dragon, excellent creature!

Sedem's toothy grin definitely broadens. An impressive golden crest lifts on the top of his head.

"Nice master," Sedem hisses. He flicks a long pink tongue down to caress—or taste—my cheek.

I'm very glad that I'm wearing this bracelet. That warm wave of air redolent of old earth and sulfur in the dragon's breath suggests that without it I'd be bathed in flame.

I reach out to touch each of my companions in turn. *"Kamarat, kamarat, kamarat, kamarat."* I pat Ucta and Odvaha, touch Black Yanosh and Paulek on their shoulders. *"Kamaratka,"* I add, taking the hands of Appollina and her sister. Close friends, all. "No hurt!"

Sedem nods his huge head twice. "No hurt," he repeats, though he sounds a bit disappointed.

I make a wide gesture that takes in all the others in the hall from the disordered warriors to the two authors of all our woes who are standing with hunched shoulders on the dais.

"Zly!" I say. "Bad!"

"Dobre," Sedem growls as he gapes his jaws wide in a pleased yawn. "Good." He turns to look at the baron and his wife.

Poteshenie lifts up the rune sword in both hands. Her body quivers as she gathers herself. *"Blesky!"* she shrills.

An impressive green bolt leaps from the sword's tip. Sedem opens his mouth and swallows the lightning.

"Nice." Sedem burps. "Taste good."

Temny raises himself to his full height. He elevates both of his hands over his head. The dramatic effect is rather spoiled by the cloth that he wrapped around his wounded hand. It's come loose and is dangling in front of his face.

"I am Temny!" he screams in a high voice that sounds a bit hysterical. "None can stand against me. I am Lord of the Dark Ways!"

"I hungry," Sedem replies.

Then he strikes—with incredible speed for one so huge.

Sedem starts at the podium, then makes a circuit of the room like a hungry guest circling a banquet table. When Sedem is done—our great hall is empty of all save my comrades, the great worm, and me.

Sedem turns toward us and begins to lower his head. There's still hunger in the dragon's eyes.

"Hold up your sword," I say to my brother out of the side of my mouth. Then, as Paulek does just that, I lift my arm that bears the bracelet.

"*Prestan!*" I command. Sedem stops.

Sedem settles back on his haunches. "I stop," the great beast hisses. "See. No choke." The dragon bears his teeth in what is probably meant to be a friendly grin. Then he lifts his right foot up to use a long middle claw to dislodge a piece of gold and black chain armor lodged between his front teeth.

"*Dobre,*" Sedem adds with a satisfied burp. "*Spat znova?* Sleep again?"

"*Ano,*" I agree, gesturing downward. "*Spat.* Sleep."

Sedem turns. As he slithers toward the hole in the wall, his tail makes an absentminded swipe in our direction. I have already foreseen that and quickly herded our small party over to duck down on the other side of the dais. The dragon's tail swishes over us.

Sedem looks back over his shoulder, a bit hopefully, it seems.

I stand up, Paulek next to me.

"Sorry," Sedem hisses. "Tail bad."

I tap the bronze bracelet with one finger.

"*Spat!*" I say, putting more iron into my words. "Now."

Sedem eyes the bracelet and nods. "I go now. Sleep."

The last we see of him is the tip of his glittering tail vanishing through the gaping hole in the wall.

Black Yanosh strokes his mustache as he looks at me and Paulek. "I would say that you both did rather well."

It's the highest praise I've ever heard from his lips.

Paulek nods. Then, instead of hitting me in a big-brotherly way, he reaches over and takes me by the hand.

"Brother," he says, "I am proud of you."

Tears come to my eyes. I squeeze his hand and nod to my good, brave brother, my true *kamarat*.

Georgi comes through the doorway that leads to the back stairs as soon as the dragon disappears. He's followed by the three Graces, Charity, and most of our other retainers, including Zelezo, Jazda, and Hreben.

I'm a bit taken aback. How has Georgi managed to retrieve everyone so quickly? I thought all of them had taken refuge far from Hladka Hvorka. And why does Georgi put me in mind of a certain Gypsy juggler? What would he look like with a mustache on his face and a pillow stuffed under his shirt? I am going to have to have a long talk with him.

Grace, Grace, Grace, and Charity move to the sides of Appollina and Valentina.

"Come with us," the oldest of our Graces says.

"You need to freshen up a bit," says the second Grace.

"Wouldn't a bit of tea be lovely now?" Charity asks.

And just like that, as if they had not been engulfed in a storm of revenge and treachery, magic and bloodshed moments ago, the two martial sisters put down their weapons. They allow themselves to be led from the hall. They're actually giggling as they chatter about clean clothes and bathing and drinking tea. I do not understand women.

Georgi casts a critical eye at the broken and no longer concealed doorway, the disarranged but undamaged tapestry, the floor, the walls, and the dais of the great hall. All bear reminders of Sedem's feast. Even the high ceiling has not escaped the occasional spray of blood and gout of torn flesh. Dragons are, I have discovered, decidedly messy eaters.

Georgi taps the ends of his fingers together, then nods and gestures to our other capable servants, who are carrying brushes, shovels, and pails of water.

"There is a bit of work to do," Georgi says, "cleaning away these, ah, leftovers."

CHAPTER SEVENTEEN

In Order

MY PARENTS RETURNED just as the evening torches were being lit. When Georgi came to our chamber to tell us of their arrival, Paulek and I were engaging in conversation with the princesses. True princesses—that is what Appollina and Valentina are. Now that the sisters have bathed and dressed themselves in better clothing, my brother and I found it hard to believe that those two striking young women could ever have been taken for men or itinerant entertainers, good as they were at playing that role. When they first walked into the room where Paulek and I were waiting, their loveliness took our breaths away.

We bade them to sit, which they did quite gracefully and properly. Then there followed some awkward minutes while the four of us tried to find something to say. The fight we'd just survived had been so terrible that none of us wished to be the first to bring it up. Then Ucta walked over and put his head into Valentina's lap. That led to Paulek relating how our four-legged brothers came to us, followed by Valentina's tale of how the old sheepdog that was their childhood companion once saved her from drowning.

We soon discovered that royal blood and juggling were not all that we had in common. Appollina's wry sense of humor is much like my own. Valentina is, indeed, just as vigorous and fond of animals as my kind-hearted, athletic brother. Soon Valentina and my brother were wrestling on the floor with Ucta and Odvaha.

"At times I wish I could be like that," Appollina whispered. "I spend far too much time thinking and worrying."

"I know exactly what you mean."

"Look at them," Appollina added. "They are so loyal. And all they ask to be happy is to be well fed and petted."

"Yes," I agreed, "and that is also true of the dogs."

We were both trying not to laugh out loud when Georgi came to tell us of my parents' return.

"Go," Appollina said. Valentina nodded. "You will want time with them. You have much to tell. We wait here until you are ready to introduce us."

* * * * *

IT TURNED OUT that Father and Mother had, indeed, heard my call for them to return and immediately left the grand affair.

"We are so sorry, but we must be going."

"Lovely party, but the children need us."

With amazing ease and no loss of time, they left the Silver Lands and rode straight home.

They might have been here sooner had they not been slowed by various groups of people who stopped them along the way. Some of them were merchants and landowners who'd fled the hall before the fighting and fervently wished to reassure my parents of their continued loyalty. Others were mercenaries who'd managed to escape out the doors before our scaly ally had his afternoon repast.

"Rather a bother," Father says, "having to deal with one bruised and terrified armored man after another hurling himself on his belly to beg us for mercy."

"Yes, yes, it's quite all right," Father and Mother told each of them. "Just leave our land and never return again, that's a good fellow."

The one who took the most of their time was the baron's no longer haughty herald, who'd watched from outside and seen through the open doors all the events that transpired. Truba's confession of guilt included a detailed account of what the plans of the late Temny and his consort had been. More detailed than necessary, according to my mother.

"The fellow could hardly stop talking long enough for us to pardon him," Mother says. "Some people just seem to enjoy hearing themselves talk."

I walk with them into the great hall. Already, there's now little to show of what occurred. Georgi and our servants have, with amazing speed, mopped up nearly all traces of the carnage. All that remains is the sword mark on the corner of the dais. The secret doorway has been repaired—or did it repair itself?

"Well done," Father says, clapping Paulek and me on our shoulders. Then Mother enfolds us in an embrace.

"Now take us to our guests," Mother says.

As soon as my mother spies Appollina and Valentina, her smile lights up so brightly that it seems as if the sun has entered the room.

"You lovely young ladies must be the daughters of my dear old friend Katina! Welcome, dears! How are she and your father, King Karel?"

The sad looks that come over the faces of Appollina and her sister are more eloquent than any words.

Then, as she often does, despite her lack of intellectual brilliance, Mother knows what to do. She spreads her arms wide to the two orphaned girls.

"My poor dears, come here to me."

And just like that, they do.

As my mother listens they sob out the story of their parents' murders. They tell how they made their escape with the help of the good Gypsies whom their father (like our own parents) had never treated with cruelty and disdain. Those Traveling People—from whom they had learned juggling years ago—rescued them, gave them shelter. Then, when the leader of those Gypsies returned, he agreed to help them plan their revenge against the evil man who killed their parents.

By the time their story is done it's so late that everyone needs to retire.

My parents go up to their own room, after we see Appollina and Valentina to the guest chamber prepared for them by our dutiful servants.

"We'll talk more tomorrow," Appollina says, then leans forward to place a kiss on my cheek.

I can't think of a word to say as she smiles and then closes the door. But I am looking forward to tomorrow and I suspect the smile on my face is as broad as the one that Paulek is wearing as we go down the hall to our own room.

Soon Paulek is slumbering in our shared bedroom,

but I am still wide awake. And if my guess is right, I am not the only one still awake. With Ucta and Odvaha by my side, I go down to the servants' quarters. There, just as expected, I find four chairs pulled up to the great kitchen table. Two are empty and two are occupied.

Baba Anya is in the first chair. She beams up at me like a mischievous child. Next to her, one great arm around her shoulder is Uncle Jozef.

"Sit," Uncle Jozef says.

I sit and look over at the remaining empty chair.

Baba Anya and Uncle Jozef turn their heads toward the door.

A mustached Gypsy enters carrying two bottles. He takes the chair at the table's head, leans his elbows on the table, taps his fingers together, and then, with a small smile, removes his head scarf and the hair that had been pasted to his upper lip. Just as I suspected, it's Georgi.

I eye the bottles that he places on the table.

"Our oldest wine?" I said. "The hundred-year-old vintage?"

"Rashko," Baba Anya said, "we've been waiting longer than that."

Uncle Jozef nods. "As the one who bottled it, my cousin has earned at least a sip or two."

Georgi raises one eyebrow, as self-contained as

a cat who's caught the rat that was stealing grain.

"A friend can never be judged by the coat he wears," I say, quoting one of Father's proverbs. "But sometimes the coat prevents you from recognizing that friend right away."

Baba Anya, Uncle Jozef, and Georgi all exchange a look.

"What if," Georgi asks, "we were to tell you that we are In-betweeners."

"In-betweeners?"

"Children of human fathers and Faerie mothers?" he says.

"Ones who have chosen," Baba Anya adds, "to belong not to the Silver Lands, which never change, but to this world of changes?"

"This more interesting world," Uncle Jozef rumbles.

"Ones," Georgi continues, "who decided to be as much a part of this land as trees of Stary Les and the hill from which Hladka Hvorka grew."

"Ah," I say.

But why, I think, *why disguise your true nature?*

"Of course," Baba Anya says, her voice taking on the cadence of storytelling, "if we were such beings as that, we might hide our near-immortality, which might stir resentment in the hearts of ordinary humans whose lives are as brief and as bright as butterflies." She smiles at me, a hint of sadness in her smile.

"Instead," Uncle Jozef says, "we might chose to wait and watch, to help those who, like Pavol, hold the potential for wisdom, who may grasp the Way and stay true of heart and purpose."

I don't say anything. Silence, it seems, may be my wisest answer right now.

Georgi produces four glasses with a flourish, and opens the bottle of wine.

"To Cesta?" he says as he pours.

I take my glass and raise it. "To the Way."

WHEN WE'VE SHARED that drink, I nod to all of them and leave the kitchen. I don't go up to my room. I have one more errand to run. I enter the great hall and look at the tapestry. One torch is burning next to it, but it also, as is often the case, seems to glow with its own light. For a moment I seem to see something in it. It's a figure that resembles my brother, Paulek, standing in a doorway that looks like that of our kitchen. Our two dogs by his side, he is about to enter and sit down at the table with Georgi, Uncle Jozef, and Baba Anya.

I blink my eyes and that image is gone. I must have imagined it. I'm sure if I go upstairs I will find him snoring along with Ucta and Odvaha. Just a few doors down from the room where our two princesses now rest. That broad smile returns to my face again as I think of Appollina—the same way, I am sure, that Paulek is thinking of her sister. Time will tell what stories we may share together, but as I look again at the tapestry I think I see two couples holding hands and sitting together on four thrones. Then, as usual, I lose that vision. Wishful thinking, mayhap. But a most pleasant wish.

I go through the hidden door and descend the long stairs. As I do so I think of the story that I was just told.

Are Georgi and Baba Anya and Uncle Jozef truly that old? Or are they merely the offspring of those who came before them, passing the teachings on down? I don't need to know the answer to that. If I've learned one thing in the last few days it is that every question does not need to be answered. A story is not true just because if its literal veracity. It is the message, what it teaches, that counts.

I know now that I have as many faults as anyone. One of them has been being too quick to judge others, especially my parents and my brother, Paulek—who is more like my father than I realized, in the best ways. And Father, I now see, is more than I thought he was. To say nothing of my mother. If I am to continue carrying some part of Pavol's spirit in this time, I must work to be worthy of the gifts my family and I have been given.

Thinking of carrying gifts, I have carried this one far enough. There, in front of me, is the stool where I first saw it. I place Pavol's pouch back in its place. It will be here waiting should I need it again, here deep in the heart of Hladka Hvorka, our ancestral home that also has another name. It is one that we do not share with everyone.

Dratchie Hrad. Dragon Castle.

Sestnast

PAVOL THE GOOD and Karoline the Wise sat looking back at the kingdom they had ruled together with kindness and wisdom for so many years. On the other side of the river, the glittering fields of the Silver Lands waited.

"Now it is the turn of our children," said Pavol.

"And their children's children after them," said Karoline.

"May peace and justice be with them, said Pavol.

"And also our good friends who remain to guide them," said Karoline.

"And our very big friend too," a slightly sarcastic voice added from next to them.

Pavol reached over to pat the neck of Jedovaty.

"True enough," said Pavol.

"And you will be with them, also, my lord,"

Karoline said, leaning over to place a kiss on her husband's cheek. "Pavol will return when he is needed."

Pavol nodded. "You, as well, my love," he said, returning the kiss.

"What about me?" Jedovaty asked. "After all I've done, have I not earned the right for part of my spirit to remain and guide them?"

Pavol nodded again. "You are right, my friend. A faithful horse may be of use when, as it seems inevitable, the Dark Lord will seek to return."

Jedovaty shook his head. "Not a horse. How about a dog? A dog gets to sit inside and sleep at the foot of the bed."

"A very big dog?" Karoline asked.

"Why not *two* dogs?" Jedovaty added.

Pavol raised an eyebrow. "But with only half of your sarcasm?" Then he nodded a third time. "Why not, indeed. And, for that matter, why not two Pavols?"

Karoline smiled. "Or two princesses?"

Then they crossed the river.

⊰ Cast of Characters ⊱

Rashko: Prince of Hladka Hvorka

Paulek: Prince of Hladka Hvorka, Rashko's his younger brother

Father: King

Mother: Queen

Georgi: head retainer at Hladka Hvorka

Black Yanosh: weapons master

Zelezo: castle blacksmith

Jazda: head groom

Hreben: stableboy, Jazda's son

Grace, Grace, Grace, and Charity: castle maids

Uncle Jozef: village wise man

Baba Anya: village herbalist, storyteller, and midwife

Teraz (Appollina): first juggler

Zatchni (Valentina): second juggler

Prince Pavol the Good (or Foolish)

The Dark Lord: his adversary

Uncle Tomas: Pavol's mentor

Baba Marta: Tomas's wife

Jedovaty: Pavol's steed

Sedem: the seven-headed dragon

Baron Temny

Princess Poteshenie

Laska: the princess's cat

Truba: Temny's herald

Peklo: bald, scar-faced mercenary

Smotana: blond spade-bearded mercenary

⊰ PLACES ⊱

CIERNY LES: the Black Forest
HLADKA HVORKA: Smooth Hill, their castle
MESTO: nearby (and only) town in the kingdom
STARY LES: the Old Forest

⊰ SLOVAK VOCABULARY ⊱

Ahoj: hello
Ako ti je: how are you?
Ano: yes
Babovka: a type of cake
Bezhte: run
Blbec: Idiot
Blyskat: lightning
Boj: fight
Brana: gate
Bratcek: small brother
Capitan: captain
Cas: time
Chlieb/Chleba: bread
Cierny: black
Citaj: read
Csakaj: wait
Dakujem: thank you
Davaj pozor: be careful
Dobre: good
Dospej: grow up

Dost: enough
Do videnia: good-bye
Dvere: door
Dvihat: to raise
Dvihatch: gateman
Dyka: knife
Hotovo: ready
Hreben: comb
Hyb sa: move
Jazda: ride
Jedovaty: poisonous
Je mi luto: I am sorry.
Kamarat: comrade
Kolac: pastries
Kruzit: to circle
Lepshi: better
Les: forest
Matka: mother
Mesto: town
Milacik: darling

Napred: forward

Nerozumiem: I do not understand

Nie: no

Odvaha: courage

Otec: father

Otvorte: open

Pan: sir, mister

Petcheny chlieb: baked bread

Pockaj: wait

Pod: come

Pomoc: help

Poteshenie: pleasure

Pozri: look

Prejdi: pass

Prepac: sorry

Prestan: stop

Prosim: please

Pridi: come

Pyrva: first

Sadni si: sit down

Sedem: seven

Sedliak: peasant

Skala: big rock or boulder

Smrt: death

Spat: sleep

Stary: old

Stavka: strike

Strom: tree

Svetlo: light

Synovec: nephew

Tam: there

Temny: dark

Teraz: now

Trojky: triad

Truba: trumpet

Ucta: honor

Udriet: hit

Ukashte sa: show yourselves

Utok: attack

Vd'aka: thank you

Velke: big

Vietor: wind

Vitaj: welcome

Vyborne: wonderful

Yedz: eat

Zachinat: to begin

Za nitch: it is nothing (you're welcome)

Zapekane rezne: Wiener Schnitzels

Zastav: stop

Zelezo: iron

Zial: sorrow

Zly: bad

Zmiznut: to disappear

Znova: again

Zobudit: to wake up

⊰ NUMBERS ⊱

Jeden/Jedna/Raz: One

Dva/Dve: Two

Traja/Tri: Three

Styria/Styri: Four

Pat: Five

Sest: Six

Sedem: Seven

Osem: Eight

Devat: Nine

Desat: Ten

Author's Note

BY JOSEPH BRUCHAC

DRAGON CASTLE is a fantasy novel. Its plot and characters are products of the author's imagination. However, the language of its characters and the overall country in which its imaginary kingdom is located are both very real and part of my own heritage. My father's parents, Joseph Bruchac and Appolina Hrdlicka, came to the United States from the city of Trnava in Slovakia—which was then a very small part of the Austro-Hungarian empire. Like thousands of other Slovaks seeking opportunity and freedom in a new land, they passed through Ellis Island in the early twentieth century and became American citizens.

Slovakia, which has often been called by its people "the Heart of Europe," is, indeed, located in the geographic center of Europe. To the east of the Alps, south of Poland, and north of Hungary, where the great Danube River forms a wide plain, Slovakia's capital of Bratislava has been a crossroads for both war and trade for thousands of years. Although its people long saw themselves as a separate nation, for much of its history Slovakia was ruled by others. The many castles of Slovakia are a visible record of that long history—and of the frequent domination of the Slovak people by such stronger powers as Hungary. The fact that the Slovak nation and language exist at all is a measure of the devotion of its people to their own history and culture. Even after throwing off Hungarian rule, for seventy-five years Slovakia was not a nation of its own but part of the country of Czechoslovakia, which was itself dominated by the Soviet Union for several decades after World War II. Slovakia quite literally had to fight for centuries not only for its borders, but for its own mother tongue. Those who ruled the Slovak people tried at various times to force the people to speak German, Latin, or Hungarian rather than Slovak.

One of my favorite stories about Slovakia has to do with that language.

Long ago, it is said, all of the nations gathered at the throne of God. Each nation asked for great gifts. Some wanted fertile land. Some wanted strength and power to rule other lands. Others asked for splendor and glory. And the Lord gave each nation what it requested.

The last nation of all was that of the Slovaks.

"My children," the Lord said, "welcome. Why are you the last to come before me?"

"Father," the Slovaks answered, "the bigger nations pushed us aside."

"What then shall I give you? The other nations have taken all of the most fertile lands, the power, and the glory."

"All that we ask for, Lord," the Slovaks replied, "is your love."

God nodded his head and smiled. "You shall have it, my children. And I shall give you other gifts as well."

Then God wet his finger in the well of Paradise and touched each of their tongues.

"Here," he said, "I am giving you the most beautiful language in the world. It will be as lovely as the singing of angels, the sun shining on the dew, the laugh of an innocent child."

The Lord smiled, turned again to the well of Paradise, and dipped in his hand.

"And next I am giving you the most beautiful songs. When your women sing, the birds will fall silent and listen. The brooks and the hills will dance and your land will be a paradise."

Then the Lord smiled a third time. "Because all good things come in threes," he said, "I am giving you a beautiful land to live in. There, under the Tatra Mountains, you will find your homes, work in your fields, raise your families, keep your language and your faith. There, even though you may suffer, never give up, for I will always remember you with a father's heart."

And so it remains to this day.

THERE ARE A number of people to whom I owe a debt of gratitude. Without them this book would never have come to be. The first are my Slovak grandparents, Joseph (whose name was passed down to me) and Appolina (who real name I never learned until she was in her eighties). Though they were reticent to pass the Slovak language on to their grandchildren, I often heard it spoken in their home, and the echo of its gentle music lingers with me still.

The next person I need to mention is my friend, the artist Anna Vojtech, who illustrated *The First Strawberries,* my retelling of a Cherokee traditional tale. Anna, who was born in what is now the Czech Republic, urged me to find out more about the rich folklore on the Slovak side of my heritage. She also introduced me to Marta Zora, who did me the great favor of reading the early draft of this book and correcting the Slovak language that appears in it. *Dakujem,* Marta. *Som zaviazany!*

Over the last two decades, I've been fortunate enough to have a number of things I've written translated into several European languages. In 1996, I was contacted by Vlasta Chylkova about translating some of my stories into Czech. She and her husband, who was then the Czech ambassador to Canada, came to visit me at my home and brought with them the gift of several books of folktales from the Czech Republic and Slovakia. And what a gift that was!

One of those treasured books Vlasta gave me was a small, beautifully illustrated guide to the nation. Called (of course) *Slovakia, the Heart of Europe,* it contains a version of that story I just retold and also these words about the heroes of the Slovak nation: "Every nation honors its forefathers. Those of the Slovaks include no fighters and leaders who exterminated smaller nations, destroying their towns and culture. The Slovaks were a peaceful, hardworking, and religious people who always proudly defended their rights against more powerful nations."

That, one might say, is the underlying theme of *Dragon Castle,* and of the following folk song with lyrics by Janko Matuska, "There is Lightning on the Tatras," which is the Slovak national anthem.

Nad Tatrou sa blyska,
hrony di-vo bi-ju.
Nad Tatrou sa blyska,
hrony di-vo bi-ju.
Zastavm ich, bratia,
ved'sa o-ny stratia
Slavaci o-zi-ju!
Slavaci o-zi-ju!

There's lightning on the Tatras,
the wild thunder roars.
There's lightning on the Tatras,
the wild thunder roars.
Let us stop it, brother.
Look, it is disappearing.
The Slovaks are reviving.
The Slovaks are reviving.

It can be argued that the best-known European folk tales are the stories published by the Brothers Grimm in their famous volume *Kinder-und Hausmarchen (Domestic and Children's Tales).* However, Slovak folklore is just as diverse and marvelous. Epic heroes, clever maidens, dragons, and lucky fools are all to be found in stories that are by turns exciting, amusing and informative. Like American Indian stories, Slovak tales are often lesson stories—entertaining on the one hand and inspiring or instructive on the other. There is even a Slovak Robin Hood named Janosik, who took from the rich and gave to the poor (and deserves a book in English of his own). I was fortunate enough to also be given (in that stack of books from the Chylkovas) *Janko Hrasko (Johnny Littlepea)* a volume of Slovak folktales by Pavol Dobsinsky (1828–1885), the most important collector of Slovak folk stories. That book and David Cooper's *Traditional Slovak Folktales* (a well-edited and annotated translation of Dobsinsky's Slovak stories) were tremendously helpful and inspiring. The following quote from Cooper's introduction to *Traditional Slovak Folktales* may indicate just how helpful:

"Perhaps the most important animal helper in Slovak tales is the fairy horse . . . The heroes often receive magic objects from their helpers, including golden wands, magic rings, and sabers."

Lastly, though much of this novel is the product of my imagination, traditional Slovak folklore and proverbs guided me along every step of the way. The wise words of the elders in my tale are frequently drawn from proverbs still in common use in Slovakia today. Such sayings as "Small fish taste sweetest," "If a fool could keep quiet, he would not be a fool," and "A good name is the best inheritance" offer us a glimpse into traditional Slovak values . . . and remind us of basic truths that go far beyond national borders. I am grateful for those lessons.

I hope, that in some small way, the journeys of my characters in *Dragon Castle* may also offer readers the sort of delight and instruction that my own journey into the Slovak half of my heritage has given me.

Na mier a priatel'stvo!
To peace and friendship!
Zelam vam dobru cestu.
I wish you a good journey.

Bruchac